AF226230

JESSICA K. FOSTER

NEW YORK   LOS ANGELES

This is a work of fiction. Names, characters, places, and incidents are either products of the author's imagination or, if real, are used fictitiously.

Copyright 2026 by Jessica K. Foster

All rights reserved, including the right of reproduction in whole or in part in any form. If you would like permission to use any material from this book other than review purposes, please ask via contact@windingroadstories.com. Thank you for respecting the rights and intellectual property of authors and creatives.

Jacket design by Rejenne Pavon
Jacket Copyright 2026 by Winding Road Stories
Interior book design by A Raven Design
ISBN#: 978-1-960724-54-0 (pbk)
ISBN#: 978-1-960724-55-7 (ebook)

Published by Winding Road Stories
www.windingroadstories.com

To Coley J. for not only cheering this book on from the beginning, but also for suffering through way too many dream stories on the bus in middle school so we could get to this point.

1

WASTE OF TIME

THE CLASSROOM INTERCOM crackled with less than twenty minutes to go until lunch. "Virginia Benson to the dean's office, please."

I tapped in a new equation on my graphing calculator. One more problem and I'd be done.

"Virginia," Mr. Newcastle said in a mild voice when I didn't get up.

I held up a finger for him to wait. I couldn't lose momentum, or I'd have to redo the whole thing.

"Virginia," he warned.

"One second," I mumbled. With one last scratch of my pencil, I had it.

I smiled at Mr. Newcastle, but his raised eyebrows told me he wasn't impressed. *Whatever.* He should know better than anyone that you can't stop mid-problem.

Trina nodded to me from the corner of the front row, and I smiled back. At least someone understood.

I dropped my books into my bag and slung it over my shoulder on my way to the door. The dean called me down to his office on a regular basis. I was always in the spotlight.

Anyone else could be too, if they entered as many contests as I did. Awards were given to people who deserved them, and I worked hard to be one of those people.

But come on. They had to call me out of the classroom farthest from the office during a core subject? I picked up the pace, practically flying through Holder Academy's wide, winding halls. Maroon flags and golden plaques of rich old family names winked at me as I passed by, people whose donations made all the marble and mahogany possible. My parents had two of those engraved plaques. Someday, my name would shine on the wall, too. I'd like nothing better than to give back to the institution that launched my Ivy League law career.

I expected a quiet walk because class was still in session, but when I skipped down one of the staircases to the first floor, I rounded a corner and almost slammed into a stepladder.

Gabriella was hanging an Anti-Vaping sign for the Student Council that read PROTECT YOURSELF AND OTHERS. It was our big campaign this year. She teetered on the top rung trying to drape it over the doorway to the cafeteria.

I steadied the ladder. "A little to the left," I said. She was the treasurer. I don't know why she didn't make one of the freshmen do this.

"Thanks," she said drily.

Someone was in a mood. *Whatever, not my problem.* "While I have you, I'm going to need you to email me the most recent numbers for our budget so we can make some decisions about the class gift."

Gabriella finished securing the banner. "I sent them over last week," she huffed as she climbed down the ladder.

"I know, but where did the money for…" I trailed off as Mr. Darryn approached us. I'd been trying to avoid the Drama Club director since tryouts last week. Maybe he'd be in his own little world and wouldn't even notice me.

"Look it over and get me the numbers again," I hissed.

Gabriella rolled her eyes as I tried to escape Mr. Darryn by speed walking in the opposite direction.

"Ah, Ms. Benson. We missed you at tryouts last night."

Dang it. I turned to face him. "I didn't sign up this year."

He arched an eyebrow. "Do you still want an audition?" It was impossible to tell whether his smile was real or fake. Actors.

"Uh no, thank you." One year was more than enough for me.

"Ah, that's too bad," he said, shuffling the papers he held in his hands.

I breezed by him. The drama club would be fine without me, even if I had a pretty decent voice. "It's good to see you, Mr. Darryn!" I didn't wait to hear his response before I ducked into the front office.

Ms. Anderson looked up from her computer. "Virginia. Dean Alton will see you in a minute."

"Do you know why I'm here?" It had to be the Americanism essay. Took him long enough. I busted my butt on that one, visiting all those nursing homes to interview veterans about the conditions of their base camps. They'd had war stories for days. It was the perfect essay from start to finish. Even my mom had no comments to add when I sent it to her, and she wasn't one to hold back criticism.

Ms. Anderson shrugged, turning her eyes to the papers on her desk. Okay, then. I took the seat closest to the dean's door. It would cut down on time—and time was precious.

Five minutes passed. The dean was probably on a conference call or yelling at some poor kid too stupid to know how to follow simple school rules. That would make him doubly happy to see me. I'd be a nice break from all that.

I rotated my shoulders. God, my neck was tight. I needed to stretch. Better yet, I should see if I could get to my chiropractor for a massage.

I ran through my daily checklist in my head. With so much to do and so little time to do it each day, it'd become a habit.

Then I remembered: the letter of recommendation for Yale! What better time to ask if the dean had finished it than when I was front and center, accepting an award from him? He probably already finished it, and *that's* why I was here. Perfect.

"Has Virginia arrived yet?" Dean Alton sputtered through the ancient desk intercom.

Rather than answer right away, Ms. Anderson pressed her lips into a straight line and smoothed her frizzy red updo with practiced fingers.

At length, she finally pressed a button. "Yes, sir."

"Well, any day now."

Weird. Last year, they'd been more friendly with each other. Too friendly, if the rumors were true. And I mean, I got it. He was good-looking for a dean. He still had all his hair and kept himself fit. The dark suits he wore never had a wrinkle or a seam out of place. Dean Alton might be the actual definition of put-together.

Ms. Anderson's eyes flicked in my direction like she could read my thoughts. I pretended to study my French manicure. It was none of my business.

"Ms. Benson? The dean will see you now," she said.

"Thank you, Ms. Anderson." I gave her a glowing, megawatt smile. My dad often reminded me to be polite to assistants, that they were the front line. Even young assistants with short skirts and wow, could her shirt be any tighter? Those buttons were working overtime.

I opened the heavy door with a strong hand and strode across the room, planting myself in one of the chairs across from Dean Alton. He was a serious kind of guy, intimidating to students, especially troublemakers. Thankfully, I never fell into that category. He was one of my biggest supporters.

The dean stood in the light of the window behind his desk, squinting at a handful of papers through reading glasses. He didn't even look at me. It had been thirty seconds since I sat down. *Hello?*

First, he calls me in here, then he makes me wait while I'm *missing class*, and now, when he asks Ms. Anderson to let me in, he doesn't even talk to me? I cleared my throat.

He looked up, and I graced him with a winning smile.

Virginia, here's your letter of recommendation. It was an honor to write.

He laid the papers down instead of handing me one. *Strange.* Then he centered his gaze on me. His very stern, unpleasant gaze that he reserved for someone annoying who had done something that was a "big deal."

"Let's take a walk, Virginia."

"I'm sorry?" My smile dimmed. "Take a walk where?"

"To your locker."

"Okay?" I barely ever used my locker. I rose to follow him out the door and down the hallway. My locker stood less than twenty yards from his office.

His keys jingled as he found the tiny silver one that would unlock any locker. He didn't have to do that. I could've put my combination in myself if his gross invasion of my privacy wasn't making my hands tremble.

I clenched them into fists. I'd done nothing wrong. I snuck a look down each side of the hall. I had no reason to feel nervous right now.

My locker swung open. I noticed nothing out of the ordinary about the contents until I spied a few spray paint cans lying on their sides on the bottom of it. What—where did those come from?

The dean gave a somber nod, like he'd expected this all along. He picked up each of the cans and put them under his arm. "Now, I know it's your senior year, and many high school students start to feel a little rebellious when they see the light at the end of the high school tunnel, but this is—"

"Those aren't mine," I said. Crap, I shouldn't have done that. Interrupting was rude, but I needed him to stop. This spray paint meant I was in trouble, but who cared if someone stored it in my locker? It could be for an art project or something.

"Then whose are they?" He pocketed his keys, putting on a show that he had all the time in the world. Adults loved to do that, but not the dean. Not with me.

"I don't know."

The bell rang long and loud, and students spilled into the hall.

The dean sighed, pinching the bridge of his nose.

My blood froze. Whatever those paint cans had done, now I looked guilty to everyone who walked by me and Dean Alton. "Can we..." My throat went dry. I could already hear the whispers.

"Is that Virginia?"

"Like, *the* Virginia? Straight A Virginia?"

"But she's never in trouble."

"What did she *do*?"

Dean Alton ran a hand through his hair and pretended to ignore the whispers and the way the crowd skirted around us, their beady little eyes scanning us for clues. "Does anyone else have the combination to your locker?"

"Um..." My locker stood in the central hall, which was prime real estate. When I was a freshman, people begged for my combination to stash their stuff. What was I going to say, no? Anyone could have it now.

"Virginia?"

"I might have shared it with a few people," I muttered, feeling like I was confessing to a terrible crime, even though everyone else broke the same rules. I flashed a bright smile to a group of girls and waved. *Everything is fine*, I willed them to think. *I'm not in trouble.*

"Exactly as I thought." The dean frowned as silence stretched between us. *Yes, think it through. Whatever you're mad about wasn't me. Obviously.*

He ran his hand through his hair again, oblivious of the fact that it ruffled his perfectly neat appearance. "Follow me."

I forced my face into a politely puzzled frown, even though my insides quaked. Didn't we just take a walk? Whatever he thought I had done, he was wrong. I'd never jeopardize my future.

Without another word, he swept us down the bustling hall. More than one of my classmates raised their eyebrows at me. I shrugged, my expression bored. Blood pounded in my head as I tried to think of something, anything I'd done wrong. I came up empty. Rules were important.

The hall emptied out quickly—too quickly. Had everyone rushed to class to escape the tardy bell, or did they know something I didn't know? Rumors were probably already flying about why we were out here. Holder Academy ran on gossip.

"What's going on?" I asked.

The dean shook his head and kept walking until we paused next to the boys' locker room. A hastily scrawled Out-of-Order sign was taped to the door. *Uh, what?*

"I'm not supposed to go in there," I reminded him. This better not be some elaborate joke, because the heart attack he threatened to give me right now wasn't funny. At all.

"That," he said, "is a fact I am well-aware of, yet here we are." He gestured to the door.

I used the elbow of my sweater to push through it. Boys were gross and didn't wash their hands half the time. Lord only knew what kinds of germs grew on the doors they touched.

I crossed my arms when he took forever making sure the door was firmly shut behind us.

When I finally turned to look at the boys' locker room, it was kind of a let-down. Tile and porcelain, sinks and toilets, all of it mimicked the girls' room. The only difference was a wall of urinals, and gross, what was that smell? It reeked of mildew mixed with B.O. mixed with… paint.

Then I saw it. The reason Dean Alton dragged me out of math and into this testosterone-filled germ factory. Big, colorful lettering on the wall about six feet above the sinks:

DEAN ALTON IS AN ASSHAT

2

THE SLOPPIEST CRIME EVER

THE DEAN PUFFED up like an agitated owl beside me while I smothered my laughter. Who wrote in this jagged, half-cursive, half-print style? It wasn't even level. The last half drooped like the vandal had gotten tired at the end. If I reached my arm up as high as I could, I still wouldn't be able to touch the dried drips on the wall. Did someone hang from the ceiling like a burglar to write this all-important message?

Poor Dean Alton. Someone wanted to make his life miserable. Wait...

"You think *I* did that? I can't reach that high!" Not even a stepladder could get me up there.

He arched an eyebrow, and we both went back to staring at the wall like it was chanting at us: *Asshat, Asshat, Asshat.*

"I'm bad at art, too," I added. He had to see reason here. Sure, it might be suspicious that the same color of paint was in my locker, but didn't they have security cameras? "That lettering is..."

"Virginia, we both know you have a perfect GPA. The design is not that complicated."

"Well, that's..." Not untrue. But a lot of extra credit was

involved in that Art A. "I didn't do it." My fingernails dug into my palms. *Never let them see you struggle.*

"It does seem out of character for you," Dean Alton admitted to the wall, "but the evidence is incriminating. We have a real problem here." I'd never heard this edge to his voice before.

I didn't know what to say. I thought the dean understood me. Liked me. He knew how hard I was working to get into Yale. I didn't even leave my dorm room most nights. My roommate teased me regularly for being glued to my desk. How could he accuse me of the sloppiest crime ever? Logistics aside, I didn't have the *time* to be so stupid.

Our short walk back to his office was painfully silent. I knew every step I took would be dissected by the vipers watching me through the tiny windows of each classroom. I concentrated on my breathing, unable to sort through the jumble of thoughts in my brain as I mindlessly floated along in Dean Alton's wake. Was I going into shock?

As soon as the dean shut the door to his office, the interrogation began anew. "Where were you last night?"

"Don't you guys have cameras in the halls?" I asked. "You have to know it wasn't me."

He drew in a breath and let it out in a prolonged exhale. Was he trying to keep from yelling at me? He never yelled. "Answer the question please, Ms. Benson," he said in an unnaturally quiet voice.

Don't get defensive. It will make it worse. "I was in my dorm room studying."

He braced his hands on his desk like a cop in a crappy movie. "Can anyone corroborate that?"

The only person who would've been able to was my roommate Agnes, and she'd been out, like always. She said the dorms were "suffocating." "Do you even know what time the graffiti happened?"

He sighed. "It seems the tape has mysteriously vanished."

A tape? Like a VHS tape from the 1900's?

"You have access to the gym after hours."

For fencing. So? I wasn't the only one in that sport. "Practice hasn't even started yet."

"And you're telling me you were not aware that the closet between this office and the gym labeled 'Surveillance' has hallway footage stored in it?"

"I don't think anyone could've guessed you'd still be using tech from the '90s."

"Virginia, this isn't funny," he snapped.

Like I could laugh right now. "Obviously, I've been framed!"

He shook his head in disappointment.

I refused to confess to something I didn't do. If it weren't a horrible idea for several reasons, I would involve my mom. He wouldn't be stupid enough to punish me in front of her steely lawyer face without actual proof. I met his stare without blinking. I wasn't guilty, and I had no intention of looking that way by crying or doing something else equally brainless.

As if reading my thoughts, he said, "I've already left a message for your parents detailing this unfortunate incident."

The room contracted; all the air was sucked out of my lungs by that one statement. He did *not*.

Ms. Anderson hurried into the room and handed him a slip of paper. He squinted at it for a moment, then mouthed a word I didn't catch. She nodded.

He stood. "Excuse me a moment."

I watched him leave. It was so unfair! He'd already called my parents when he had no actual proof that I wasn't in my dorm room last night? Everyone here shared lockers. He knew that. Why didn't anyone else get called down to his office? There had to be someone who hated him, someone he'd suspended or snapped at. What motive did I have? None.

I slumped in my chair. He'd never write me a recommendation letter now. And being expelled would be enough to get me kicked out of Yale before they even admitted me.

I had to figure a way out of this.

The door opened, and Dean Alton returned, his mood even darker than before. The lines on his forehead had deepened, and his mouth turned down so much it was almost funny. Almost.

After a long moment, he said, "I can appreciate the... investment you and your parents have made in your education here. This is a grave matter. It must be dealt with carefully."

Was he speaking to himself? He didn't even meet my eye.

He took a deep breath. "I think it's best to reconvene to discuss punishment in two weeks. Perhaps evidence will surface to exonerate you before then."

Well, that was a switch. I'd been halfway certain he planned to kick me out on the spot.

He sat down and loosened his tie with an agitated hand. "Ms. Anderson, I'm going to need a new locker for Ms. Benson," he buzzed through the intercom without taking his eyes off me.

Who'd been on the phone? Was it—wait. *Investment.* My parents had called back to buy me time.

My face went numb, and I did what I always did when everything crashed in on me: I shut down. Dean Alton kept talking, but I didn't hear a word he said. I just nodded, at a loss for words, until he calmed down enough to slump back in his chair.

How had I been naive enough to think that our meeting would be about my Yale letter? *Because it should've been.*

Ms. Anderson reappeared with new locker information for me, and Dean Alton waved me out. Like I didn't win the last three essay contests and the Science Scholarship. Like I annoyed him, and he needed me to leave. *Unbelievable.*

As I left his office, my public mask snapped into place even as my chest caved in with the effort of looking calm. It would be fine. I was innocent. I didn't spray paint DEAN ALTON IS AN ASSHAT on the wall of the boys' locker room.

Anger churned in my gut. *What an asshat.*

I tried to return Ms. Anderson's smile as I shut the outer office door, but my mouth wouldn't cooperate, so I grimaced instead. She appeared concerned, but I didn't care.

I walked back to class at the pace of a tired turtle. My late pass wrinkled between my fingers; the tiny sound magnified in the now silent hallway. Someone was trying to frame me. God only knew why.

I stopped and leaned against a wall of lockers. Maybe I could fake sick for the rest of the day. No doubt everyone knew Dean Alton blamed me for the stupid prank. All the popularity I'd racked up, all the academic respect I'd worked so hard for... slipping right through my fingers.

No. Stop it. None of my classmates would believe I'd paint a wall in the boys' locker room. I was so far above that. I could find a way to clear my name—I had two whole weeks. Dean Alton would be so embarrassed that he'd write me the best recommendation letter ever. I wouldn't be expelled; I'd be *congratulated* for tracking down the real culprit. I might even get an award! I pushed off the lockers and practically skipped back to class.

Four steps from the door, the bell rang. Students spilled into the hallway, talking over each other on their way to lockers and lunch.

"What's wrong?" Agnes rushed forward, dark curls bouncing, and pulled me to the side.

"Nothing." I faked a small smile.

"Bullshit, but okay." She grabbed my arm. "Let's eat."

In the lunch line, Agnes loaded up her plate with pizza and cookies. I filled half my plate with salad as we waited to scan our cards to pay. Too much cheese. My mom would have a fit. I could almost see her waving her finger at the lunch staff, griping about how they should let students sprinkle it on top instead of mixing it in like that.

"Class was super boring after you left," Agnes said as we sat down. She broke her cookie in half. "Think everyone was wondering why the dean called you down."

A hint, and not a subtle one. When I didn't respond immediately, she narrowed her eyes.

I waved her off. It was our signal for being overwhelmed, that we weren't ready to talk yet. Neither of us wanted to show weakness by crying in public.

"Did I miss any notes?" I managed to ask. I scraped little bits of cheese out of the salad and into the corner of my tray.

Her expression softened a fraction. "What are you doing?"

I followed her gaze to my plate. *Oh.* I pushed the cheese back into my salad. "Nothing. Habit." It wasn't like my mom was standing over my shoulder.

Agnes narrowed her eyes again, but let it pass. Good, because I didn't have it in me to nod through another "Mother doesn't always know best" speech. "You're in luck," she said instead. "I already copied my notes for you. You can have them when we get back to the room."

"Wow, it must have been really boring." Normally, Agnes would have flirted during any downtime in class.

She took a huge bite of her cookie. "You have no idea."

I sighed.

Agnes swallowed. "Just tell me," she said. "You know you want to. It's not like you're in trouble or something."

I pressed my fingers to my temples and let my hair fall forward to cover my suddenly very hot face.

"Are you?"

"I'm so screwed," I muttered, mostly to myself. My parents were going to kill me. Maybe they'd even go biblical on me and stone me in the courtyard like a true heathen. One who would graffiti swearwords on walls.

"What did you do, submit two essays for the same contest or —no." She snapped her fingers. "The graffiti?"

I nodded, frustration clogging my throat. It wasn't surprising that Agnes already knew about the stupid graffiti. Her middle name was gossip.

"Well, it isn't like you did it," she said in a flippant voice. "You never leave your desk."

Not this again. Not everyone wanted to go to every single party. Some of us had to work for our grades. "Studying isn't a crime." I peered up at her through my hair.

"But graffiti is. I heard it said that Dean Alton could go suck—"

"It doesn't say that. And can you lower your voice?" I hissed.

"Well, it's not like I could get in to see it." Agnes folded her arms and leaned back.

"Yeah, well I got the full tour." And a full dressing down, even though I didn't do anything. Ugh, this was such a mess.

Agnes suppressed a smile. "I can just imagine you in a place where boys pee. Did you faint?"

I pressed my hands against the table. "It's not funny. I'm going to get expelled."

That sobered her up. "No, you're not. You didn't do it."

"The paint was found in my locker."

"What? But you don't even use that locker!"

I glared at her.

She lowered her voice. "Can't they roll back the camera footage and get the real guy?"

"They don't have footage, I guess."

Her eyes widened. "Oh God. Your parents…"

I didn't have time to appreciate that her thought process was almost identical to mine. "I know," I whispered. "I'm dead."

"No, you're not," she said in a firm voice.

"I am," I moaned.

"No, you're not. We'll figure this out. Just let me think."

"Okay."

But she didn't come up with a plan before the end of lunch. We left for Economics together in a solemn, desperate silence.

And as we walked into class, it was hard not to analyze every possible suspect. Todd from the Art Club waved at me, and I smiled and gave him a small wave back. His face scrunched up in an awkward smile. Too timid to be the bad guy.

"Hey, Tamara," I said as I passed by. It was important to act normal. Just because my life was falling apart didn't mean everyone needed to witness it. Tamara adjusted the glasses on her short nose and pulled her eyes from the complete works of Sylvia Plath long enough to echo my greeting in a soft voice. I hoped we'd get partnered in Science for the next lab. If I got put with one of the brainless girls again, I would scream. Tamara didn't have any time for anything but her dorm room experiments outside of class. Every other day, smoke or some sort of smell spilled into the hall. Not the bad guy. Also not a good candidate to help me track down the graffiti villain.

Graham chilled at the back of the room, leg shaking as he tried to hide the fact that he was texting under his desk. He was slammed too. His tutoring app had taken off, and he'd told his family he had no intention of going to college. If I tried something like that, my parents would kill me.

I knew all of them. Every single one. But I didn't know who graffitied the locker room, and I didn't know who would be able to do more than I could when it came to sussing out the spray paint bandit. I needed someone who knew me and everyone who had my locker combination. A senior. Unless someone shared my information. Then everyone in the school would be a suspect.

What I didn't understand was *why* someone would want to frame me. I never did anything to anybody. I didn't gossip. I just hung out with Agnes and kept my head down. I stayed friendly with everyone; they all knew I prioritized studying.

No one ever yelled at me or accused me of stealing their boyfriend. Why would they? I didn't date anymore. But someone hated me enough to want to ruin my life. Dean Alton had been my friend too, until he wasn't.

I sat down in the seat I always chose, in the center of the class where the acoustics were perfect to listen to the lecture. No one would confess anything to me. I hated asking for help, but the wheels in my brain were already turning. *Someone everyone talks to. Agnes. No, not Agnes. They'd know she was reporting back to me. Someone I normally wouldn't be seen with.*

Xander Hearst blocked the doorway, talking to a trio of his not-so-funny friends. He probably thought that his wrinkled shirt and the way he slung his bag over one shoulder made him look cool. He looked sloppy. The fact that he refused to cut his wavy brown hair didn't help. I bet he kept it long so he could flip it back to flirt.

Students bumped into him as they tried to get past him to their seats. How self-centered. Couldn't he see he was in the way?

Like some Hollywood celebrity, he said hello to about a half-dozen students on his way to the desk in front of me, knocking knuckles with a guy he *just* talked to and bestowing a brazen glance at Claire's mostly exposed boobs. From her seat in the corner, she bit her pencil, and he arched an eyebrow.

I snorted. *Get a room.*

He leveled a cool glance at me before slumping into his seat. Like I cared what Xander thought of me anymore. It wasn't my fault we broke up freshman year. Yale demanded excellence, and he was a distraction.

Girls were always hugging him, shoving him playfully, running their hands along his muscles in the hallway. I wouldn't be surprised if he'd dated half the school since me. He wasn't exactly suffering.

Was being an obnoxious flirt the same as being stupid

enough to paint a swear word about the dean on a locker room wall? I set my books on the desk and opened my laptop.

"Psst!"

I signed back into my home page and clicked on the folder with all my Economics notes.

"Psst!"

I glanced up to see Agnes motioning to Xander. Why would she—

I shook my head. He didn't do it. Xander was a lot of things, but I felt confident graffiti was below him. I never would have dated him if he was that stupid.

No, Agnes mouthed. She scribbled something down and then threw a wadded up piece of paper at my face. I caught it before it bounced off my forehead.

He knows everyone. Get him to help. He can't hate you that much.

If only she knew. There was no way I was asking him for help. Absolutely zero chance.

Except... No one would expect us to work together.

I glanced at the clock above the whiteboard. Two minutes, and we'd be neck deep in lecture. What choice did I have?

3

WHEN HELL FREEZES OVER

"Xander!" I hissed.

He didn't react.

I leaned forward and poked his shoulder with the eraser of my pencil. "Xander!"

He turned around slowly. "Yes, Virgin?"

Oh God. I didn't think this through.

I bit my tongue to keep from snapping back at him. Was there such a thing as reverse slut-shaming? It wasn't even a clever nickname.

A few girls near us let out dainty giggles. I glared at them.

Agnes lifted her eyebrows. Did she think I wouldn't do it? I would do anything to clear my name.

But why would I talk to him in such a public place? Panic? This was such a bad idea.

"Forget it," I muttered.

He leaned forward and placed a hand on my desk. "The Ice Queen deigns to acknowledge my presence, and I'm supposed to forget that?"

Whatever. He didn't have to be such a drama king. I talked to him. Sometimes. Well, I did for group projects in class to divide the work.

I looked pointedly at his oversized hand. A few seconds later, the teacher began to lecture.

Xander snaked his arm back in and swiveled his chair to face forward.

I pressed my fingers against my computer keys harder than was necessary as I copied the board. I would've spent the hour cursing myself for being so stupid, but the material was more important. I took a ton of notes so I could rewrite and highlight them by hand later to help me remember. Nothing mattered more than my grade. Even embarrassing myself in front of one of the most popular guys in school. A guy I'd kissed. A guy who'd—

No. Focus. I resumed typing, underlining what I didn't understand. The teacher talked too fast. I'd have to look it up later.

After class, I found Xander leaning on the lockers outside the door, waiting.

I swept by him, but he fell into step beside me. I couldn't hide behind my laptop and pretend not to look at the back of his head now.

"Let me guess. You've realized your mistake freshman year and are really, deeply in love with me." He bent his head down to look me in the eye. God, he was tall.

I weaved between people, trying to ignore that half of them stared at me, probably thinking I was guilty of the stupidest crime of the century. The hallway overflowed with navy jackets and name-brand shoulder bags. It was like trying to swim upstream. Surely I could lose Xander by rounding a few more corners. Once I dodged him, I would ask someone else to help me with the case. A girl. Yes, definitely a girl.

He followed me.

"You can go away now," I said.

He didn't go away.

I needed to grab my stuff from my old locker and take it to my new one. I speed walked, but he was relentless. His annoying tall-person strides made me look like a squirrel running next to an elephant.

I rounded on him where the hall poured into the cafeteria. "Let's just drop it. I don't know why I even thought you'd help me." As soon as the words left my mouth, I wanted to reel them back in.

He stopped, and a freshman clipped his shoulder as she rushed past. "You need help?" Xander asked with exaggerated disbelief. "What could you possibly need from me? You have everything."

I rolled my eyes. Based on his fangirls, it took him about three seconds to recover from the tiny dip his popularity took freshman year after we split. His immaturity knew no bounds.

I opened my mouth to tell him off, but across the hall, a few girls from our class craned their necks while pretending not to watch us. "We can't do this here." I tilted my head in their direction. Over my dead body would we feed the overactive rumors in this school.

He didn't look at them as he scanned me from head to toe. "Even more intriguing. What are you hiding, my dear Virgin?" He winked. Who did that? Just threw winks around like confetti?

I tightened the backpack straps on my shoulders. "Call me that again, and you'll never find out." I kept my voice low and measured, but I stood my ground. So what if it was a part of my name? There were lines. Solid ones he should know better than to cross.

A few seconds passed. Seconds I needed to get to class.

He folded his arms. I swallowed, my throat dry. The movement pulled his shirt tight. He shouldn't have that kind of body in high school. Twenty-five-year-old men had those arms.

"My car. After school." He smirked. *Crap, he caught me staring.*

I opened my mouth to object. People would talk if they saw us together in his car. I didn't need that right now. Not to mention, Xander and me in a small space? My heart slammed against my ribs.

"We'll drive someplace quiet. You can tell me all your dirty secrets." He flashed a flirty smile and leaned over until his mouth hovered inches from my ear. "Unless you'd rather show me."

"When hell freezes over," I said through clenched teeth. He always knew what to say to get to me.

He laughed and stepped back. "After school," he said over his shoulder as he rejoined the girls who had launched themselves at him earlier. I knew he saw them!

One yanked on his arm to pull him down to her level so she could touch his stupid shaggy hair. And *he let her.*

What did I get myself into?

The expression on Dean Alton's face as he lectured me about how my "crime spree" better not continue flashed through my mind. A black sort of desperation settled onto my shoulders—I'd do whatever I had to.

By the time I sprinted to my locker to make up for the time Xander had wasted, Agnes was already there waiting for me. I pulled out all my textbooks and shoved them in my backpack.

She tapped her fingers against the metal. "So how did it go?"

"Let's not." I spared a second to check my hair in the mirror on the locker door. It fell in waves to my armpits. Washing it was a pain and styling it took forever, but appearances mattered. Adults always told us not to judge a book by its cover, but come on. In what world? My hair was an asset. After smoothing a few errant strands, I pocketed the mirror. Whoever got my locker next would have to get their own.

Agnes didn't leave. Her hawk eyes watched me as I zipped

up my bag, pinching my finger in my panic to get to class on time.

"Seriously, I can't right now."

She snorted. "I still don't get why Dean Alton thinks *you* did it. So what if he found the paint in your locker? You'd die before going in the boys' locker room."

"Right?" This was the proper response; the response Dean Alton should have had the second he searched lockers and found what he did. *Of course Virginia didn't do it.*

I glanced down at the slip of paper from Ms. Anderson. "I'm stuck in locker 23 now. Is that in the—"

"Freshman hall." Agnes's lip curled. "Gross."

I should have known the dean would exile me to the ninth-grade wing. I started in that direction.

"So, what are you gonna do?" Agnes applied her lip gloss blindly as we walked.

"Go to the freshman hall?" I pasted on a fake smile and waved to Gina from AP Bio, who looked a little too interested in our conversation. She moved along.

"No, I mean about Xander," Agnes said. "And have you heard from your parents yet? Are they coming here?"

I shook my head and tried to push her words away. Having someone ask that out loud made my skin crawl all over again. At this rate, I'd end up with a full-body rash.

"I don't think so," I said, though I had no idea. Would this be enough for them to fly out here? Why hadn't they texted me yet? The dean had called them. This was a big deal. "But I have to figure out who did it so I can clear my name." Dean Alton needed to understand that I didn't do this. This extended beyond the letter of recommendation. He thought I hated him. That I would call him an... No. I refused to be hurt by his assumption. I could almost hear my mom's voice in my head telling me to stop dwelling and focus. Nothing existed besides Yale.

"Back to Xander." Agnes wouldn't let me dodge. "Is he going to help you or not? I know you guys aren't like...friendly anymore," she said, "but he's kind of perfect for it. He knows everyone. But wait. Are we sure he's not the one who did it?"

I threw down my bag next to locker 23 and a few freshmen jumped back in surprise. I dialed in my combination: 01-01-10. It wasn't exactly difficult.

"He wouldn't do that to me." I don't know why I was so sure Xander wasn't involved, but I was. He had as much reason to frame me as anyone. More, actually, since I'd dumped him. Especially the way I'd dumped him. It hadn't been my finest moment, but we were freshmen. I refused to relive that mess.

When my locker opened, a burnt popcorn smell invaded my nostrils. Something brown and sticky clung to the bottom of it, too.

"Ugh." I bent over to pull some tissue out of the front pocket of my backpack. I didn't have time for this!

Apparently, neither did Agnes. "See you later," she said. She turned and disappeared in less than two seconds.

4

EATING WITH THE ENEMY

I REFUSED to be alone with Xander in his car, so I texted Agnes to ask him to meet off campus. Fish would fly before I admitted I still had his number.

Thankfully, she didn't comment on it, even though I bet she secretly found me ridiculous. Instead, she shot back the name of a diner on the other side of town.

I weaved through the ever-present traffic in my recently detailed car as the sun began to sink over the lines of specialized shops and entrances to mid-level subdivisions. Driving in the vehicle my dad had purchased for me when I won student of the year calmed me enough that I entered the restaurant in a determined state of mind. If my parents knew about the graffiti, their clock was ticking faster than the dean's little deadline. I would not lose their approval over this, or anything else.

I slid into the bright red booth across from where Xander was snarfing down cheesy fries. His dress shirt looked more wrinkled than ever; the sleeves scrunched up as he bent over the table to shovel another pile of greasy food into his mouth.

"Thanks for waiting," I said dryly.

He flipped his hair back from his face. "What? It's not like this is a date. Come on, Virgin." Cheese clung to the corner of his mouth as he flashed me one of his half-smiles that made most girls go crazy. "We've been down that road, remember?"

I remembered.

"So, what's this big problem you have that only I can help you solve? Are you actually admitting there's something you can't do?" He grabbed the ketchup and smeared it on the side of his plate.

I resisted the urge to gag. He needed cheese *and* ketchup?

"I don't have time for your ego." Why did it bother guys that I was smarter than them? "I asked for your help, but if you're just going to insult me, then..." I started to scoot out of the booth.

Xander pointed his fork at me. "Have you ever asked someone for help before? Because this isn't how you do it." He shoved another greasy handful of fries into his mouth and pulled the straw of his drink toward him, slurping so loudly that the table across the aisle looked over. I did not remember him eating like this when we were dating. He had to be doing it on purpose.

I paused on the edge of my seat. I didn't have a whole lot of other options. I needed him.

"Alexander." I used his full name, hoping that would show the gravity of the situation. "You're friends with a lot of people."

He squinted at me. "And?" Of course, he wouldn't make this easy. He needed to stop leaning toward me while we talked, too. It looked intimate, the way his eyes crinkled when he spoke. His hand inched too close to mine, too. It was almost...date-like.

"And those people know other people." I leaned back against the padded seat. If I could do this myself, I would, but Xander was... Xander. He put everyone at ease. Everyone respected me, but it didn't give me the same kinds of connections.

"That is generally how it goes." He patted the corner of his mouth with a paper napkin as if that excused his lack of table manners, his mouth quirking up in an unspoken challenge.

He would *not* get to me. "I need to find out who graffitied the boys' locker room," I said through gritted teeth.

Xander played with the straw of his drink. "You need to know who the 'Asshat' artist is? Why?"

"Because the dean thinks I did it!" I whispered fiercely. The problem with meeting in a public place was that it was, well, public.

Xander let out a bark of laughter. "Seriously? Have you ever even sworn out loud before?"

"Shut up," I ground out. He had a point, though. It's not like I judged other people for swearing, but I refused to lower my own vocabulary. If I wouldn't say dirty words out loud, why would I write them?

I should have brought that up to the dean today. Maybe it would have wiped a trace of that condescending look from his face.

"Benson." He signaled the waitress with two fingers. "No one in their right mind would think you did that."

"He found the spray paint in my locker. I'm being framed!" My voice rose in a half-shriek. "He said if anything else happens..." *Stay calm.* "Xander, I could lose everything." I couldn't let anything screw me up now. Not when colleges would send out early acceptances later in the semester.

His teasing expression softened.

An elderly waitress with dimples and puffy hair sidled up to the table in old-fashioned roller skates and a poodle skirt. "I see your girlfriend has arrived," she said to Xander with a smile.

"Oh, I'm not—"

Without a flicker of hesitation, Xander slipped into a fake Prince Charming personality. "It's okay, babe. She won't tell anyone." He covered one of my hands with his. Warmth shot through my fingers even as I subtly tried to twist my wrist and pinch him.

"It's our anniversary. We've been dating for two whole weeks and she's embarrassed." He turned to the old lady, who melted under the full force of his megawatt smile.

Well, fine, if he wanted to play it that way, who was I to stop him? My *date* could pay for the food.

"And since you started without me, sweetheart," I said through gritted teeth, "it looks like I have some catching up to do."

He gestured to the menu. *How generous.*

I quickly scanned the entrees. Betty, our cook at home, called this type of food "fluffy stuff." Under my mom's hawk eyes, I wouldn't even consider touching it. "I'll have the barbeque burger and a large order of fries. Two large fries! And a side of tater tots, and the macaroni salad, and oh! I also want a strawberry milkshake. And the soup of the day, and a hot fudge sundae. The big one on the back." I pointed to the menu. *Take that, Xander!*

"Sure thing. Two spoons when that sundae comes out?" she asked without batting an eye, her pencil scratching my order into her little notepad.

"You bet!" he cut in before I had the chance to speak.

I pulled my hand away and kicked him under the table the second the waitress turned and glided back to the kitchen on her skates.

He doubled over. "Ow, Benson." The toe of his shoe tapped me back.

Oh, no he didn't. I went to kick him again, but he dodged, tapping my knee with his other foot.

I scrunched down to be able to get more reach and power behind my swing when my sweater suddenly loosened.

I sat up with a jolt, cheeks blazing hot. My hand flew to my top where a button had come undone, my elbow accidentally knocking over a saltshaker.

Xander pressed his lips together, trying not to laugh. *Someone kill me. Right now.*

"Don't you dare," I hissed at him, trying to button my sweater with one hand and block his stupid guy gaze with the other.

"Come on, Virgin. There's no way someone like you doesn't have a shirt on under that. Have a sense of humor."

I glared at him. Wearing a tank top under a sweater didn't make me a prude.

He heaved a long-suffering sigh and became fascinated with the wallpaper for a second while I fiddled with my sweater. By the time he'd turned back, I'd buttoned it all the way up to my neck.

"Seriously?"

Yeah, seriously. Call me a virgin one more time, I wanted to say. But I didn't. I couldn't. Our foot war had triggered the memory of a night I'd tried hard to forget…

His mouth on my neck, making my toes curl. His fingers tracing my collarbone, the sound of our heavy breathing lost under the hum of crickets.

His chest heaving, eyes panicked. "I'm sor—"

"And hey, thanks for the extra fries." He laughed.

I jumped, my heart hammering like I'd just run a 5K. Extra fries. God, he was so cocky. How did I ever date him? "How do you know what I will and won't eat?" It didn't matter that I hadn't eaten a whole order of fries in… Well, ever. Too many snacks like that and my mom would be all over me.

"You're so controlled. I know you." He used one finger to

swipe at some cheese left on his plate and popped it in his mouth.

I almost gagged. "I'm not even going to dignify that with a response." I straightened my spine. He would not get to me.

"You just did."

"And like, what, are you spying on my eating habits now?" I tried to sound like I didn't care. Was he seriously watching me?

"Spy on you, Virgin?" he drawled. "Now why would I do a thing like that?"

Silence settled over the booth as we stared each other down, neither one of us willing to break eye contact for fear of losing. Losing what, I didn't know, but man, he knew how to get to me. Always had.

A chill ran up my arms that had nothing to do with the temperature. Tension crackled, changing our childish game. He quit smiling and went all intense. His face inched closer to mine, but I didn't retreat.

Within seconds, we were less than a breath away from each other. I should be disgusted. How many times had I seen him in the hall, girls hanging all over him? Then there was that time near my locker when his tongue had to be halfway down the esophagus of that freshman. He was so gross.

But I couldn't look away.

It was like he could see through me. Like he could peer into the past, into everything we'd sworn to forget. That I'd sworn to forget. Another centimeter disappeared between us. His breath feathered hot on my lips.

I needed to take control of this situation before I forgot what I came here for. "I still don't know why the dean is making such a big deal out of it," I whispered. Hadn't Robbie spray painted a Smurf on each of his friends' lockers last year? He only got community service. "It's probably because he was personally attacked."

"Nah," Xander said, giving me some space.

"Nah?" My breathing eased with every inch he retreated.

"He's up for review this year, Virgin." He said it like it was the most obvious thing in the world.

"How would you know that?"

"How do you *not* know that? He's been in a bad mood the whole school year. Everything by the book. How would it look to the board if he couldn't catch the student who did it?"

I blinked. Well, that was… I couldn't even begin to… "Are you going to help me or not?" At this point, a part of me wanted him to say no.

"Tell you what," he said. "I'll help you if you eat even half of what you ordered. Loosen up, Benson. It won't kill you."

A challenge. It was so Xander. For a second, I flashed back to the way he'd been during our freshman year, the reason he'd interested me so much. He was so *fun*. Everything was a game. Being near him after living the way that I had my whole life was like walking in sunshine. In freedom.

But this wasn't freshman year. His challenge was brutal. Unkind. He knew how I felt about what I'd ordered. Now, the real question was, should I take the dare? My mom would have a fit if I didn't look like her perfect prodigy the next time she visited.

On the other hand, I'd been so good on my diet lately. Maybe I could double my run time tonight and Mom would never know. Just the thought of eating all of that rich, carby food had me salivating. Who cared if I'd probably have a stomachache later? It was the perfect way to show Xander he didn't know me as well as he thought he did. And I *was* hungry.

"Any day now, Benson," he taunted.

"Fine. But this isn't a date," I reminded him.

He finished off his fries. "Of course not." He licked his fingers like a caveman. "I wouldn't bring a date here."

I looked around at the records on the walls and the intimate seating. A bubblegum fifties tune about a rockin' robin played softly from an old-fashioned jukebox in the corner. The diner even had a soda counter, like in an old movie. Sure, the floor was a puce sort of green tile, and the pink wallpaper was peeling at the edges, but it was retro. I sort of loved it. "Why not? It's actually pretty cool."

Xander leaned back in his seat, observing me as I stole his drink, slurping on the straw. Ugh! It was like drinking fizzy sugar! I gagged and pushed it away. Arguing with him had made me thirsty; I'd forgotten how soda was the literal definition of disgusting.

He cocked his head to the side. "Who *are* you?"

"What?" Where was the waitress with my water? Had I ordered any water? Shouldn't they just bring you water? I needed this taste out of my mouth *now*.

"Nothing." He shook his head as if he was trying to get rid of a thought. "Just... Nothing." He pulled his drink back across the table. "So, let's talk about the bridges you've burned, Virgin. I can already tell you a few off the top of my head."

My mouth dropped open in shock. He couldn't have suspects already. "People don't hate me. I don't hang out with anyone but Agnes."

Our waitress rounded the corner, weighed down by a tray sporting the disaster of food I'd ordered. No water in sight. I swallowed hard as she slid the plates in front of me.

Xander leaned forward and stole a fry. I shot him a murderous glance. How could he still be hungry after that messy mountain he ate? He had to be doing it to make me mad.

"Thank you." I unrolled a napkin from around my silverware to place in my lap.

"That's part of the problem, you know," Xander said through a mouthful of food as soon as she left. "You're stuck up."

"I am *not*," I gasped.

His fingers inched toward my plate again, and I pointed my fork at him. I was not above stabbing his hand.

He retreated to his side of the table. "The tone you just said that in was the snottiest thing ever. You go around talking to people like that all the time. It's not going to be easy to figure out who's got it out for you. You've probably ticked off half the school."

"Oh my God, you're such an...an..." I didn't finish. I turned my attention back to the plate of grease that passed for food.

"Just say it. What am I? Because that's another thing. You act like you're above swearing when we all know you're thinking it anyway. What's that about?"

"It's about having some class," I said. People didn't hate me. I was the head of their student council, one of the top fencers at our school. I was academic and completely drama-free. They adored me.

Xander nodded like I'd just proved his point.

"I don't have to justify anything to you." He was obviously raised in a barn. I picked up a fry and popped it in my mouth. The taste of salt and vegetable oil exploded on my tongue in the worst, most delicious way.

"Yeah, but you're going to have to justify your actions to somebody." He leaned over to take another fry before I could impale him. "Otherwise, how are you going to figure out who wants you expelled?"

I didn't have an answer for that. The number of variables in this case compounded every second. The dean's reputation, Xander's lips close and distracting, enemies exploding from behind unknown corners.

I did the only thing I could. I grabbed the greasy burger piled high with deep fried onion rings and barbeque sauce and bit down on it, hard. Flavor flooded my mouth, making me groan in sheer bliss. Breaking the diet was downright delicious.

An hour later, I'd eaten half of the food I'd ordered, and all of that amazing strawberry shake. My stomach bulged against my waistband, and nausea swirled at the back of my throat.

"You should probably start with Jenna," Xander said. He folded his hands behind his head. "She was so mad at you last year. The whole school knew it."

"That's not possible," I said.

"And why is that?" He winked at a girl in the booth across from us. She gave him a shy smile in return.

Ugh, could he concentrate for even one second? Time to get back on track. "If the whole school knew she was mad at me, then I would've known, too." *Right?*

Xander ripped his attention from the blonde and refocused on our conversation. "There's no way you didn't know. She talked down to you every time you spoke. She still avoids you in the hall."

Maybe I'd noticed that she'd been cold to me, but I'd written it off as her having a rough time with her friends or grades. Now I was starting to rethink everything.

"Okay," I said, willing to concede that to him. "But why? I didn't do anything to her."

"I think it's more about what you took from her." Xander stared at me, willing me to remember. And okay, yes, my parents might have donated to the school last year for the new theater seats they needed, and yes, I got the lead the same year that Jenna tried out for it, but... Oh.

"She wouldn't hold a grudge like that." There was more than one lead in *Les Mis* anyway, and she'd gotten another one. Was it really that big of a deal?

Xander's eyes drifted skyward, and he muttered under his breath. "Do you ever think about anyone besides yourself? Maybe you *should* be expelled."

How *dare* he?

"We can find the people who are mad at you, but no one can make you human, Ice Queen."

"Yeah? Well, I'd rather be an ice queen than what you are," I spat back.

"And what am I, Virgin?"

I stood, bracing my hands on the table, ready to let him have it.

Xander surged to his feet, too.

I glared at him. "Please, Xander. Like the whole world doesn't know about your *sex life*." My voice lowered to a whisper.

"You can't even say the word sex!" He exploded into laughter as he sank back onto his side of the booth. I straightened my back, mad that I ate all that greasy food for nothing. I knew it had been crazy to think Xander was the right one to help me.

This was over. I was almost to the door when his hand caught my arm.

My body responded instantly, sparks and fire. Our eyes met, and for once he didn't look like he wanted to crack a joke or kill me. He swallowed once, his hand light on my skin, the heat from his fingers a brand I would never be able to shower off.

"R-Release me immediately."

His touch disappeared, and he cleared his throat. "See you tomorrow after school."

"Excuse me?" I folded my arms so he wouldn't get any more bright ideas.

"At the auditorium. Or did you really want to talk to Jenna on your own?"

He still wanted to help me?

Of all the... I didn't know how to process it, so I didn't even try. I had to focus on the reason I needed him in the first place and not get caught up in...Xander.

I couldn't look at him as I pushed through the door of the diner. Even with a wall separating us, I felt his words chisel into my heart. *No one can make you human, Ice Queen.* That was how he saw me. My fingers curled into fists as I walked to my car and slid into the driver's seat. I didn't care what Xander Hearst thought. I was innocent, and he was a means to an end. I never said I'd go, but we both knew I'd be at the auditorium, ready to accept whatever help he could give me. I had to get to the bottom of this, or...

There was no "or." I had to fix it.

When I got back to my dorm room, Agnes was lounging on the futon, waiting for me. "How'd it go? Was Xander a complete jerk?"

Maybe? I rifled through my drawers for my running clothes. I could already feel the grease flowing through my veins, slowing me down. My bed looked more enticing than ever.

"Xander was Xander. I need to think. Back in an hour." I synced my earbuds to my phone.

"Are you okay?"

I sighed, the rigid posture I'd held all day collapsing under her concern. "I don't know. He's so... And I didn't do it."

She nodded, understanding the tone of my half sentences. I was mad. Confused. Frustrated.

"So...running."

"Running," I confirmed.

"Okay. You do you. Have fun getting all...sweaty."

I rolled my eyes. We couldn't all have accepting, body positive moms.

I took up jogging my freshman year to help me with conditioning for fencing, but I stuck with it for its obvious benefits. It kept me within my mom's acceptable weight range, and it required enough concentration to keep going while still allowing me the ability to think about my problems. Kind of the perfect exercise.

As soon as my running shoes hit the pavement, the tension in my neck and shoulders slipped away. People were hard, always saying one thing and meaning another. Running wasn't like that. You got what you put in. It was constant.

I breathed in the warm, dry California air and synchronized my steps to my music. No one to compete with out here. Only me.

The sun shone down, hotter and more unforgiving than was normal for this time of year, but the sweat sliding down my back felt right, a purge of the poisonous day. I licked my salty lips and grinned as the first hill came into view. Then I skipped to a new song on my playlist so the drums could drown out Alexander stinking Hearst and everything I didn't want to do with him.

But the hill didn't treat me well. The food rolled in my stomach as I ran, each step heavier than the last. Not only that, but I couldn't help the memories that flashed through my stupid brain. Not the ones of a Xander who looked down on me and sighed every time we had to work together in group projects. The ones of the Xander who taught me how to play foosball and pool. The Xander who stood behind me and helped me figure out how to shoot a basketball. The Xander who saw *me*. Not my grades. Not my accomplishments. Not my failures. Me.

But that Xander didn't exist anymore. And neither did that silly, pathetic freshman girl who swooned every time he was near. I knew better now. And every time he called me Virgin, he cemented what a great decision it had been to dump him.

I gasped through a stitch in my side, slowing my steps. I hadn't realized I'd been sprinting. But that's what Xander did. He pushed me, made me feel too much. How was I going to work with him?

By the time I got back to campus, I was in full nausea mode. My whole body was melting, and the stitch in my side felt like a stab wound. Still, I forced myself to jog up the stairs and all the way to my door. It was worth a bad run to see the look on Xander's face when I ate that burger.

"Yuck," Agnes complained from her desk as I huffed into the room.

I gave her a limp wave as I raised my arms over my head to open my chest and make room for more air. At this rate, I'd sweat right through my shower. "Can you...hand me...water?" I puffed.

Agnes reached into the mini-fridge next to her for a bottle. When she tossed it to me, beads of sweat poured down the sides. Was it hot in here, too?

As if in response to my unspoken question, she said, "They're working on the air conditioning again."

Their timing sucked. I sprawled on the couch, still not trusting myself to speak clearly.

But did you die? That was my family's motto when it came to pushing for perfection. Of course, I didn't die, but from the ache in my lungs and the pain in my calves, I was darn close. As my breathing slowed, sweat running down my back and chest made my skin itch. I needed to stretch, but moving even one more muscle would be torture. Agnes had gone back to studying, so I forced myself to walk over to the mini-fridge and grab another bottle of water.

I passed it to her. "Don't get dehydrated." Someone had to look out for that girl, especially with the air down again. If she had her way, she'd exist on nothing but iced coffee and sugar.

She cracked her gum at me and unscrewed the lid. "Thanks, V."

At least I had one person I could count on.

5

JENNA'S VENDETTA

THE NEXT DAY passed in a nervous blur, and I barely registered anything my teachers said. Oh, I took perfect notes, of course, but the information went in one ear and got stuck somewhere in the back of my mind while more important questions swirled around. Would Xander actually show up tonight to help me? I had no idea what to say to Jenna about last year. Why did I have to say anything? I was the one who got the part, and I did everything I was supposed to. How embarrassing was this going to be? Probably very.

At lunch, Agnes pounced on me. "What's wrong with you? You've been like a zombie all day."

I stabbed my plastic fork into my salad, and it wedged into the Styrofoam.

Agnes took a swig of her Diet Coke. "I'm getting kind of worried about you, V."

I pulled the fork out and laid it down next to my tray. "I'm okay. Just having a weird day." Acting normal was easier than trying to describe how I felt about Jenna and Xander and just… everything.

She squinted at me. "Fine, don't tell me. Just be careful with Xander, okay?"

I followed her gaze to where he was laughing so hard his chair shook. "Why? What did you hear?" I whispered, even though he couldn't hear us talking about him from across the cafeteria.

"Just..." She stared at me. "I remember what freshman year did to you. You know?"

I sat back in my seat.

"Xander is a weak spot for you, and he's different now. He gets with everyone. Just don't get played, okay?"

"He's not a weak spot. And I know what he's like." I laughed, but it sounded off. Fake. There would always be something between us, something unfinished, but that didn't mean we had to act on it.

"Uh huh." Agnes turned back to her food.

What was that supposed to mean?

As soon as classes ended, I realized I hadn't finished a paper for History. It was due tomorrow. I wanted to blame Xander and the dean for distracting me, but I knew it was my responsibility to do my work. My fault.

I dashed back to my dorm and set up shop at my computer. From there, it was as it always was when it came to homework: difficult.

Agnes called me the Color-Coding Queen when we were freshmen, and it still held true. She laughed about it, but different colors made sense to me. It sorted the information, and I'd never been great at chunks of text. Hours and hours of study had gotten me this far. Once I understood the material, the words could flow. But this paper? It wouldn't. It came to me in bursts and jerks until I was ready to rip my hair out. Well, not really. My hair was the one thing that made me beautiful. I'd never sacrifice that. But still, my brain cells were practically dead.

Agnes breezed through the door. I waved absently at her, chewing on the end of my green highlighter. The cursor blinked at me, taunting me from the mostly blank doc. What would my mom think of this paper? *Trash.*

But it was *trash* that was due tomorrow.

"You okay?"

"What?" I turned to her. "Did you say something?"

"I asked if you need help. You're going to get a mouthful of neon green."

I yanked the highlighter from my mouth and saw she was right. It was ten seconds away from exploding all over me.

"I've got it," I said. I didn't have it. But another hour made a difference, and when I shut my laptop, I knew I'd be okay. I smoothed the massive, perfectly centered Yale sticker on the cover of my computer. Then I checked my phone and groaned at the time.

Five minutes later, I made my way down to the auditorium in the main building of campus. I imagined a dirge playing in time with my steps, like walking to a funeral.

Xander leaned against the outside of the building. His dark hair fell over one eye. The sleeves of his shirt were rolled up like he'd never heard the word *crease* before. Why did he bother wearing long-sleeved shirts if he didn't plan to take care of them?

I ignored the way he smirked when he saw the plaid skirt and white blouse I'd been wearing all day. What? I didn't need to change for him.

"I haven't even done anything with the drama club since last year," I complained as we pushed through the auditorium door. "Are you sure Jenna's still mad at me?"

At the center of the stage, students swarmed around a set

wall that the art department had constructed for the new *Guys 'n Dolls* production next month. At the far end, Jenna slapped a gray base coat of paint on the thin plywood. I always thought set construction was the worst part of drama, but she seemed content as she moved the brush over the rough wood. Other kids gathered props, and Mr. Darryn spat out orders from the loft above the stage where students came and went, wearing varying degrees of costume accessories.

It impressed me how our school could put on so many productions every year. I found it impossible to memorize all the lines in a few weeks, let alone flip the set that fast. I'd learned that the hard way last year.

"Hey, Jenna," Xander called over the music the AV guys filtered through the stage speakers.

Jenna turned, a smile stretching across her face, exposing her large white teeth. She had the perfect face for drama. All her features were exaggerated: wide brown eyes, broad mouth, hair for days. When she saw me, her expression visibly cooled.

"Xander," she acknowledged and turned back to the wall she was painting. *Ouch.*

He raised a judgy eyebrow as I trudged toward the stage. Okay, fine, she wasn't over it.

He flopped into a seat a few rows back, watching my walk of shame. This was how he planned to support me? How Xander.

The stairs leading up to the stage had been moved for some reason I assumed had to do with the production, so I braced my palms on the stage to jump up, but I could already tell it would be the wrong angle. Because of my stubby little legs, I couldn't get the leverage I needed and keep my skirt down. A snort came from behind me as I wiggled, scrambling for a better hold.

"You could help me!" I hissed through gritted teeth when I fell back to the floor.

He flipped his hair off his forehead. "And ruin the view?" he shot back.

What a pig. When I turned to the stage and tried to climb it again, I started with a small jump and managed to get a good hold. God only knew how much of my butt I flashed, but I made quick work of it this time and rolled myself onto the stage. Jenna didn't look directly at me, but the corners of her mouth lifted slightly.

Trying to salvage whatever dignity I had left, I scrambled to my feet and walked over to her. "So, how's set construction going?" I asked. Like stopping by and making a fool of myself was a regular thing.

Jenna didn't answer or even pause while painting. Awkward.

I shifted my weight from one foot to the other as the silence stretched. What was I supposed to do now?

Xander cleared his throat loudly from his seat. I glared at him and raised my hands in a *Help me* gesture toward Jenna. He pointed at her. He had his feet propped on the seat ahead of him, looking as relaxed here as he was in sports and in class. It was insanely annoying.

"Um. So, about last year…"

She stopped painting, turned toward me, and dropped her brush into the can on the ground. The paint splashed up over my shoes and onto the tarp covering the stage.

I looked down in horror, then back at her. My hands clenched into fists. "I guess I deserved that," I muttered.

"You guess." She folded her arms as she faced me. "Why are you here, Virginia?"

The lights above us radiated heat as I wiped my sweaty palms on my skirt. "To say I'm sorry." I pretended to check out the other pieces of the set instead of freaking out that my shoes were probably ruined forever.

"What was that?" she asked, her stage voice echoing across the auditorium. A few crew members stopped what they were doing in the wings and turned toward us.

I ignored them and faced Jenna head-on. The sooner I did

this, the sooner I could leave. I had what I wanted to say memorized, so I needed to get it out, even though it wasn't that big of a deal. "I'm sorry for what happened last year. I really wanted the lead role, and I didn't think—"

"No, you didn't think. All you thought about was you. You didn't stop to consider that other people actually cared about the production. About this club." Her hands flew as she spoke, like she could physically push her anger at me.

I cringed. Eponine was the best female part of *Les Misérables* even though Cosette got more singing time. I'd been type-cast last year because I looked like the girl from the movie version Mr. Darryn was obsessed with. I don't know how that was my fault, though. And she'd been perfect as Cosette, so really, it had been a win-win situation.

"Did you step up and help your understudy? Or work on the set? You didn't even show up to sound check before the lights went down on opening night. You think you're so far above us —" She cut herself off and wiped her forehead with her sleeve, leaving behind a streak of paint. "You know what? I'm not doing this. Just steer clear of this club and me, and everything will be fine." She picked up her paintbrush and got back to work. It was a clear and painful dismissal.

My face burned as I started to slink away. Of course I didn't help with all the other stuff. No one told me that I had to, and I had trouble enough memorizing lines. Mr. Darryn showed me the sign-up sheet, but he made it sound like it was volunteer work, so I didn't sign up. Did everyone else? Maybe Jenna was right. I didn't belong here.

Before I could escape, Xander's lanky frame vaulted over the side of the stage in one smooth movement. I guess if you were over six feet tall, it was easy to hop up on stages. He pushed me back toward Jenna with gentle hands.

"Make it right," he whispered. "We need her!" He wasn't wrong. If I worked alongside Jenna, helping her out, maybe I could talk to her friends and find out if she was the one who framed me. It wasn't such a far leap from stage paint to spray paint. I needed to stay focused.

"I...um. What can I do?" I asked her. "To make it up to you?" My words came out garbled, halting. *Yale*, I reminded myself. *Yale is worth any embarrassment.*

She opened her mouth, but desperation made me beat her to it.

"I don't want to ruin your play or get a part, or even be on the crew and screw up the energy you've got going on here, but..." I crouched down on the stage and dunked my hand into the bucket of paint, fishing out the saturated brush. Nasty grey goop slid down my fingers, but I didn't flinch. I wanted to make a point here. "Can I help you with the set now? I really am sorry, Jenna. I want to make it right."

She braced one hand against an unpainted section of the wall. "Fine. We're in a time crunch and could use two extra sets of hands. You can finish the base coat of this wall, and Xander, you can follow me."

Xander shuffled back a step. He obviously didn't expect to get roped in too. He gifted her with a flash of his perfect, straight teeth. "Oh, I'm just here to—"

"To gawk at an embarrassing situation that you're only making worse. You have time to waste, or you wouldn't be here, and there's a lot of construction that still needs to happen. Let's go." Jenna whirled around and walked away, expecting Xander to follow.

I stifled a giggle as he stood frozen, a puzzled expression on his face. Someone besides me who wasn't affected by his charm? The horror!

He did as he was told, trailing behind Jenna like a puppy. As if he could sense my amusement, he scowled at me before they headed backstage.

I had bigger things to worry about than Xander. Mainly,

Jenna's sheer level of investment in the production. Was it enough for her to try and get me kicked out of school? Now that I had a chance to think about it, the graffiti had appeared the week of auditions. Was she scared I would take another lead part from her?

Guilt gnawed at me as I tried to smooth the grey paint over the wood. What if I really did screw her over last year?

By the time set construction was over for the day, I felt a small sense of accomplishment. I finished the base coat of the wall and painted red bricks in different shades of red to give it an old-school vibe. Once that was done, I moved on to about a million signs that had to be created to shout things like GIRLS, GIRLS, GIRLS and EAT AT JOE'S to give it a street feel. Well, a theater street feel, anyway. I had just finished outlining the music notes on a jazz sign when Xander appeared.

He squatted down next to me. "You know everyone's gone, right?"

I looked around. He was right. The auditorium was empty, and the music I'd been humming to was no longer playing. The only one left besides us was Mr. Darryn, who muttered to himself as he locked up the control booth.

"Guess I got caught up." I smiled as I tapped the top of a paint can back on with a hammer and left the sign I'd been working on to dry on a tarp. When I came back from washing the paintbrushes, Xander sat on the stage, swinging his legs back and forth. Was he waiting for me?

His mouth tilted into a half-smile. "You have paint all over you." He pointed to my head. "It's even in your hair."

Oh, God. My hair! But when I glanced at Xander, his eyebrows were raised, waiting for me to make a big deal out of it. So instead of complaining, I struck a modeling pose. "And don't I make it look fabulous?" It was only Xander, after all.

He frowned, then looked down. Guess not.

"It's that bad?" I dropped my stance to look down at myself. The grey paint on my shoes from when Jenna had splashed me hadn't disappeared. And now red and gold decorated my hands, and even a black streak marred my skirt. Would it wash off? I sighed. Probably not. Was that why he was being weird?

"Come on, Picasso." His eyes crinkled at the edges. "Let's go get some food. I'm starving."

I couldn't make my feet move to follow him. I was hungry, too, and the dorm cafeteria would be closed by now. But I'd skipped meals before. My chest tightened with anticipation. Being alone with Xander was not a good idea.

He walked halfway down the aisle of the auditorium before he realized I wasn't behind him. He sighed dramatically.

"What?" I folded my arms.

"You know what."

I stared at the ceiling.

"Don't make it weird. It's not a date, Virgin."

Great. Now if I didn't go, he'd win. I had no choice.

I followed him out of the auditorium to his car. Most of the paint on me had dried, but I hoped I didn't ruin his upholstery.

He turned the music up on a top 40 station and started singing off-key to the lyrics of the cheesiest song on the air as he pulled into traffic. Then he cut off suddenly. "Oh, man." His hands pushed aside his seatbelt as he checked his pockets while we drove. The steering wheel swiveled.

I lurched forward and grabbed it with one hand. "What?" He'd kill us both if he kept it up.

"My wallet. Detour, Benson. I must've left it at home." He settled back into his seat and flipped his signal to turn left.

I let go of the wheel, but my heart picked up speed. What if we ran into his parents and I looked like this? The thought of being seen by any authority figures without my shirt perfectly pressed and spotless made my skin prickle. I knew what *my* parents would say if they saw me like this.

I dug into my pocket. "I've got it." I had a preloaded card with more than enough money for whatever he wanted to eat.

"Don't be ridiculous. You know I live local. It'll take five minutes."

I swallowed. Maybe he'd leave me in the car.

We pulled into a circular driveway of a beautiful white house with a man-made pond beside it. The drought this year had turned most grass brown, but the lawn here was an immaculate emerald green, neatly cut and watered. Greco-Roman columns held up a sweeping front porch, and a wall of windows faced us, twinkling in the last rays of the setting sun. It wasn't weird that Xander's parents were in the same tax bracket as mine. You had to be kind of rich to go to our school. Even scholarship kids had a bit of money. But with money came expectations.

When I didn't get out of the car, Xander came to the passenger side and opened it for me. "You'll die in this heat. Come on."

I could have told him that if he left me with the keys I'd be fine, but now I wondered why I'd even gotten in his car in the first place. We weren't dating. We weren't even friends... Were we? Why did we need to eat together? He was right—even at this late hour, the temperatures hadn't dropped. My hands squeezed into fists as I climbed out of the passenger's seat and followed him to his door. Ten seconds around Xander and I'd fallen into his trap. It had been three years, and I still hadn't learned how to control myself.

He punched in the code next to the front door and swung it open, exposing a large foyer accented in a pale marble. Simple paintings hung on the walls, but I knew how much they were worth. Old money. My mom could replicate this type of casual wealth in our house, but it would never have the same presence as a long-standing family home of money.

"Wait here for a minute," he said and jogged up the stairs, probably to grab his wallet from his room. *Good.* Being alone with Xander in his room might be a dangerous move. Even though, to be honest, I was a little curious about it. We hadn't dated long enough freshman year for me to have visited his house. I imagined clothes and books and sporting equipment scattered all over the floor. That would be very Xander.

I shifted my weight from foot to foot. Why was I even thinking about Xander's bedroom? How long did it take to grab a wallet? That's when I heard the music. A popular radio station was playing, maybe the same one we listened to in the car. I recognized one of the songs from my playlist echoing down the hallway to my left.

I weighed my options, and then figured that bumping into someone intimidating, like one of Xander's parents, was more likely if I stayed near the front door when they got home from work. He could come get me when he found his wallet.

As I made my way through the winding hallway, the music pulsed louder. I pushed open a door on the right to find a middle-aged woman in a black apron dancing while preparing a meal in the kitchen. Flour covered the granite counters and coated the floors. She even had a little in her greying hair. The room was a complete mess, but it smelled amazing. Like cinnamon and beef stew mixed together.

A comfortable ease settled over me, and I bobbed my head to the music. Our cook at home baked like this: ingredients everywhere, music turned up. How many afternoons had I snuck downstairs to peek through the crack in the door as Betty bustled around?

When the lady in Xander's kitchen turned my way, I flinched. I shouldn't be here. This wasn't my house. My mom told me over and over it was inappropriate to interrupt others while they worked. I peeled my feet off the floor to back away, but the woman gestured to a stool at the breakfast bar, her kind grey eyes sparkling with amusement. I hesitated a moment, but then slid onto the seat before I could feel too weird about it. A bowl of berries sat on the counter in front of me, and when she turned around, I popped one in my mouth.

The chorus of the song swelled, and I mouthed the words as she belted it out, laughing. When it was over, she turned down the volume.

"I'm Peg," she said to me. "I'd shake your hand, but…" She shrugged and showed me her dough-covered fingers as she worked on what looked like a loaf of bread. "Are you a friend of Alexander's?"

For some reason I didn't feel the need to lie to this woman. I picked up another berry, studying it. "Not really."

"Well, I'm happy to meet a new girlfriend," she said in a light tone, a curious gleam in her eyes. Oh God, she thought I was one of his groupies from school.

"We're not…" My hand curled into a fist on the counter, but I relaxed my fingers when I realized I was squishing my fruit. "We're not…that."

"Interesting." Her mouth lifted into a half-smile as she watched my reaction.

"He doesn't think so." I popped the mutilated berry in my mouth. As soon as I said it, I wished I could take it back. Now I sounded like I wanted him to be my boyfriend, and that wasn't what was happening here at all. "He's helping me with something," I offered grudgingly, picking at a fleck of white paint on my knuckle.

She laughed. "I like you…" She placed a glass of milk in front of me and paused, waiting for my name.

I picked it up and took a small, polite sip. "Virginia."

"Not freshman-year Virginia?"

Apparently, I was famous. I winced at what Xander must've

said about me after our abrupt breakup. The help always heard everything. Time to play it off. I raised my glass in a toast to her. "The same."

"*Very* interesting." She pulled cling wrap from a drawer to cover the dish that held the bread dough. I raised the glass of milk to my lips again to take another sip.

"What's interesting?" Xander's voice took me by surprise, and I choked on the milk.

Peg wiped her hands on her apron. "Just meeting Virginia."

"Uh huh. Sure."

She shrugged, her expression innocent.

"Let's go, Benson." Xander grabbed my sleeve and pulled me off the stool. "Bye, Mom."

6

THE NILE PILE

THE COOK WAS HIS MOM? And I'd just... *Oh my God*. I never would have talked to her so casually. They didn't keep a staff? Their house was enormous! Drifting along in Xander's wake, I wallowed in silent shame all the way to the car.

I opened my mouth half a dozen times as he threw the car into gear and started driving, but I didn't know what to say. My fingers twisted together. Now that I thought about it, it made perfect sense that she was his mom. They had the same mischievous gleam in their eyes, the same wavy brown hair. I was an idiot.

When he stopped at a red light and glanced over at me, I pulled my hands apart. He frowned, looking at my hands, then back at me.

I licked my lips and stared straight ahead. Darned dry heat.

When he shifted in his seat, the car seemed to suddenly condense. His tan hand gripped the gearshift only a few inches from my thigh, the space between us somehow less than before.

The light changed.

"It's green," I practically yelled. We needed to get to wherever it was we were going.

He faced the road again and pressed the gas pedal.

I pulled my hair over my shoulder, a thick wall between me and his intense, knowing eyes. It didn't help. Even when he wasn't staring at me, it was still like he was noticing every little thing. That was one of the reasons I'd started dating him. He'd always seen me. The good, the bad, everything. And he'd accepted it. Liked it, even. But now that we weren't dating anymore, I didn't know what to do with it. I wanted to know what he was thinking, but at the same time, I really, really didn't. So we sat in a silence filled with all the words we couldn't say as he weaved between traffic with strong, capable hands.

When he stopped the car, I craned my neck to peer through the windshield. A giant cut-out of the King Tut of Putt-Putt loomed over us. His skin was orange, and he held up a neon pink putter in victory. The paint was peeling around his fingers and face, making his smile look both creepy and sad at the same time as he advertised a two-for-one deal on mini-golf. The real King Tut was probably rolling over in his grave. I'd never seen anything so tacky in my entire life.

"This isn't a food place," I said as we got out of the car.

"You're kidding." He shut his door. "You've never had the Great Pyramid of Pizza?"

I shook my head as we walked toward what could only be described as a shack.

"Not even a Scroll Roll?" he asked with disbelief.

I burst out laughing.

He didn't. Was he serious? "How have you lived here for as long as you have and not tried the Nile Pile?"

Well, that sounded disgusting. Still, I had to know. "What's a Nile Pile?"

"It's nachos. But like, *nachos*, you know? Good God, we have to get the works. This is ridiculous." He led me through the doors to one of only three booths. Then he made his way back to the front to speak with the cashier, who of course fell all over herself to get him anything he wanted.

He flipped his hair as he talked to her, bracing his hand on the beat-up counter. She leaned in and whispered something in his ear, the neckline of her tank top sliding down an inch. His easygoing laugh at whatever she said echoed in the small area.

I read the laminated menu in front of me before their flirting killed my appetite. How many ways could a person fry a potato? There was nothing here I should eat, at least according to my mom. Still, the sheer amount of alliteration was enough to make me want to order *something*.

Seconds later, Xander slid in across from me. I raised my eyebrows.

"What?"

He knew what. I had half a mind to tell him exactly how he looked, flirting with that girl while I sat here waiting for him in a booth, but... But I shouldn't be bothered by it. We weren't dating. It wasn't my business who he flirted with. I swallowed the lump in my throat. "Are you a fan of greasy food or something? How do you eat all that and still look..." I broke off, my face warming.

"Still look what? Decidedly dashing? Horrifyingly handsome? Babeliciously buff?" He flexed an arm and arched an eyebrow.

The sight of his muscles straining against his T-shirt matched perfectly with the huge sign over the door declaring that the Nefertiti Niblets were half price. I laughed. "You hang out here too often."

"And you don't hang out at all," he fired back.

Which is how I ended up eating half of the greasy chips from a pile of nachos that allegedly hailed from the Nile and playing putt-putt. The decorations were clapboard and tacky, but I got to choose a purple golf ball—my favorite color. My stomach was full in the best possible way, and when Xander bent over the first shot of every hole, his eyebrows pulled together in concentration, it was hard to contain my smile. It was like he was convinced there were professional putt-putters or something. It had been a long time since I'd seen *this* Xander, his brow furrowed, his tongue touching the corner of his mouth as he concentrated. It was weird to think he might still have a real side to him still, something behind that lazy, flirtatious exterior.

Involuntarily, I remembered the day Xander had asked me out freshman year. We'd been chatting a while, texting at night and talking between classes. Still, I was taken aback at how direct he was.

"Go out with me, Virginia. Please? I want you to be my girlfriend."

At the time, such straightforwardness was a relief to me in a school where I always had to try to figure out what was going on. Home tutors didn't prepare me for friends or teachers, or, well, anything but facts and numbers. Xander's earnest, direct speech was one of the reasons I liked him so much. I never had to guess where I stood. Not like now.

We wandered along by the sun-bleached signs of the mini-golf course, both of us lost in thought and the deepening shadows that crept in past dusk. My score was... Okay, it was crazy high, and it didn't improve as the game continued. Xander kept his sarcastic comments to himself, but from the set of his shoulders and the way he kept turning his back to me every time I made a shot, I could tell it was killing him.

"What?" I said at one point.

"Nothing. You're golden." He met my eyes and grinned.

My stomach tightened. I swallowed. To have his full attention was to be the only girl in the world at that moment. A flirty, fun Xander? There was nothing more distracting, and he knew it.

When my ball bounced into the Sahara Desert sand trap for the second time on hole twelve, I hacked at the stupid thing. It flew out, smacked into Cleopatra's face, and rolled back to the black starting mat. Seriously?

Xander snorted. My head whipped up, but he was the picture of innocence as the lights above us snapped on to illuminate the course.

I scowled. When we got to hole fourteen, I hit the ball so hard it bounced off the fake hieroglyphics under the cat sign and into the grass.

Xander finally broke. He bent over, bracing his hands on his knees as he exploded with laughter. I ground my teeth together.

"It's not possible to be this bad at putt-putt," he wheezed, wiping tears from under his eyes.

"Shut up," I said as I picked up my ball and plunked it a little too hard back on the worn green carpet. "I've got this."

"Want me to teach you how to do it?" he asked, wiggling his eyebrows.

"Like that's ever going to happen."

"Only in my dreams," he sing-songed as he abandoned his position at the beginning of the next hole and walked toward me.

"Like you want me," I shot back, only half-joking. "Why don't you go ask the basically naked cashier? Seems more your type."

"Oh really?" Xander ran a hand through his hair, gracing me with one of his filthier smirks.

I ignored the way my stomach tightened and looked away.

"And what is my type, Benson?" he said in a silky smooth voice.

I huffed. His shadow blocked my aim. "You know."

"I don't. I think you're jealous."

I made an exasperated noise, unsure if it was for Xander or for me. I shouldn't have said anything. He filled me up with chips and jokes, and my filter malfunctioned. I lined up the little tick on the putter with the center of the ball. "You're not supposed to step on the green."

"That's not a rule, sweetheart, or the ball would never make it in the hole."

"Don't call me sweetheart." He could save his little pet names for the girls at school who dangled from his arms.

He held up his hands in mock surrender, his smile unreadable.

I huffed. Like I wanted to read his facial expressions anyway. He was just trying to throw me off my game. I wiggled into a better form, trying to line up my shot, but I couldn't concentrate. I didn't want Xander to think he had the upper hand, that he knew me better than I knew myself. I didn't want him to think I was pining for him like a pathetic little dweeb for the past three years. I broke up with *him*. He didn't have the first clue what I was feeling, and I...

I shook my head like I could physically dismiss everything between us. Then I took my shot. Miracle of all miracles, the ball went in the hole. For a moment, I stood there frozen with shock, but it didn't last long.

"Victory!" I jumped and danced around him. "Yeah! Eat my dust, Xander!"

He raised his hands in surrender again, his face stretching into a wide smile. Then he took his stance in front of his ball, using more time to line up his shot than he normally did. He got it in the hole in two hits, which was twice the number I'd needed. Never mind that I was putting six on every other hole.

"Hole in one! Hole in one!" I crowed at him like a child while he placed his ball on the next starting mat.

He didn't tell me to shut up or stop acting like a kid. He grinned bigger and more genuinely than he had the whole time we'd hung out and took a terrible shot.

When it was my turn, his big feet stepped in the way of my ball. I looked up at where he stood, so very close to me now. A light breeze pushed against his wavy hair and his eyes had darkened with something at once familiar and dangerous. My breath caught in my throat and my grin dissolved as he reached for me, his intent clear. He was going to kiss me. It had been so long since he kissed me.

"Virgin," he whispered, placing his hand around mine where I grasped the club.

And with that one little word, the moment was gone. I was the virgin.

I shook him off. "In your dreams, remember?" My words came out only a little weaker than they should have. "I'm getting bored. We should call it."

Xander stepped back, a small frown of concern pulling down the sides of his mouth. But he recovered quickly. "We're so close to finishing, though. Don't worry, I'll beat you quickly."

"Sure. Fine." Far be it from me to not see it through.

"Okay." His voice became teasing again as he bent over in a one-armed bow. "Lead on, Putt-Putt Princess."

Xander could always lighten a mood. It was one of his gifts. I just couldn't enjoy the activity as much as I had before. Now, every scrape of my putter against the fake green turf was grating, every shot I missed somehow laced with double meaning. Inexperienced. Innocent. Virginal. For all Xander's teasing, he was probably actually thinking about how stuck up and pure I was. Did he remember our first kiss and think *God, that girl could use some practice?* I couldn't find it in me to believe anything else.

We putted our way to the end quickly, and Xander was as good as his word. He owned me in this sad excuse for a game. Again and again, he tried to tease me back into the comfortable conversation we'd enjoyed earlier, but I couldn't. Not anymore.

I sighed and picked at a bit of red paint wedged under one of my nails. When we started this game, the gray of dusk was just giving way to night. Now, the stars glimmered in the black sky.

Under any other circumstances, I would think it was romantic. Instead, Xander's "Virgin" comment and the fact that I had forgotten it was a weeknight made panic well within me. He would *not* make me miss curfew.

On the last hole, he sank his ball in one putt, winning the game. Like it was even close. Then sarcastic Xander returned, smiling that self-important half-smile.

"But I was still good at one of them," I felt compelled to say as he marked our strokes on the little scorecard. He didn't win *everything*.

His mouth twitched. "Sure," he said. "You rocked it, Virgin."

Yeah, he could take me home right now.

We returned our clubs in silence and headed to the car twenty minutes before curfew. I'd make it back to the dorms before I got in trouble.

As Xander started the ignition, he glanced at me. "I'm sorry."

I stared straight out at the mostly empty parking lot. "Why?"

"I know you're stressed. I'll help you find the graffiti guy. Promise."

I closed my eyes against his earnest voice, the one that had made freshman me believe I was beautiful, smart, funny, seen. He couldn't be the Xander who called me Virgin and Xander the Putt Putt King at the same time. I didn't know how to make those two people coexist.

"Thanks," I said. And left it at that.

The next morning, I found myself humming as I got dressed. Instead of putting my hair back into my normal tight ponytail or straightening it, I let it go free, pulling my hands through the natural waves. Of course, my hair cooperated. We had a good relationship.

Agnes smiled as we grabbed our bags on our way out the

door. "Do tell." Her tone dropped to the same level it always did when we gossiped. "Is it a Xander thing?"

"No. I dumped *him*, remember?" The caffeine in my cup from our forbidden coffeemaker hadn't kicked in yet, so I was still a little snappy.

"Yes, but why was that again? Something about your parents? They never come here, and you only go home for Christmas, so why would they care?" She blew on her own coffee.

"They care." I didn't take it personally; this was classic Agnes. I turned away from her to hop in the breakfast line. Sometimes living together made it easy to forget how different our families were, but Agnes and I had something deeper in common.

She'd earned a scholarship and had to maintain a certain GPA, but no one expected her to understand or play the games that members of families from old money did. My dad was from a respectable family, but they'd disowned him for eloping with my mom. It was the first and last spontaneous thing he'd ever done, throwing over the match his parents had made for him for a scholarship girl with a will of steel. My grandparents' anger had fueled my parents' ambition to the point where they were now richer than their parents had ever been.

Because of that, Agnes and I understood each other. She would never fit in. And my family could no longer belong. It didn't matter that we were sent to an academy where everyone was supposed to feed right into an Ivy League school. We were outsiders with reputations to create and protect. The loyalty we found in each other that year and the years since—it couldn't be bought. Agnes had even backed me when I broke up with Xander, though she didn't understand my decision.

Most of my classes were silent and studious that morning. We were coming up on big projects and papers, so the teachers gave us time to work. Unfortunately, it was mindless enough that it also gave me too much time to think about Agnes, and

Xander, and the graffiti. My English teacher had to repeat my name three times before I heard her. Of course, I'd done the reading, so I could easily answer her question, but that was beside the point.

It was Xander's fault. Being near him again was easy. Too easy. He was definitely a distraction. Yale required every bit of studying and dedication I had in me. I couldn't jeopardize a future my parents had worked so hard to make possible for me. Even if last night was the most fun I'd had in a long time before his Virgin comment, I needed to focus. No more Egyptian-themed food or fake golf. Xander and me and whatever was or wasn't between us anymore didn't matter. I had to clear my name in case someone woke up paint-happy again. If it was Jenna, then great. Case solved. If it wasn't her... I didn't want to think about it not being Jenna.

When I got to lunch, I was fully prepared to let Agnes in on all the ridiculousness of the past day. But as I slid into the seat in front of her, that plan dissolved. She stabbed at her chicken like she was trying to kill it again and glared up at me. What did *I* do?

Thankfully, with Agnes, I never had to ask. I just had to wait.

"I thought we were done with the drama club thing," she accused after about three seconds. "Why didn't you ask me to go, too?" She folded her napkin into a deliberate triangle and used it to wipe the corner of her mouth, which wasn't even dirty.

I sighed. Someone must've told her about my cameo appearance at set construction last night while we were separated in the food line.

"It's a thing for the graffiti case," I said. "You can help if you want to, but I didn't think you'd like it."

She picked at her Styrofoam plate. "Trina told me she saw you and Xander sharing nachos together last night too. I thought you didn't eat that kind of stuff."

"I don't. He basically dragged me there." The words tasted wrong coming out, but I had to fix this with Agnes. She had to understand. "It's...you know, Xander."

"Whatever." She didn't look up at me.

Was she really upset? Honestly, it never crossed my mind to ask her to help with something for theater. She hated getting her hands dirty.

"Like I want to get paint all over me, anyway," she confirmed. Her attention shifted to the top of my head, and I panicked a little, wondering if I still had paint in my hair.

"So why are we having this conversation, then?" I popped a forkful of salad into my mouth.

"We're not." Agnes left to get rid of her trash, swinging her curly hair behind her. She didn't even finish her lunch, so I must have ticked her off. When she didn't return to the table, I looked down at what was left of my salad. Whatever her problem was, I didn't have time for it right now. She'd have to tell me or back off. I had bigger things to worry about.

Classes passed in a blur. I went directly to each of them because I needed the extra time to study for the English test tomorrow, not because I was avoiding Agnes or anything. Before I knew it, the last bell rang, and I had to rush off for fencing practice.

"It wouldn't kill any of you to have a little strip practice," our instructor informed us as we filed into the gym. "So, we'll pair up some of our veteran fencers with our freshmen to mentor them on the basics. Don't forget to teach the salutation rules," he added. "No dueling just yet. Let's get the process down first."

I swallowed a groan. The first practice always involved teaching the newbies the basics. How did I forget that? It was necessary, but with all that had happened lately, I was itching to strike at someone, do something physical.

I glanced over to where Xander was helping a freshman girl with her grip. His forehead wrinkled with concentration, oblivious to how the girl was totally spaced out, like a doe in sexy Xander headlights. And yeah, I guess when I looked at him through that lens in his white jacket, his dark hair brushed and slicked back, he was handsome.

He smiled, and she almost swooned into his arms.

God, I was so glad I was above that kind of crap now. His boyish charm and squared jaw might have tempted me when we were freshman, but now I knew what a player he was.

His eyes flicked toward me.

I quickly shifted my gaze to the mat, my heart pounding a mile a minute. I chose that moment to inspect the corner of the room where freshmen still waited for an upperclassman to help them. A petite girl with a bob haircut stood off to the side, studying her shoes. A feather could have knocked her over, let alone a foil. Her shoulders hunched as student after student in front of her was chosen to pair up. She scooted toward the blank gray wall of the gym until her back was up against it.

Something in me wrenched a little, and I remembered how tall the seniors had appeared to me as a freshman, how intimidating. I covered the ground between us in record time and pulled her onto a practice mat, jumping into showing her the basics. Her name was Amy, and she was a quick study. We were able to run through a bunch of moves before the end of practice.

As we were leaving the gym, she fell into step beside me. "Thanks," she whispered.

I had to crane my neck to hear her. Talk about shy. Maybe fencing would help her with that.

"No problem. You're doing great." I'd thought it would be a chore to help someone with the basics, but the look on Amy's face as confidence found its way into her steps wasn't something I'd anticipated. Helping her was oddly energizing. We were in off-season now, but later, we'd duel against other schools. The rush of winning one of those competitions was intense. If I could help her get to that point...

She beamed and bounced off to the locker room, a drastic change from the girl afraid to look at anyone an hour ago. Good for her. Maybe she could build her confidence up and bring it to the mat when the matches started.

As I hauled my gear back to the storage room, Xander passed by me, having already shelved his stuff. "Set design in ten?" he called over his shoulder. I hadn't expected him to remember or help again.

I licked my lips. "I'll be there."

He nodded and went to change.

Exactly nine and a half minutes later, I skidded into the auditorium, my hair only half dry from my shower.

He showed up on time. I didn't know what to make of the fact that he hadn't flaked on me yet. It's not like he had ever done that to me freshman year, but...

I focused on the instructions Jenna was giving us, trying not to be distracted by Xander's equally damp hair, the way it was drying messier than it had looked this morning. That meant he did, in fact, brush it. I wasn't supposed to notice stuff like that. I wasn't supposed to watch the way his back flexed as we finished smoothing paint over the last set piece, or how his eyes lit up when someone talked to him. I hated how much I cared that my stilted, borderline rude comments made his face scrunch in concern. I shouldn't care when he kept calling me Virgin. It was an unending torture. Even when we wrapped up the painting, we were assigned to clean-up duty together.

An uncomfortable silence padded the air between us as we gathered the paintbrushes. The crew left to meet in the dance studio for a meeting. The cast members had things to memorize, I guess.

That's how Xander and I ended up by ourselves at the dinkiest sink known to man in the backstage closet.

"Your big, pointy arms are in my space!" I complained when he edged me out of the way yet again.

"I can't help it if your paintbrush-washing skills are inferior to my manly muscles," Xander retorted.

I flicked water at him. "What do muscles have to do with paintbrush cleaning?"

"What do tiny little chicken arms have to do with it?" He splashed my arm with dirty paintbrush water. "You've been in a mood all day."

"You did not just call my arms chickeny. Chickens don't even have arms!"

Xander's shoulders shook with laughter, and I used his weak moment to nudge him aside again. This was ridiculous. Acting like human pretzels in this dingy closet wouldn't help me get the kind of spy time I needed to find out if Jenna was the spray-paint culprit.

"Can we focus on why we're here in the first place, please? We should sneak into the wings to see if they talk about the graffiti." I shoved his hands over in the sink.

"They'd see us, Benson. They're literally right there."

Right. Duh. "Well, I don't see you coming up with any great ideas to find the graffitier." I turned to grab another paintbrush from the small mountain we had to clean.

His dark eyes assessed me. He nodded, seeming to decide something. "Come with me." He pulled on the sleeve of my shirt, and I smacked him. He was leaving water stains all over me, and some of us actually liked our clothing!

He rolled his eyes and put his finger to his lips, like I didn't already know to be quiet when sneaking around. "The loft is right over where they're rehearsing. Maybe we'll hear something," he whispered. "There's a vent." He led me around to the back of the stage where a rickety metal ladder stretched up into the loft.

"Uh..." When was the last time a safety inspector had seen this thing? Did it even have all its screws?

"Afraid of heights?" he taunted.

"More afraid of tetanus," I hissed back. I gingerly eased my toe onto the first rung. I'd seen Jenna go up and down this thing with no fear whatsoever, but I just knew I'd be the first to get some kind of disease or huge, gaping gash from this neglected piece of crap. If it stayed together.

"Are you going to stand there forever? They're talking," he whispered.

I glared at him. Then I squeezed my eyes shut and climbed the darn ladder.

7

YOU REALLY WANT TO DO THIS RIGHT NOW?

SURPRISINGLY, I didn't fall to my death, and the ladder didn't so much as squeak. I counted my blessings as I flattened my body at the top and crawled until I was lying on the dusty wood floor next to the vent. Xander joined me a moment later. He wiggled until his side rested against mine. Did he have to be this close to me? A piece of hair escaped my ponytail, and I blew it away from my face.

"... letting her help. You can't be serious, J."

J must be Jenna. I didn't recognize the other voice. All I could see was the dusty grill of the vent. Were they talking about me? I arched an eyebrow at Xander, but he motioned for me to listen.

"Why not? It's not like she did last year. She and Xander are doing a pretty good job, right? Why not take the free labor?" Jenna asked.

I nodded.

"But I mean, aren't you still mad at her?" the voice asked.

With careful, silent movements, I scooted closer to the edge. This was the important part. Did she still hold that grudge? How far would she go to get me out of school? If it was her, I could try to prove it. I pulled my cell phone from my pocket. I had no idea whether it would record a conversation this far away, but if I could hear it clearly, couldn't my phone? I tapped the button, and seconds of silence passed before Jenna said something.

"I shouldn't have been surprised last year. You know how she is. And at the end of the day, she did an okay job playing her part."

"You would have been much better. If it was me, I'd—"

"Well, it wasn't you. And she's helping this year, so I'll take what I can get. Now, let's rehearse Act Two the way we told Mr. Darryn we would. Where are the rest of the Debutantes? Jill! Stacy! Ugh, I'll go find them myself." Footsteps. Guess she'd gone off to do just that.

I clicked the button to stop recording. I'd been expecting... I didn't know what I'd been expecting. This new evidence didn't scream guilty, but what was that pause for?

Xander shifted, and I flinched when he pressed his side more firmly against mine. My breathing accelerated in the cramped space. I was hyper-aware when his shoulder brushed mine. The warmth of his body seeped into my clothes. My skin. For a long minute we stayed frozen, the small movements of our breaths forcing our bodies to meld together.

Then a door slammed, and the spell was broken. I avoided looking at him as I shimmied back over to the ladder of death, stretching my right foot down until it connected with the first rung. We snuck back to the washroom. I rolled up my sleeves and cranked the ancient faucet on the sink to continue washing the paint supplies.

"Did you hear what you wanted to hear?" Xander asked, his low voice rumbling through the small room as he handed me a paintbrush to rinse. Red paint swirled in the bottom of the sink, fading to a light pink as I pushed my fingers through the bristles. When the water ran clear, I handed it to him. He laid it on a paper towel on the floor to dry.

"The word on the wall didn't seem like one she'd say." I cleared my throat. "I mean she swears a lot, but she usually just uses the 'd' word."

Xander paused in tearing more paper towel off a roll. "The 'd' word? Seriously?"

I didn't reply. Swearing was for people who couldn't articulate in more descriptive words. It was emotional, primal. My mom had drummed into me since birth that above all, it sounded uneducated.

"I still don't know if Jenna did it," he said after a minute. "Maybe she just wouldn't say it out loud. What do you think?"

"I think…" I let the water run over my hands for a moment. "I think I shouldn't have taken that part," I murmured, mostly to myself.

It had been a pressure-filled year for me, the last one before Yale would start to look at me as a potential student. I needed as many extracurricular activities as I could manage. Or at least, that's what my mom told me. Over Christmas break, she'd cornered me, and I'd reluctantly agreed to try out for the school musical. I had exactly zero experience with theater, and it wasn't until after my audition that I found out no one got that kind of one-on-one time with the director. My parents had paid a hefty sum to get me into yet another activity, and it made everything awkward. I never broke into the drama clique, so I steered clear when the production concluded. And that was that.

Except I never thought about how it affected everyone else. My means to an end was Jenna's dream. Her angry face flashed in my head. She knew exactly how to embody the characters she played, and she worked really hard to make sure the production came off without a hitch, even volunteering her time to help with the set. I tried to swallow back my guilt.

"Because you think she did it?" Xander asked.

It took me a moment to remember what we were talking about. "I don't think Jenna spray-painted the locker room." I squeezed green paint out of a roller under the water. "She doesn't seem like she has time for something so petty. I respect that."

It was a hopeless conclusion that I wasn't entirely sure of. If she hadn't done it, we were back to square one. I only had twelve days until my meeting with the dean. Would he stand by his word and keep me here that long? Was he even trying to find the real criminal? I was still reeling over how fast he moved from loving me to hating my guts.

Oh, God.

The roller slipped out of my hands and clattered against the sink. What if the dean... What if it was like the play? My parents' phone call... What if Dean Alton never liked me? What if *everyone* was tolerating me for my parents' money? I stood there frozen, the scalding water pouring over my hands. My teachers' faces flashed before me, their approving smiles when I'd solved a tough problem or given a thorough presentation. The essay contests I won, the awards I had gotten... How much of it was actually mine? My stomach cramped with nausea.

After a moment, Xander leaned across me to pick up the roller. Quietly, he showed me an easier way to strip the paint. He added a little soap, and I took over again. Our bare arms slid against each other, and I jerked away before I could stop myself.

"If we're going to work together, you could at least pretend not to hate me so much," he said.

I swallowed and finished washing the roller, then handed it to him. He turned to take care of it. When his back was to me, it was easier to talk. "I don't hate you."

"Sure seems like it," he grumbled.

"Do you really want to do this right now? We were fourteen."

"Kind of, actually." Xander turned to face me. "You didn't even give me a reason for breaking up."

My heart stumbled a beat. A full-on confrontation was not what I expected. I'd thought the direct Xander I'd known was gone, but apparently, that wasn't true. I pushed down my rising panic. Trying to keep it light, I rolled my eyes. "Yes, I did."

"No, you didn't. Not a real one," he said in a husky voice. Why did he sound hurt? It reminded me too much of the Xander from freshman year.

"You remember what I said?" I tried to look like I was focused on cleaning the sink. Apparently, we *were* doing this right now. At least it was in private.

"You wanted to 'concentrate on your academics,'" he air-quoted. "We were freshman, Virgin. We had all four years to do that. It was the wimpiest excuse ever. You know what I think?"

I swallowed. "You're going to tell me anyway." I couldn't believe he was still hurt over it—that he was ever hurt over it. I mean, when it happened, I'd expected him to make a bigger deal out of it than he had, but he'd just nodded and moved on. Maybe this was a delayed reaction. Incredibly delayed.

"I think you were afraid," he accused.

Everything stopped. The silence hung thick between us. Then I scoffed. "Afraid of what? Of you?"

Xander stood over me, his height almost comical in the tight space of the washroom. "Of what you felt for me."

That was it. I was done trying to play nice. "Oh my God. Get over yourself, Alexander."

"You remember that night. I know you do."

My face burned as I met his eyes. "Stop," I hissed through gritted teeth.

"Which is exactly what you said then," Xander's voice cracked. "And I did. I didn't mean..." He pushed a shaky hand through his hair. "I didn't mean to make you feel uncomfortable. I thought... I thought we were okay."

I shook my head. "We *were* okay. It wasn't that. Not at all." Panic clawed at my throat. He couldn't think... All this time, he couldn't think that I'd broken up with him for *that*.

He blew out a breath. "Okay. Then what?"

"I told you."

"But it can't be true," he ground out. "You broke up with me *the next day*."

I didn't owe him an explanation. I didn't. But he was right. It looked bad. The fact that he'd been obsessing over this, maybe for years... I didn't know he'd felt that way. It really wasn't about that night.

I jabbed at the faucet, turning the knobs to off. "I didn't lie then, and I'm not lying now. We broke up because I had to focus on my future and not some freshman fling." I stared at a green paint fleck on the wall. Someone should come in here and scrub this whole room.

"Fine. Don't tell me." He turned to leave.

My fragile control broke, and I whipped around. "Have you seen me date anyone else? Anyone at all, in the past three years?"

His looked over his shoulder at me, his expression unreadable.

"I have priorities, Xander. Why are you trying to make drama when there isn't any?" I threw my hands up, water flying off my fingers at him. "You are so...so...frustrating!" I wanted to punch him in the throat—he was such a jerk. And maybe cry after, because I might be a jerk, too.

His mouth twitched. "You're kind of hot when you're mad. I missed that."

"Well, I didn't miss you and your..." *Chest, arms, hair, smile.* "Get out of my way." I tried to brush past him.

"Wait. Virgin, stop."

I winced. He prided himself on being a gentleman, got so upset when he thought I'd broken up with him when he knew it wasn't his fault, and then he called me that. Yet I paused, frozen in the doorway. Waiting.

"You're right. This is stupid." His voice was earnest. "It's okay if you didn't like me as much as I liked you then. We're older now, right? We can admit that's why it didn't work out. Be friends. Truce?"

But that wasn't it, either. It would be so easy to agree with him, to say I hadn't liked him enough. But it was a lie. It was a betrayal to freshman me, to him. With everything blowing up in my face, when I wasn't sure who and what was real anymore, I couldn't handle even one more lie.

"Okay?" he said when my silence stretched out longer than was comfortable.

"I liked you," I said. "A lot. But I couldn't date you." It was as close to the truth as I could get. At the end of the day, I had been the one to ruin things between Xander and me. And he'd thought it was because...

"Okay," he said in a quiet voice. A frown wrinkled his forehead as he thought. "Okay," he repeated. "So, truce?"

I closed my eyes. Everything was just as painful as freshman year. I'd thought we both moved on, but our wounds had only festered. I didn't want a truce with Xander. We'd broken up. I didn't have time for this boy-girl drama. I needed to find out who was mad enough to frame me. Who might be on the warpath, looking to get me kicked out of school, destroying everything I'd worked so hard for. Could I do that without him?

"Truce," I whispered. I couldn't lose him. I mean, I couldn't lose his connections. I needed them for my search.

He grabbed a towel off the counter and handed it to game. "I don't see why we can't be friends, Benson." The way he stared at me, so intense. God, this room was small.

"Sure." I took my time drying my hands. "You're friends with everyone, right?"

"It's a great way to be." He smiled wide, extending his hands.

Just like that, he transformed back into everyone's golden boy. He might fool other girls with that act, but not me. He was hurt and trying to cover. Earnest, direct Xander was gone again.

"Maybe for you," I said before slipping out the door. I couldn't comfort him when I'd been the one who created his pain. He wouldn't want that from me.

I ran down the steps and didn't turn back when Jenna called my name. I'd email her about handing out programs tomorrow. Xander could put the set pieces together tonight. Right now, in this moment, I'd had enough.

As I lay in bed that night, I couldn't stop myself from remembering Xander freshman year. Heat flooded my body as I relived the feeling of when we were first dating.

It was easy to fit in with Xander's friends then. After he asked me out, we spent every free second we could get together and texted every night after curfew. When we were both nominated as representatives for our class for Homecoming, I was shocked. I mean, Xander, sure. But me? The support of my peers was something that would look good to my parents, and it was going to be so fun! Xander and I would get to sit together on a float, our relationship out in the open for everyone to see. My first boyfriend.

After we helped with the float construction, it was natural to hang back on the bleachers as the sun set, sitting together. Just talking. Sharing wasn't something that came naturally to me, but everything was easier with Xander. I could tell him about my day, about how I was trying to make friends. We talked about fencing and our classes and our teachers, and it felt like such important stuff in the moment. Real stuff.

And then, before I knew it, we were on the float at half-time that night, waving at the crowd, smiling even though it was far too cold to wear the sleeveless red dress I'd chosen. Of course, my parents couldn't make it. Mom was working on another high-profile court case, and Dad never went anywhere without her. My school was so far away from them, so it was okay. I had everything I wanted.

Instead of sitting with his parents afterwards, Xander excused himself to steal me from Agnes. I felt so special, so singled out.

It was different that night, somehow. Maybe the formalwear and the promise of slow dancing with him later made me nervous, and I fell silent, slowly chewing on a Starburst candy Xander had given me as the cheers from the crowd rippled over the football field. One or two candies wouldn't kill my body. I was burning a ton of calories in the cold tonight, anyway.

"Want anything to drink?" Xander asked in the fourth quarter. His eyes were still on the field, where the score had been tied 14 to 14 for most of the game. Not that I'd been paying much attention. Xander's face was far more interesting. He admitted to me that he rarely watched football, yet every time we lost yards or fumbled the ball, his face would scrunch up like a little sad puppy. Whenever we were close to scoring, he'd hug me tighter and smile. What would he do if we won?

"Or do you want to, like...get out of here?" He winced. "I'm sorry. That was cheesy."

I smoothed the collar of his white shirt. "I like cheesy," I whispered. Was I doing this right? All I knew was that I didn't want to be up here in the stands in the cold wind, even though he'd so nicely given me his jacket.

"Yeah?" he croaked.

"Yeah."

He threaded his fingers through mine, bringing my hand up to his lips and grazing my knuckles with a small kiss. I shivered.

Xander pulled me up. "Then let's go."

He led me under the emptying bleachers and held me tight, resting his chin on my hair. I drew back, afraid of getting makeup on his shirt, but he just held me closer. "You're freezing."

I didn't feel cold, but he didn't have to know that. "Then warm me up." I was so much braver when I didn't have to see his face.

His grip on me loosened, and I stared up at him. His lower lip was a little bigger than his top. Electricity flowed through me. He closed his eyes, so I did too.

Until that moment, we had said we were dating, but it wasn't anything more than conversation and shared space. A handhold here and there. Maybe he'd sensed how nervous I was, that I'd never done something like this before. But now... Now, it was my first kiss, and it was so gentle. It was like he thought I was fragile, that I'd break if he breathed the wrong way. I couldn't get enough. When he went to pull away, I kissed him again. He smiled against my lips and his mouth tilted. This time it was a little harder, a little more aggressive. I threw myself into it. I trusted him. If the world exploded, I wouldn't have cared.

Time ceased to exist. Xander's arms around me, his mouth against mine, the staccato beat of my heart as I dragged in breath, my blood simmering with a feeling so foreign and desperate, it was like I would die if my lips detached from his. Then he migrated to my neck, and that was an entirely new experience for me. My skin tingled, and I gasped. He tightened his grip on my hips, and I leaned into him. There was nothing better than this. There was nothing better than him. I melted.

Then one of his hands drifted up to cup my breast. He thrust his tongue into my mouth.

When his fingers started to inch under the fabric of my neckline, I panicked.

"Stop," I choked out, though I wasn't really sure that's what I wanted.

Immediately, he froze. Then he stepped back, his face red.

"I'm sor—Virginia, I'm sorry."

I breathed deeply, pushing back my embarrassment. "No, it's okay. I'm just not—I can't—"

"No, no. I totally get it. Do you just want to—what do you want to do?" He gave me a sheepish smile.

My heart swelled.

The wind kicked up, blasting my hair forward and whipping my thin dress against my legs. The crickets singing in the grass quieted, waiting for our next move. "Will you walk me to the dance?"

He held out his arm, and I took it.

No, that wasn't why I broke up with him. It was the next morning, when everything came crashing down.

My parents showed up on campus after receiving my progress report from the school. They'd fly across the country for two B's, but not to see their daughter ride on a float.

"I don't understand," Mom said. She handed me the printout. "You were doing so well at home."

I wiped my hands on my skirt before taking the report as I stood before them in my dorm room. On the cork board above my desk was a photo of Xander and me, a fun selfie of us he'd taken before the game last night. I'd printed it barely ten minutes prior to my parents' visit, and now I couldn't help but stare at it. Xander's arm stretched casually over my shoulder as he bent to kiss my cheek. My expression was a little surprised as I smiled at the camera.

Mom followed my stare and walked over to the picture, ripping it sharply out from under the tack. "This is the problem, isn't it? This boy."

"Xander," I whispered.

Mom nodded, as if this explained everything. "I knew we shouldn't have let you go to this school. The tutors in Boston are—"

"We brought her here for socialization," Dad finally chimed in.

I may as well have not even been in the room.

"Well, she's aced that," Mom said flatly.

"I can handle it," I said in a small voice.

"She can't handle it," Mom continued, as if she hadn't heard me.

"I'm sure this is just an aberration." Dad continued scrolling through his phone. "The boy is probably just a friend. One she'll be

spending less time with now that she realizes how it may impact her *future." His eyes drifted* up until they met mine.

I knew what he was telling me. I had a chance. To stay, I'd have to cut Xander out.

I licked a bead of sweat from my upper lip as I said the next words that ended my relationship with Xander before it even had a chance to take off. "He's just a friend. I'll take care of it."

My fear of failing my parents was greater than whatever I felt for Xander, and that's all there was to it. At the end of the day, I didn't have to answer to him. Our relationship was so fresh, I knew he'd get over me. Even though I curled into a ball and cried myself to sleep for weeks, it was for the best. From the many, many girls I'd seen him with since, he hadn't suffered much.

But his face flashed before me, serious and sad as we squared off against each other in the theater. *I thought we were okay.*

It was a long time before I finally fell asleep.

8

ANOTHER DAY OLDER

WAKING up to my eighteenth birthday was kind of a letdown. Though I could now gamble and buy lottery tickets, I had zero intention of doing either of those things. When I climbed out of bed, I half expected Agnes to be twirling her car keys at me, ready to force me into some sort of eighteen-year-old ritual.

But she wasn't. And she didn't. Agnes was nowhere to be found. I blinked back surprise. She was the birthday queen. She never let anyone's go uncelebrated, especially mine. Balloons, cards as big as my bed, glitter I had to wash out of my super thick hair for a week—that was Agnes.

It was fine. I mean, what was so exciting about being another day older? What was so different between yesterday and today? Nothing. My parents never made a big deal out of birthdays.

It was whatever. I dressed normal, felt normal, and did all my normal morning things, including checking for my mail in the entryway before heading to breakfast. It was more habit than anything else. I rarely got anything except college junk mail. Unsurprisingly, there was nothing there for me. That was also fine. It wasn't like I needed a card or anything. My dad had already deposited my birthday money into my account, anyway.

After I got my food, my pocket buzzed. I swiped into my phone as I sat down...and blanched when I saw who it was from. I picked at my cold hard-boiled egg, staring at the screen until it faded to black, trying to control my breathing. I knew better than to think it was a birthday text. My dad never texted me unless I was in trouble. Had he found out about the graffiti? Yes, of course he had. The dean said he called my parents. I had figured their radio silence was to give me time to clear my name. I hadn't done that yet. Was this text a reminder—or something worse? When not knowing got scarier than knowing, I wiped my hands on my napkin and read it.

> Virginia, your mother and I will be visiting on the 4th to discuss your behavior.

The fourth. Tomorrow.

My hands shook as I flipped my phone over. I stared at my fingers, twisted and pale and afraid. My parents were going to be so mad. I blew out a shaky breath, but it did nothing to calm me. Nothing would.

A large pair of hands covered mine. Through my blurry vision, Xander's concerned face loomed. He kept one hand on mine and picked up my phone with the other. After scanning the text, he looked at me.

"They found out about the graffiti?" he asked.

I nodded. I didn't know why I was reacting so strongly right now. I'd been waiting for this moment.

"So explain to them that it wasn't you."

I blinked away the moisture in my eyes and looked across the cafeteria to the Exit sign. "You don't get it."

"Help me get it," he said earnestly. "Talk to me."

I didn't want to. It was all I could do not to scream and push away from him. Maybe if I could get him to understand, he'd leave.

"There are...expectations I haven't met." I whispered the last part.

"Expectations?" He snorted. "Virgin, they sent you to a boarding school. They have to know they're not getting the whole story about anything that goes on."

"That would be logical," I agreed.

"You didn't do it," he said in the same chill tone. "So I don't know what you're worried about." Like it was that easy. Maybe in his world, it was.

"It doesn't matter." I slipped my hands out from under his. Twice now, he'd almost seen me cry. I couldn't remember the last time I let any tears fall. Maybe... Maybe when I broke up with him. I stood to leave.

"Benson," he said softly.

I shook my head as I turned and speed-walked out of the cafeteria. I didn't need his pity. The egg sat like a lead weight in my stomach. I needed to go for a run before class.

But the pounding of my feet on the trail behind our school didn't do anything to calm my fears, and the run was difficult for some reason. By the time the first bell rang, I was exhausted. Too exhausted to remember to turn my phone to silent.

When I got a text a few minutes into the hour, it chimed for everyone to hear. My heart jumped into my throat, and it took everything I had not to dive for my bag. Thankfully, the teacher couldn't pinpoint the culprit from one text alone. Even though everyone around me knew it was mine, no one snitched. We all stood in solidarity against the school's no-phone policy during school hours.

I was always so careful, though. Only Agnes and my parents texted me, and none of them would text me in class. Agnes and I were both too afraid our phones would be confiscated, and my parents knew my schedule. They'd never interrupt my learning. I drummed my fingers against the desk for the rest of the hour, curiosity gnawing at me. As soon as the teacher turned her back at the end of the period, I booked it to the hall.

My fingers fumbled for the zipper of my bag as students knocked into me. When I finally unlocked my phone, Xander's name flashed on the screen. Adrenaline flooded my body.

I never deleted his number after we stopped dating. I didn't want to be surprised if he ever texted me again. He never did. Until now. Was he ditching me? *Sorry, Virgin, but you're a basket case.*

I shouldn't have let him see that text message from my dad.. I stared at his name on my phone, foreign after so long. The little emoji hearts I'd put around *Xander* needed to be deleted, for sure.

I dodged the beefy linebacker standing in the middle of the hallway. It was now or wait another hour. I swiped into his text.

> Party at Nikki's tonight. Good time to find some suspects. See u at 10?

Ah, Nikki's. Where all the most scandalous events of our small school went down every month. Her parents left for business like clockwork, and though her house wasn't as large as most, she was local. Almost everyone went.

Except me. Not even freshman year. Nikki's parties were after curfew, and I was nothing if not a rule follower. But Agnes told me they were pretty wild. Xander was right; this would be a great way to figure out who hated me. Show up to something I'd never gone to before, and people were bound to talk.

When I returned to the dorm room, Agnes stood in front of the full-length mirror fine-tuning her vampy makeup. She wore a tight pair of hip-hugging jeans that were faded and ripped all the way up to the front pockets, and her loose black crop top gave her a casual, yet sexy vibe. She'd let her brown hair go wild, not even trying to tame her curls. The final effect was amazing.

When she saw me sizing up her outfit, she said, "I'd invite

you, but you always turn me down." She smirked at the mirror as she finished applying mascara to her left eye.

"Well, I'm going tonight." I straightened the books scattered across her bed into a small pile.

She shoved the mascara wand back into the tube. "Because it's your birthday?" she sing-songed.

I hid a smile. "You remembered."

Agnes nodded to her desk. "You've been so MIA, I haven't even run into you."

MIA? I was right here. "What is it?" I walked to the desk, where a small silver box waited for me. "Jewelry?"

"Hardly."

Now my curiosity was killing me. I popped the lid off the box and laughed.

"Gold-plated highlighters?" All my colors were laid out on a bed of satin.

She finally grinned. "Great, right?"

I held the pink one up to the light. "You're ridiculous. Thank you." I blinked back the sudden moisture building in my eyes. Agnes didn't forget me. She got me a present she knew I'd use. One that probably cost her more money than she had.

She put her hands on her hips. "Just try to bite through those. They're refillable, too. You'd better get ready if you're coming with me."

"I am ready."

"You—" She broke off laughing.

Did I look weird or something? I looked down at my black skirt and fitted white shirt. What was so bad about it? It was cute, put together, very me. "What?"

"You look like you're going to serve everyone dinner."

I blinked. "Do I need to undo a button or something?"

"You're kidding." She glanced at me. "You're not kidding."

I looked down again. This shirt was tighter than the one I wore for our uniform.

"And you're going with a scraped-back ponytail and no makeup?"

"I have makeup on!" Sure, it was light, but that was my style.

"Looks like we're going to be a little later than I thought." She pulled out her phone and texted someone. Then she turned to her closet and rifled through it, finally pulling out a white dress. "Another gift for you. Happy birthday."

I backed up a few steps. "No," I whispered. "There's no way. I can't wear that."

"Yes, you can," she said. "If you don't want to embarrass yourself, you'll let me help you. Now pull that hair down and let me see what I can do."

I grumbled and did as she asked.

An hour and a half later, we entered Nikki's house. I fidgeted, uncomfortable with the stares directed my way, but Agnes was right: My other outfit never would've worked here. Still, did we have to go this far with it?

I pulled down the hem of the white Bodycon dress. Seriously, it would not stay put. Agnes had curled my hair and pinned it to the side to spill over my right shoulder in a long wave. It was far beyond anything I'd ever been able to do with it. I'd stood in the mirror for a full minute before we left, watching the way the light played off the strands. This hairstyle was made for me.

The look didn't stop there. I had so much eye makeup on that I doubted anyone would recognize me. Besides that, I was a full four inches taller in spiked heels that were death waiting to happen. Agnes said they made my legs look longer, so I went with it.

I might feel like an imposter, but I knew confidence was enough to get me through most situations. I took a deep breath, went into the living room, and checked out the scene everyone made such a big deal about.

A keg sat in the corner with signature red cups sitting on a

TV dinner stand next to it. Bottles of liquor lined the kitchen counter, and a couple of guys were yelling at their friends to do a shot. The furniture had been pushed to the side for dancing, but not many people were; mostly, they just stood around. Lots of low light. Lots of girls in short dresses or tight jeans clumped together talking, joking, and laughing. The house was filled with seniors, but a lot of the students on sports teams littered the sparse seating near the walls. It wasn't especially classy or trashy. It was just a party.

I spied Xander talking to—surprise, surprise—a group of girls. His dark grey T-shirt stretched across his thick shoulders and fell over black fitted jeans. His hair was as crazy as ever, but it appeared he'd at least attempted to comb it—maybe with his fingers. Guys had it so easy. Why did I have to wear a dress and heels?

"So where do you want to start?" Agnes asked me. "I assume you're only here because of the case."

I nodded, already moving toward Xander. "I'll see you later."

When I was a few feet away, Xander looked up from the red cup he was drinking from. His eyes slid all the way down my body and up again. When they reached my face, he did a literal double-take. He stepped back, scanning me from head to toe again, his mouth hanging open. I couldn't tell if he was making fun of me or not.

I straightened my shoulders. Agnes had said I looked hot, and I agreed, even if Xander was acting like I was some kind of freak.

"So?" I yelled to be heard over the music. "What's the plan?"

He took my elbow and guided me away from the girls. One flipped her hair in my direction, and another gave me a death glare. I wiggled my fingers in a sarcastic wave. A sick part of me wanted to let them think I was competition, even as Xander's tugging made me stumble over my feet.

"Geez, calm down," I said when he finally stopped in a dark corner.

He bent down to get closer to my level. "What are you doing?" he hissed, his breath hot in my ear. "You look..." He shook his head. We were close enough now that I could really see his face, how wide his eyes were, how his jaw flexed. It was almost like...

A slow smile spread across my face. This dress was so form-fitting it was like another skin, a far cry from anything he'd ever seen me in. He liked it. Liked it a lot.

"It's not funny, Virgin. How are we supposed to blend in and find out anything when you look... When you look like..." He waved his hand at my entire body.

"Like you shouldn't be calling me 'Virgin'?" I tried to keep a straight face. This was too good. Power surged through me. I'd taken Xander by surprise. Happy birthday to me.

He shook his head, looked away, then took a sip from the red cup in his hand.

"Xander, you're the one who invited me." *Because of the case,* I reminded myself. *That's why we're here.* "This might actually work. You wanted people to talk about me. Maybe you can be the listener, and my dress can be the bait!"

"Sounds like a lot of work for me," he muttered.

"No, this will be great. Go back to your groupies." I nudged him toward them. "I'm sure they'll have a lot to say about me now."

"My what?"

Crap. I didn't mean to say that out loud. "I need one of those." I pointed to his cup. "I need to participate." I craned my neck around, trying to decide which type of alcohol I wanted to try tonight. *Oh, that's right.* The keg was in the corner. I started in that direction, but Xander stepped in my path.

"Wait—have you ever even had a drink before?"

It wasn't that weird that I hadn't, right? Everyone started

sometime. I shrugged, grinning at him. It was my birthday, and I wanted to do something new. Something fun. My parents were coming tomorrow. Who knew what would happen then? I didn't want to think about it, or anything to do with that, on my special day. I was allowed to have *one* day, right?

"Just be careful," he warned.

I twirled on my heel and marched over to the keg. A helpful guy filled a cup for me, and I took a big swig of beer. *Ugh, disgusting.* How could something taste stale and sour at the same time? No way I could finish this.

I found a seat on a sofa with a couple of underclassmen who appeared safe enough, and we ate green Jello out of little plastic cups. Kind of cute that this party had such a cheap and funny dessert chilling around like that.

It wasn't much fun for long. The boys kept reaching over me and brushing against my chest. Maybe sitting in the middle wasn't the best idea. It had been at least an hour. Our plan should be in full effect by now. I needed to find Xander and say goodbye, then seek out Agnes to get a ride back to campus. But when I stood up, the room tilted.

"Whoa, there." One of the underclassmen steadied me. What was his name again? Something that started with a B. His hand was warm, and the sudden urge to dance took over.

"Come on," I said. We stumbled to the middle of the living room, squeezing between other couples to get to a clear space. A popular slow song was playing, which was a relief. I didn't want to try to fast-dance. The heels felt more like stilts now, and the room lurched under me. Swaying felt like a good idea, since the room felt like it was rocking anyway. I must be really tired.

The dude pulled me into his arms, and I wrinkled my nose. He smelled sour in the same way the beer had. Still, I liked the way we swayed, the way his hands molded themselves to my back. But then they drifted lower.

"Hey, now." I laughed. "Keep it PG."

Then someone grabbed my arm gently and pulled me back. Xander hovered over me, his brows drawn together. I gave him a watered-down smile, swaying a little in his grasp. "You're so frowny," I told him.

"Goodbye, Brad," he said through gritted teeth.

I was right! B for Brad!

Weak-willed, handsy Brad gave me an apologetic smile and disappeared in an instant.

"What are you doing?" Xander asked. His tone wasn't very nice.

"Dancing," I said. *Duh.*

"It looked more like you were letting a freshman grope you in a short skirt." His voice was all judgy. He sounded like a dad.

"Freshman? He looked taller than that," I said. I walked my fingers up his chest.

Xander stood stiffly in front of me.

"And it's a dress," I twirled around to show him and stumbled. *Whoops.* That was a little fast.

His hands shot out to steady me. "Jesus."

"Shut up and dance with me, Xander." I looped my arms around his neck. Always so angry. "It's my birthday, you know," I murmured. I liked that he was taller than me. His body was warm, too.

"No, I didn't know," he said as I nuzzled into his shirt. "Is that why you're so dressed up?"

I nodded against his chest. "Agnes's present to me. You like it?"

The song changed to another slow tune, and Xander's hands finally found my waist. I pulled him in until we were hugging and swaying at the same time. Hug dancing was the best way to dance.

"You really do look nice tonight," he said.

I raised my head. "Oh? Suddenly you like it? What happened to 'What are you doing, Virgin? You're blowing up the plan with your dress'?" I tried to pitch my voice as low as his.

"I never said you were blowing up the plan."

"Uh huh."

We were silent a moment as the music flowed over us, practically a lullaby. "You like my dress," I murmured.

"I like your dress," he repeated, but the way he said it did something to my stomach. My pulse picked up speed. His face was close to mine in the low light of the living room, and...

I rested my head on his chest again. The room was too spinny. "Mmm," I mumbled against his shirt.

He pulled me tighter. "Just out of curiosity, how much have you had to drink?" he teased.

"One." I nuzzled into his chest, but his body was too hard for me to get comfortable.

"One Jello shot?" he asked.

"No. One beer. Lots of little Jello cup thingies." The song ended and another kicked up, this time with a faster tempo.

He sucked in a breath, his feet stopping. "You didn't—Virgin, those had alcohol in them!"

I giggled. "Must be why they tasted kind of weird. Oh, well."

"'Oh, well'? You're drunk." He pulled away to look down at me, his lips twisted into an expression I couldn't put my finger on. Amused? Disappointed? It was too hard to figure out tonight.

Why weren't we dancing anymore? I glanced around at the other couples, some shaking their bodies, some making out, and a few dancing in that dirty grinding way I'd always wanted to try. Okay, maybe not always. But right now. Right now, I wanted to try it with Xander.

"Let's be friends, Xander. Like, real ones." I smiled up at him.

That weird, unreadable expression deepened, turned sadder. "I don't want to be your friend, Virginia." He released me from his arms. Well, that was rude. I only repeated what he said at set construction. I opened my mouth to say as much, but he'd stalked off across the room to down another cup of beer.

I stood in the middle of the dance floor where he'd left me and watched him drink. If I told him I wasn't a virgin, would that be an acceptable kind of lie? Would he stop calling me that? A twinge of pain twisted through my gut. Ugh, I didn't feel very good.

Someone tapped my shoulder. "Hey." It was Agnes. "Xander said you needed me." A wide smile stretched across her face, like she wanted to laugh. When did Xander tell Agnes that? What a control-freak. I was fine. I'd show him. I was going to—

I was going to throw up.

Oh, God. I didn't know where the bathrooms were in this house. Vomit pushed into my throat, burning hot. I pushed people out of the way, spilling drinks all over in my mad dash to the door.

"Virginia!" I heard a girl squeal, but I couldn't concentrate on it. I rushed outside and puked all over the rose bush in the front yard.

"Sick," I could hear Agnes say to someone else. A hushed conversation went on behind me, but I couldn't concentrate on it or care. "No, I've got it," she told whoever it was. "You've done enough."

The next few hours were a blur. The inside of Agnes's car, the inside of our dorm room, the inside of a toilet bowl.

The next morning, I woke up on the tiled bathroom floor. Sweat slicked my hair, and the white dress was hiked up to my butt. A bunched-up towel cradled my face, which was inches away from the base of the toilet.

"*Uhhng.*" I braced my hands against the sink and pushed myself up to a standing position. My makeup was ghoulish. Streaks of black and purple tracked down my face.

Agnes burst through the door. "Finally. I have to pee."

I turned my head toward her, even that small movement painful.

"I forgive you. Birthday rules. Now get out before my bladder explodes." She pushed me out the door.

I returned to my room and collapsed on my bed. What was wrong with me? It had to be all the sugar from the Jello. My body was rejecting it. So stupid. I couldn't afford to be sick right now!

The dress wasn't helping. It bunched up around my hips and pulled at my stomach. I wiggled out of it under the covers. I was better for five whole seconds before nausea had me bending over the side of the bed.

But there wasn't anything left. All I did was gag through a throat on fire before flopping back onto my pillow holding my side. Everything hurt. The whoosh of a toilet flushing barely punched through the rush of blood pounding in my head.

"I'm going to take a shower!" Agnes called.

I didn't reply. The click of the door closing was louder, sharper than it should have been. Then, nothing but blissful silence.

My eyelids drooped. Maybe I could take an hour nap and that would help. Or like...ten minutes, even. I thrashed back and forth before I found a position that didn't make me feel like complete death. I had just begun to relax when a hand shook me.

I squinted at Agnes, who had a towel wrapped around her hair in my blindingly bright room. "Can you turn off the light?"

"Get out of bed!" she hissed. "Your parents are in the hall!"

9

THE MOM AND DAD VIBE

I SWUNG my legs off the bed and staggered to the bathroom, grabbing my clothes from yesterday off the back of my desk chair.

"Stall them!" I begged Agnes. "Please!"

I didn't wait for her to answer. I was already shimmying into my clothes. Agnes's shrill laugh bled through the door as I pulled a brush through my hair and washed my face. My makeup wasn't coming off! I scrubbed harder. What I wouldn't give for a full shower, but those were down the hall.

It might've been only one full minute of me getting ready, but it was one minute too long, and I knew it.

I swung open the door, and there they were: my parents. Of course, there wasn't a wrinkle between the two of them. I could feel them judging my appearance, lingering over the state of my hair and everything else I didn't have time to make perfect. I swallowed. *Don't throw up.* I leaned against the wall casually, trying to make it look like I didn't really need it for support.

"Hi, Mom. Dad."

"Virginia," my dad said.

Agnes cleared her throat, then crossed to the door leading to the hall. "I'm just gonna—" She didn't even finish the sentence before she left. I didn't blame her. *Take me with you.*

My dad leaned back on the white couch purchased with his money, his hands braced on his knees. Mom perched on the edge of her seat next to him, her lips pursed.

"I'm sure you are not at a loss as to why we are here?" my dad asked.

I nodded. No point in denying anything. They probably knew every detail already.

"What could you have possibly been thinking?" Mom said. "You're so close to everything you've worked so hard for. I—we—"

"We don't pay for an incredibly expensive private school, hand you a car, and fund your allowance for you to decide to become a street thug and throw away your entire future," my dad interrupted. Though his face was still set in a calm mask, I knew that was all it was: a mask. He was disappointed. Angry.

His comment took me a moment, though. Graffiti must mean I had become a street thug. To him, those two things would be related. God, my head hurt.

"I didn't do it," I said tiredly. I hadn't expected them to come to my rescue, but would a little trust be too much to ask? Hadn't I done everything they'd ever asked of me?

Mom arched one perfectly plucked eyebrow. "Then why does the dean think it was you?"

I sighed.

"And how do you plan to fix that?"

My track record of stellar behavior, of perfect grades, all the awards I had earned—none of it had been enough. One accusation was apparently all it took to make all my accomplishments meaningless to them. And now I had to fix something I didn't even do. Not for the first time, the injustice of it all made me want to scream. I kept my expression smooth, though. Hysterics would make this worse.

"I'm working to find the culprit with every spare second I have. If I can show their guilt, I'll prove my innocence."

She nodded. "Proactive." It was as close as she'd come to complimenting me. I allowed myself a small smile.

"You know what's at stake here," my dad said. "Your mom and I went to Yale, but it's no guarantee they will accept you if they consider you a risk. I'm glad you're taking this seriously."

I practically preened under his praise.

Mom switched directions. "Have you...? Stand up straight," she ordered.

Dread forced adrenaline through my body as I pushed off the wall and straightened my spine. I threw back my shoulders and tucked in my stomach the way I'd been taught, though the movement made me dizzy.

"Have you been following the nutrition recommendations my secretary passed along?" Mom asked. "You know your body type doesn't tolerate a sugar-filled diet. Sugar..."

I bowed my head. No matter how many times I heard the lecture, it never hurt less. Why didn't I notice what she was seeing? The answer was obvious. Xander. Him and his stupid dares and his Egyptian-themed nachos. But I couldn't blame him. I'd always cheated on the diet, at least a little. I'd just stopped being careful lately. What was happening now was totally avoidable. My fault.

"Virginia." My mom's voice softened a fraction. "You know what the world is like. What people are like. I don't want it to be a reality, but it's true that you and I, we're ambitious women. It's not enough to just be smart. We have to act above reproach, look above reproach. You know that."

I did. Of course I did. I nodded at the floor. "Yes, ma'am."

"Okay. Good." She blew out a breath. "I can have my personal trainer fly out here and run you through some exercises. Would that help?"

Sweat broke out on my upper lip. "I can run more."

"I'm much more concerned about this graffiti nonsense," Dad said.

I turned a fraction to face him. "I told you I didn't do it."

"Of course not," Mom said. "But remember, your behavior has to be flawless while we get to the bottom of this. Dean Alton was very clear about that."

Yes, he certainly had been. I nodded. It was so easy to fall back into the yes-ma'am, yes-sir daughter, my hands folded in front of me. It was what they expected.

"What I'd like to know is how you got yourself into this mess in the first place," my dad continued. "The dean said you haven't been keeping your locker combination private?"

"It's the same locker I had freshman year. They never change them. I was..."

My dad's expression soured.

He'd be more disappointed if I gave an excuse, so I didn't try. "I don't know what I was thinking."

"You weren't thinking. That's the problem. Everything you do has consequences." Mom's voice softened again. "Maybe now you understand that?"

I nodded like a nervous bobble head figurine. The motion pushed the headache to the front of my face. How could I sit down right now without looking weak?

"Are you sick? You don't look well." She missed nothing.

"Of...of course not." As soon as the words escaped my lips, I wanted them back. I should have just said yes. Maybe then they'd leave. Maybe then something about my appearance would be deemed appropriate in their eyes.

"Fine. Do you have your most recent tests? That English essay? We should go over them while we're here. How are your grades?"

She knew exactly what my grades were. They were on the parent portal.

"Um..."

"Your GPA has fallen in the past week."

Barely. "It's been kind of stressful with the dean's deadline and everything." I couldn't stand anymore. My head was going to explode. I scooted backwards until I was at my desk, then sank gratefully onto the hard surface of my chair.

Mom exchanged glances with Dad, whose hand had been inching toward his pocket, probably to get his cell phone. They didn't speak for a long moment.

"Yale will care more about you maintaining your GPA than what your parents had to do to keep you in school," she finally said.

So they did donate money to buy me time. A rush of emotion made my eyes burn, even though I'd suspected that might be the case. Shame that I gave out my locker combination, that the dean thought I did it. Guilt that they had to spend money to keep me here, that they thought they had to fly out here. Anger that they still hadn't even wished me a happy birthday. But it was useless. Emotions were useless. That's not how this worked.

The next hour was filled with a review and mini lecture for every question I missed on my last two tests. When we got to the essay, my mom's voice faded into a gentle hum as she studied my face. What she saw there, I don't know, but I was only surviving at that point. Even her gentle "I think we might need a review on adverb usage" felt like a slap in the face now. But it couldn't last forever. Their flight home was soon, so I would be spared the pain of an entire dinner under their hawk eyes.

I was trying to hide the relief I felt ushering them out the door when I saw Xander sauntering down the hall. *Oh no.* I couldn't believe his presence was an accident. We were in the girls' dorms, for God's sake.

"Hello. You must be Virginia's parents," he said. My mom

and dad turned as one unit toward his greeting. He was natural with them, shaking their hands one after the other.

My dad stiffened. It was impressive, since he was already more rigid than I'd ever seen him. "This is the girls' dormitory, unless I'm mistaken."

Xander's smile became a little more forced. "Of course. I got permission."

I snorted. Unlikely.

"I wanted to meet you specifically," Xander said to my dad. He finally spared me a glance.

I couldn't contain my horrified expression. *Please don't. Please.*

He frowned, then turned his attention back to my dad. "I'm the fencing captain, and Virginia told me about your generous contribution to our team. We're very grateful for your donation to our sport."

I exhaled. There was no captain, but my parents wouldn't know that.

My dad smiled formally. This was safe territory. "It's our pleasure. I hope the money is being put to good use." Of course they donated money to the fencing program. But how Xander knew that was a bit of a mystery.

"Oh, yes sir. We've purchased new padding and better equipment. Gotta keep your daughter safe." He chuckled.

What was he doing? He was acting like some cheesy television character. Next he was going to say something like "Gee whiz, Mister." I wanted to kick him.

My dad arched an eyebrow. "Indeed," he said as a shrill ringtone blared from his pocket. "It was nice to meet you…"

"Alexander Hearst," Xander said.

My mom squinted at him. *Oh my God.* She made the connection between the name Alexander and Xander from freshman year. This couldn't get any worse.

Dad's phone continued to echo through the hallway, loud

and grating. He smiled dismissively at Xander, then answered it. Mom hesitated for a brief second before gesturing for me to follow them to the exit. That was that.

I walked them to the front of the school, silence stretching between my mom and me, Dad speaking in clipped statements to whoever was on the other end of the call.

Mom pulled me to her in a stiff hug at the school exit. "I love you," she said in my ear before quickly stepping back. "Be good."

"I love you too," I whispered. "I..." I didn't know how to finish that sentence.

She touched my hair briefly, pushing it behind my ear. She'd always loved my hair. It was one of the reasons I kept it so long. One thing I could always do right.

I opened my mouth to say something, maybe apologize again, but she was already walking briskly away, her heels clicking over the blacktop of the parking lot.

"Hold on, Steve," my dad said, shouldering his cell. "Goodbye, Virginia," he said to me and held out his other arm.

With awkward movements, I gave him a half-hug. He nodded, then put his phone back to his ear as he held the car door for my mom. I watched them go down the long driveway and disappear around the corner. They'd fly to Boston and go straight back to work with no break for jet lag. The fact that my school was on the other side of the country was no accident. Out of sight, out of mind. Until I screwed up, that is.

I stared after them for a long moment before forcing myself to shuffle back to my room. It was all I could do to move at a snail's pace, energy leaking out of my body with every step. When they were here, I was wound up tight, but as soon as they left, I ticked slower and slower until they showed up again to re-wind me. Surely, that wasn't how it was supposed to be, but I didn't know how else to exist.

Even while drowning in the darkness of my thoughts, I knew when Xander fell into step with me two doors from my room. He'd been waiting. When I stared blankly at him, he frowned at me like I was a stick of dynamite about to go off.

I didn't have the energy to tell him not to worry. All I wanted to do was to take some aspirin and sleep until I didn't feel this way. "Why are you here, Xander?" He was *not* coming in my room.

He leaned on the door jamb. "Just making sure you're okay."

He was checking on me for some reason? After all that just went down with my parents, I was at my limit for caring today. I could try to understand Xander when I was less tired.

"Don't look so shocked, Benson. You want to go get ice cream or something? Purge the Mom and Dad vibe?" His head tilted down toward mine, our faces only inches apart. It was intimate. Too intimate. My stomach lurched.

"Why aren't you sick?" I accused tiredly. We spent enough time together. Shouldn't he feel like crap too?

"Sick?" His eyes burned a trail from the top of my head to my toes as he gave me a slow once-over. "Or hung over?"

I hadn't even considered that.

"You know what the best cure for a hangover is?"

"Not ice cream," I shut him down. "I have to study." Even if I had been hungry, my mom's comments about my body would be enough to keep me away from something like that for a while.

"On a Saturday? Come on. Even you can afford to take a break on the weekend for a half an hour." He gave a lopsided smile, expecting me to reconsider.

I wondered, not for the first time, what kind of grades he made. Whatever they were, he played it pretty close to the vest. His family had money, so why weren't they pressuring him about it? Maybe they were, and he just didn't show it. People weren't always the same in public as they were in private.

I studied the line between the hall and the carpet of my

dorm room. It was a barrier, one I hoped he wouldn't cross without my permission.

"Okay, no ice cream. How about a run?" he asked gently. "Maybe inside on the track? I can work on my jabs in the corner. We don't even have to listen to the same music."

"I really can't," I murmured. I didn't have the energy. Not for running, and not for... Xander. This was why I couldn't have a boyfriend. This was why Agnes was my only friend, why everyone else thought I was a prude, a snob, a... A b-word. I deserved all of that, and I deserved my parents' wrath. I wasn't thinking last night. I never should've gone to that party.

Xander searched my face, probably noticing the way I clung to the door handle. It was literally holding me up at this point.

"Okay," he said softly. "See you on Monday."

"Okay," I whispered.

After I closed the door, I pressed my forehead against it and stared at the dark wood, grains that all worked together to make this strong slab that could separate me from the world. I traced a large, dark knot with one finger. Even trees weren't perfect. I snapped off my light and curled into a ball on my couch and felt nothing. Absolutely nothing.

On Sunday, it was back to business. I would study harder, sleuth better, work out more. I woke up at six and sat down with my textbooks for a couple of hours. After, Agnes let me dress and tighten my tennis shoes in silence. I could feel the concern in her eyes as I pulled my hair back into a ponytail, but this wasn't my parents' first visit. She knew I needed down time after seeing them. That if I talked, I'd cry. And I hated crying.

It was better to keep moving. Better to run. My protein shake sat like a rock in my stomach, but it wouldn't give me a side stitch like greasy food with Xander did. Maybe I could get in two runs today. Get back on track.

As I sprinted the route with the most hills, my music couldn't drown out my cycling thoughts. I probably wasn't going to get into Yale. My mom and dad were angry with me. Being near Xander was confusing. I was no closer to finding out who framed me for the graffiti. No one believed I hadn't done it. No one was gossiping about who really had.

As the blistering sun blazed down on me, I realized I forgot to make the loop I was supposed to a half mile back. I stopped and braced my hands on my knees, struggling for breath far more than I normally would.

It wouldn't be this hard if I wasn't so stressed. *Stressed, or fat?* Mom's comment about me needing her personal trainer rang loudly in my ears.

Stop it. You're not fat. And you won't be able to run at all if you cry. Suck it up.

So I did.

But later, I couldn't stay in the dorm room while Agnes puttered around me, pretending to not want to talk, but really wanting to. I couldn't study any more with her mother-henning me. Every corner of the room reeked of my parents' disapproval. Here was where they sat when they lectured me. There was where I had to bite my tongue to keep from screaming when I pulled out another test for criticism. It was too much. I put on some shorts and a school T-shirt and walked down to the courtyard with my history textbook.

All the picnic tables in the lavish courtyard were taken, but there was a tree on the opposite side of the yard that offered a small sliver of shade. I started toward it.

"Hey, Virginia!" Brad waved sheepishly from one of the tables as I passed by.

My face flooded with heat as I waved back. How drunk was I when we danced at Nikki's party on Friday?

One of his friends shoved his shoulder, and I turned back to the tree to keep us both from any more embarrassment.

I stumbled to a halt when I saw Xander leaning against the trunk, studying a large green apple in his hand.

"If you're done flirting, you should know that going to the party worked. I've got a lead for you."

"What?" I asked faintly.

"A lead. Come on." He took a huge bite of the apple and started back toward the building.

We moved silently through the halls until it became clear he was heading for the library. Xander pushed through the doors, walking in as if he owned the place. He pitched the apple in the trash, and we wound around a few tables where other students were reading and working on homework. No one of note was here.

"What do you see?" Xander shifted his gaze to mine.

"What?"

"What do you see?" he repeated.

I glanced around. Books lined the walls in great oak shelves. Posters advertising the next book drive wallpapered the room.

"Um, books? Students?"

Xander sighed loudly. "Think, Benson," he said. "Who could be mad at you in here? Do you seriously not remember?"

I scanned the room with new eyes, and they involuntarily stopped at a skinny dark-skinned guy with glasses poring over a huge leather-bound volume: Trent.

"Bingo," Xander whispered. His lips were dangerously close to my ear, and his breath was hot. Goosebumps spread down my arms. I batted him away.

"I didn't do anything to him. He just helped me with something." Even as the words escaped my lips, they tasted wrong.

"Is that really all?"

"Yes," I whispered back. I was highly aware that there were other people who could overhear us, but did he need to be so close to me?

"Go talk to him."

"No." There was no reason why I couldn't. Maybe I hesitated because Xander had somehow found out Trent was mad at me.

"Yes," he urged.

I inched forward to sink into a seat across the table from Trent, who looked up, blinking as if he had come out of a trance.

When I turned around, Xander was gone. Guess he didn't want to stay to see how his lead turned out.

"Hi," I said. So. Awkward.

Trent looked straight at me, his expression neutral. "Yes?"

"I heard that you weren't happy with me, and I want to fix it." Direct speech was the best route, considering it was Trent.

He pushed his glasses up his nose. "You mean the fact that you stole my essay contest idea and passed it off as your own after making me think you were flirting with me? Or how you haven't spoken to me since? Did you think I wouldn't find out?" His tone was matter of fact, his words as sharp as the pencil he held.

"I..." I was at a loss. I wasn't some horrible, slutty mastermind. I did *not* flirt with him. I didn't flirt with anyone! "I never meant to do that," I said, trying to keep myself from sounding defensive.

Trent snapped his book closed. "You never *mean* to be the way you are."

"Exactly! Wait, no..." That didn't sound good. Trent turned and began walking away, his back ramrod straight. "I..." Excuses wouldn't help here. I didn't even have a good one. "I'm sorry," I whispered as he exited the library.

At the time, I'd thought we were volleying ideas back and

forth. We hit on one I could use. Until Xander brought it up, I didn't remember that Trent was the one who'd said it. I should've asked. I kind of hoped I wouldn't win the contest, because now it wouldn't feel like a real win, even though I worked hard on that paper.

But the essays had been submitted. And obviously, Trent had seen my topic above his on the entry list. I couldn't really do anything at this point. Not without getting kicked out of school myself.

I didn't know how to fix this.

"That went well," Xander said as he sidled up next to me. So he had stuck around after all.

I shook my head, looking down at the book Trent had closed. He'd worked so hard. And I hadn't been flirting... Had I? I never dated anyone. Not since...

I couldn't meet Xander's eyes, but I could feel him looming over me as we exited the library. I didn't have anything to say. Nothing to fix what I'd broken. I was... Did I really come off that way? Was I *that* girl?

When we got to the hallway, Xander touched my shoulder.

I pulled away. I didn't deserve comfort right now.

"Benson, you—"

Both our phones chimed at the same time.

Open practice 4-7. Seniors only.

As one, we turned in the same direction down the hall. It wasn't required, of course, but Xander was obsessed with fencing, and I wasn't about to miss a senior practice. They were less formal, yet somehow more competitive than normal ones.

Fencing was a difficult sport, but it involved much less physical contact than volleyball or soccer. Now that I thought about it, I couldn't remember why I chose it freshman year. Probably because parrying with a foil was much more dignified than diving for a ball. Probably more because, while there were winners and losers in all sports, my dad preferred one very clear, individual winner.

Xander didn't continue what he was about to say before we were interrupted, but I knew what he was thinking. That I used Trent, and when we dated, I used him, too. Neither was true, but hadn't my parents' visit yesterday proven that nothing true mattered? Only the outcome did.

I tried to remember exactly what I'd said to Trent two months ago.

"Ugh, I don't even have one solid idea that I haven't used in a past essay," I whined to Agnes on the way to lunch.

"Do you have to do every single contest? Maybe you can skip this one."

She wasn't serious, of course. She knew I had to do the essay. It wasn't a choice. It would look good to Yale. Who knew what could push me over the edge into acceptance? Plus, if my parents saw the announcement in the school newsletter that someone else won and I didn't even try? I shuddered. "I'm skipping lunch today to work on it."

She rolled her eyes. "Go."

After a quick trip to the bathroom, I started back down the now mostly empty hallway. Trent fell into step beside me.

"You're entering the essay contest, aren't you?"

"What was your first clue?" I waved the paper at him.

He smiled. "I'm headed to Mr. Truman's classroom to work on it if you want to come."

Study Hall was always crowded and never completely quiet, so I nodded.

When we got to Mr. Truman's class, I set down the paper and we scooched in side by side at one of the big tables to look over the fine print, our arms touching as we squinted at the rules. I'd always respected Trent. We were alike in many ways. He didn't have time for the drama of high school, either. Just studying.

After a few moments, I sat back against my chair.

Trent did, too. "So, what's your angle?"

I considered the ceiling tiles. "No idea. I'm tapped out at this point." I tried to make it a joke, but there was an edge to my voice. It was senior year, and I'd already used every innovative idea I could think of for other contests, other assignments. And yet, I couldn't afford to fail.

There was a moment of awkward silence. I lowered my gaze, realizing Trent was looking at me.

"I don't believe that. You're as smart as me."

I touched his arm as I snorted with laughter. He grinned back. I supposed in Trent's world, that was a compliment. Why he was giving me one, I had no idea. Maybe he needed help with his concept, too.

"I could write from the perspective of servicemen and women," I offered. It had probably been done before, but it would play on the committee's heartstrings. Serving our country and everything.

"Current?"

I considered the logistics of that and shook my head. "I guess not."

"You can't be generic about it anyway. You need to come up with a specific angle."

"Yeah." My brain refused to give me anything. I flipped my hair back, biting my lip.

Trent pushed his glasses up his nose. "What if..."

At the time, I didn't think I should be grateful for Trent helping me, because I'd been in academic mode. I'd thought he was, too. Did he think me accepting his invitation to work together was me being interested in him? Was sitting next to him to see the paper too close? I always looked people in the eye when I spoke to them; I hadn't read anything into it. Was touching his arm a big deal to him? And was all of it enough to make him hate me to the extent of graffiti? He'd have no problem getting into the guys' locker room. I groaned as I pushed through the gym door. How stupid could I be?

Maybe Xander was right. He hadn't said it in so many words, but I knew he thought I was self-involved. Selfish. I slapped on my fencing padding in record time.

Jenna's face popped into my head. I always knew I didn't get that part based on pure talent, but I didn't know who else wanted it because I didn't go to tryouts. I never considered that someone else would pay the price for my success. No, not mine. The success my parents paid for. I knew that's what was happening, but I didn't want to face it if it got me closer to my goal. Wasn't that the definition of self-involved?

Xander won his match and pulled the mask from his face, exposing his shaggy brown hair. It was matted with sweat. For some reason, the way he gulped back his water irked me to no end. What right did he have to make me question myself? I was doing just fine before the graffiti, and I'd do a whole lot better after this whole mess was over.

"Virginia," The instructor called. "And who else is here on foil? Ralleigh?"

"I think she's sick," someone said.

"Ah, then... Alexander. While you're still fresh."

Xander switched his sabre for a foil, jogging over to stand in the center of the room. I slammed my own mask down over my face and stood. We never matched each other because his skills were at least a level above mine. I didn't care. My anger was so close to the surface, and it was all directed at him. He was supposed to be helping me, but all he did was make me feel bad about myself. He deserved whatever I could dish out.

"*En garde*," the instructor said.

We raised our weapons.

"*Pret.*"

I squatted lower in my stance, my hand steady.

I was already in full attack when the instructor called "*Allez*," my point whipping out toward Xander's chest. He stumbled back for a moment, obviously taken by surprise, but I didn't score against him. He recovered quickly, parrying my attack and countering with a basic riposte.

"What the hell, Benson?"

He was going easy on me. My blood boiled and I advanced again, lunging with all the strength and quickness I had. It gave me a sick satisfaction when his feet inched backwards as he dodged.

His next attack was polite, but my footwork was quick. I took the right of way and went for his ribs. Anger made me sloppy, and he swatted me away.

He lunged at me once more. I blocked his attack, my teeth clenched.

"Don't take it out on me. I'm not the one you're mad at." He stepped forward in an illegal offensive move that was so complicated, it took all my concentration to dodge it.

"Halt!" Our instructor commanded.

"I don't...see anyone else here," I puffed as I flicked out my blade to attempt a touch. He brushed the tip of my sword away, obviously taken aback that I wasn't going to obey our instructor.

"You hurt people. Just apologize and be better. It's not that hard." Every word he spoke slashed at my heart.

"Shut up," I hissed through gritted teeth. I didn't care that he was probably right. It hurt.

"Alexander! Virginia! You are out of line!" The instructor was headed toward us, but I lunged at Xander's knee. The move was illegal, but he started us down that road, and I was done playing fair.

He dipped at the last second and my chest met the resistance of his weapon. He'd scored, the tip of his foil touching just above my heart. The room was silent except for the sound of us both breathing heavily. But when he stepped back and pulled the mask from his face, what I saw there was not what I expected. I was waiting for him to look at me in that judgmental, obnoxious way of his. Instead, his expression was pure concern.

He felt sorry for me.

It was all too much. I could have dealt with literally anything else from him, but not that. Before our instructor could separate us, I dropped my foil and fled the room.

10

TAKING A ME DAY

TWO MINUTES before I was supposed to leave for class the next morning, I was still in my sports bra and pajama shorts, arguing with my flat iron. The second time I burned my fingers, I stopped pretending to do my hair and threw it into a messy bun.

I sank into the mattress of my bed. It would be so easy to hide under my comforter and sleep all day. I'd never do that, of course, but instead of going through the motions like I had my whole life, all I could do was sit there and stare at nothing. It wouldn't matter if I went to school today. I wouldn't hear anything my teachers said. I'd probably screw someone else over without realizing it. My classes were better off without me. I reached for my laptop, my need for mindless RomComs suddenly overwhelming.

"Are you sick?" The massive gold hoop earrings Agnes was attaching were against dress code.

"Yes. Sick," I echoed as I searched for my favorite summer camp romance. My parents had never let me go to summer camp. Maybe I *would* sleep all day. Sleep was nice.

She folded her arms and stared me down as I nibbled on a cracker. "You don't look sick."

"And you don't look like you really care," I snapped. I picked at the edges of the Yale sticker on my laptop in the silence that followed. A therapist would say I was projecting. My parents were the ones who didn't care about my feelings.

"Whatever."

I closed my eyes. "Agnes..." but she was already gone, slamming the door on her way out. It wasn't fair to take my issues out on her, but I couldn't help it. Not today. I needed everyone to go away. I would fix it later. Right now, I needed a reset.

The opening credits to my movie rolled. I fluffed up my pillows and noticed a black streak on one starchy white side. Mascara from the morning after the party. I flipped it over. The stupid pillowcases were impossible to keep clean. Agnes's were a dark maroon, which were much more forgiving. But then, she'd been able to choose hers. Everything in my life was carefully selected for me, even this school...

The drive from the airport before the first day of freshman year was silent.

I looked from my mom to my dad in the back seat of the town car, trying hard to act reserved and respectful, the way they'd taught me. My hands were folded together in my lap, but I was excited. I'd get to meet other kids my age. Until that point, I'd been taught by tutors who answered directly to my mom. As an only child, it had been a little lonely, though I knew it was necessary. How else could my parents afford all of the great things we had unless they worked all the time? That's what they told me.

In the dorm room, the walls were bare and there was no furniture. My roommate would be arriving later.

My mom stood by the door. "Your sofa will arrive in the next few hours," she said. "I've loaded a credit card with the money you'll need to outfit the rest of this place."

I could tell she was less than impressed by my new home, but the close quarters and shared showers looked like an adventure to me. I couldn't wait to get started. "Okay, cool."

She caught my eye and immediately, I knew I'd done something wrong. "What are you doing?"

"N-nothing?"

"The second I drop you off anywhere moderately public, you use slang and forget all the proper speaking techniques Monique taught you?"

I bowed my head. "No, ma'am." All I'd said was the word "cool."

"You're here to learn, not to be cool. *Don't forget how hard you've worked, okay? You want to make a good impression on your teachers."*

"Yes, ma'am."

In the hallway, my dad was on a business call.

"Well..." Mom shifted from one foot to the other. "I'll let you get settled in, then. Have a good semester. I love you." She patted my shoulder. They spent more time with me on the way down than they had all month, and for that I was grateful. I hadn't wanted to make the trip alone.

My shoulders relaxed as they retreated down the hall, just as the door across from mine banged open and a family flowed out, talking over each other.

"Oh honey," a blonde lady sniffled. "Call me every day. Call me twice a day. I'm only two hours away if you need me."

The girl rolled her eyes as her brothers nudged her, laughing. They were big and buff and had obviously helped move furniture into the room.

"Okay, Mom, go," she said. "I've got this." She made a shooing motion with her hand.

Her mom ignored her. "I love you. I love you so much," she said as she pulled her daughter into a tight hug.

"Mom, I can't breathe," the girl gasped, and her mom let her go reluctantly.

When they finally disappeared down the hall, I still stood looking after them, gripping the door frame with white knuckles.

"Hey." The girl turned to me. "You okay?"

Caught. I didn't mean to stare at their private goodbye with my mouth hanging open. It was so rude. I should go back into my room and shut the door.

The girl laughed at my expression. "Moms, right?"

"Right."

I made friends with the girl across the hall. We had a lot in common because she was here on scholarship, and I was here for image. We understood each other because we both had a lot to lose. This year, we finally moved in together. It was still hard sometimes when Agnes's family came to pick her up for the holidays or watch her play tennis, but I had to remind myself that I was still lucky.

My family worked really hard to send me here, to earn what we had. They continued to work for it. That was love, too, right? I needed to make them proud.

Pulling the covers tighter around me, I tried to believe that. I didn't want to hate them. My eyes began to water. Stupid chick flick.

I drifted to sleep, but that was okay. I knew that in the end, the mean girl in the movie would get what was coming to her. We always did.

The next thing I heard was the door opening. Agnes must've forgotten something. I snuggled back into my pillow, searching for a spot to continue sleeping.

The bed shifted as someone sat on the corner. When I saw who it was, I stiffened. "Hey."

"Hey," Xander said slowly. He took in my sports bra and discarded laptop. "I knocked, but you didn't answer. You okay?"

"Sure." I yawned. He shouldn't be here, but I couldn't maintain this...this tension between us. It was too hard to care about anything today. "I need a 'me' day." It was as good an excuse as any.

"You never take 'me' days," he said. "In fact, I'm not sure you've ever been sick."

That wasn't true. I'd been sick plenty of times. I just wasn't sick enough to take a day off or show weakness. I reached over and patted his thigh. "I do now…" My head swirled a little, which was weird. I'd only been in bed… I checked the alarm clock in the corner… Apparently, all day.

He watched me try to orient myself. "When was the last time you ate something?"

I thought back. I'd been fasting yesterday, but today… "I had a cracker." So, not much. "It's fine. I've… I've gained weight," I said in a small voice. "I have pounds to lose."

His eyebrows pulled together in a fierce frown. "Bullshit," he said harshly.

Startled, I looked up at him from my pillow. "What?"

"I said Bull. Shit. Did your *parents*," he sneered the words, "tell you to diet?"

I didn't say anything for a moment. He was a guy, so what would he know? Maybe I should educate him. I quoted my mom. "I have a very specific body type, and—"

"This isn't healthy." He turned his back to me and started to scrounge through our cupboard.

Instead of getting angry that once again he was telling me what to do, it was all pretty funny all of a sudden. Like he could talk! I started giggling. "All you eat," I wheezed, "is grease."

"Not true. I eat a lot of protein, and I work out all the time. But I do eat," he said. When he turned back, there were more crackers in his hand. "How do you not have any real food in this room?"

"I can't do whatever this is," I used my hand to indicate the air between us, "today. I need to rest." I covered a yawn. When my hand came back down, he put a cracker in it.

"What you need is to get up."

I ate the cracker in two big bites. "Xander, why are you bothering with me right now? I'm..." I trailed off, thinking of Jenna. Of Trent. My parents. Dark didn't begin to describe my mood. I set the next cracker he handed me on the side table.

He closed the distance between us, his face now uncomfortably close to mine. "You're what?"

This was *my* bed, and I was not going to scoot back, even though I had no idea why he was mad. "What do you want from me?" My voice cracked. "I'm... I'm this horrible person. A garbage person, and..." And everyone pretended to like me! I covered my face with my hands. I didn't even know they were mad, and that made it even worse. Made me even worse. Couldn't he see that?

Xander peeled my hands away from my face.

"Virginia Benson, you are anything but garbage," he said. "You're... You're..." He couldn't seem to find the word he was looking for.

And then his mouth came down on mine.

His lips absorbed my gasp, and he was so tender, so sweet about it that it was too much to bear. I broke away from the kiss, heart pounding. "What was that?"

He ran his hand through his hair, squinting as if in pain. "I'm sorry, I—"

But that's all he got out before I flung my comforter off my body and pulled him down by his shirt, smashing my mouth against his. I wasn't thinking straight, wasn't thinking at all. All I knew was that he tasted like chocolate, and his body was warm. I pressed against him, my body aching with an unfamiliar need. I wanted to meld my body with his; I couldn't get close enough. He'd opened a door I couldn't close by making the move I hadn't been able to. All my walls were shattered now. But who was I kidding? With Xander, they'd always been flimsy at best.

At first, Xander didn't react, even though he'd been the one to kiss me first. He remained frozen under the force of my lips, his hands cradling my face as if I were made of glass. But when I bit him lightly, it was like something inside him snapped. He finally kissed me back. His lips weren't as gentle when they parted mine, and I didn't want them to be. Every cell of my body screamed *Finally, finally, finally.* It was like we picked up right where we left off freshman year, but maybe I didn't remember it clearly enough. This was so much more intense than that. We devoured each other, fighting for dominance, fighting for each other.

We might have broken up, but we weren't over. Not really. He never deleted my number from his phone. He still saw me for me. He risked the hall matron's wrath to make sure I was okay, even after we argued. He pushed me and forced me to look at things differently. Even myself. And he still wanted me.

One of his knees slipped between my legs, and his hand threaded through my hair as he angled my head to kiss me deeper. I could do anything with him. Everything. This was Xander. I could be awkward and imperfect with Xander.

My laptop clattered to the floor as we tangled together. His other hand slid down my back, and his fingers dug into my hip. I arched against him, pressing my chest against his, my whole body charged and sparking. I wanted... I don't know what I wanted, but this wasn't enough. It was as if a switch had been flipped, and now instead of hating him with every fiber of my being, all I wanted was to get close to him. Blood pounded in my ears.

"Virginia," he whispered, his voice reverent as he pulled back to look at me. His hair was a mess, his lips swollen. I knew if I had a mirror, I'd look the same right now, my chest heaving. An unspoken question floated in the air between us. It was anything but virginal.

Light flooded the room as the door to the hallway swung open.

I never moved so quickly in my entire life. One minute we were on my bed, ready to do I don't even know what. The next, Xander had my laptop and was clearing his throat, pointing at the screen in an attempt to pretend we were watching something on it.

Agnes froze in the doorway. "Xander!" she hissed. "What are you doing here? You're going to get us all in trouble!"

"Uh, yeah, sorry," he said. He handed the laptop back to me, trying to smooth his hair. It was a lost cause. Then, without even looking in my direction, he was out the door.

And I wasn't one to swear, but what in the holy hell just happened?

"Well *that* was interesting," Agnes said as she breezed into the room to sit on her bed.

"Yeah," I mumbled.

When it was clear I wasn't going to elaborate, she said, "Well, you're obviously not sick."

I flopped backwards onto my bed. "I don't... I can't. I'm sorry."

"Are you any closer to catching the graffiti person? Is that what you guys were doing? Or were you..."

I grabbed my pillow and covered my face. Why did he have to come over and kiss me when I literally looked my worst? What were we doing? Did I like Xander now? No. Maybe. No. I didn't want to. He was still a jerk. But his body against mine felt like maybe I didn't have to be Virginal Virginia forever? It wasn't like I was waiting for true love or marriage or something moral like that. It wasn't like my V-card was something I was desperately holding onto, even if that's how he made it sound.

"Hello? Earth to Virginia?" Agnes pulled the pillow off my face.

"I have no idea." I slid off the bed to stretch. The floor shifted and I reached for the bedpost.

"You okay?" She reached out to catch me. "Maybe you *are* sick."

I nodded, glancing at the crackers on my desk. I smiled at her as I grabbed one and shoved the whole thing in my mouth. Water would probably be good, too.

Agnes flopped onto the couch. "I don't know what's up with you anymore."

I shuffled to the mini fridge. She was giving me an out. A chance to say things. To be a better friend. But all I had was a water. I handed it to her and grabbed one for myself.

She snorted, and we both popped the tops and took long drinks.

"I just..." I waved my hands, unable to form the right words.

"Like, I know you're not good at talking about crap or whatever, but if you're playing a game with Xander, I'm scared you're going to lose. You know?"

I could feel her eyes on me, but I couldn't meet them. I picked at the label on my bottled water as I leaned against her desk. "I'm not playing anything." My voice dropped to a whisper. "You know how much I need Yale."

"There are other schools, V."

"Not for me." She knew Yale was the goal. The only option. It had been planned since my birth. It was going to happen. I was going to make it happen.

Except— and I felt guilty just for thinking it— there *were* other options. My dad had scoffed at the idea of me applying anywhere else, but it had been logical. I had backups if I wanted them.

And it wasn't their life. It was mine.

"You don't have to be your mom, you know," Agnes said softly. It was almost creepy how well she could read my face. "This is getting really intense lately."

I ran my fingers through my now-messy hair, trying to comfort myself. "I know." But how could it not when I could lose everything I'd worked so hard for? I couldn't have this conversation with her. It was nice that she was in my corner, but every ten seconds, she thought I was stacking my accomplishments against my mom's. I wasn't. No one could hope to compare to her.

I grabbed my towel and the clothes I'd meant to wear today. I needed a shower.

Agnes huffed, flipping one of her textbooks open to study at her desk.

As I scrubbed my stomach in one of the many cramped shower stalls, I noticed for the first time that my hips were slightly curvier. My mom had a point, and yet… I didn't hate the way that felt. In fact, I kind of liked how my body looked right now. So did Xander. My fingers brushed over my lips, remembering how he'd pressed against me, how I felt when he…

I shook my head. I shouldn't be thinking about that right now. The case was what mattered. Tomorrow, everything would go back to normal, and that kiss...make out, whatever it was, would be behind me.

I massaged shampoo into my hair and ignored the tiny corner of my brain that didn't really believe that. The part that feared that it would be hard to shut that door again with Xander now that I knew what I was missing.

By the time I left my dorm and walked down to the auditorium to see the final production of *Guys and Dolls*, my body was vibrating with anxiety. I wanted to see it now that I'd spent so much time helping with the set, but Xander would be there. Should we talk about the kiss? Did it mean anything? Did I want it to?

I shouldn't have worried, because as soon as I arrived,

Jenna put me to work folding programs, and Xander was nowhere in sight. I relaxed a tiny bit as she went through her spiel about where to stand to hand them out. When the millionth cast member passed us carrying a garment bag, I realized she was talking in circles, and her hands were shaking.

"Shouldn't you be backstage?"

Her large eyes, this time rimmed in dark eyeliner, stared down the red double doors behind me. "You know, I'm still not sure why you're doing this."

"I told you, I—"

She turned to me. "I know what you said."

I gave her a small smile. "Maybe you were right. I didn't help the way I should have last year."

She narrowed her eyes. "Two extra sets of hands *did* make set construction easier."

"I'm more suited to that than the actual stage. It was a lot less stressful. I don't know how you do it every year." A peace offering. Would she take it? I stared at the programs in my hand, afraid of what I might see if I glanced up. I'd never meant to ruin her junior year. She might not believe that, but I wished she would.

"With a lot of help," Jenna said. "If you're still looking for forgiveness, we're okay, Virginia. You and me."

"I—" I glanced up, but she'd already flitted into the auditorium for one last sound check. The corners of my mouth lifted. I didn't need to have the last word this time. I really was starting to like her.

Across the hall from my program-folding station, Xander had arrived. The parents set him up to sell tickets. Good. It would keep him busy, keep him away from me until I could figure out what to say. He was better with the public than I was, anyway. Probably better with money, too.

Fold, file. Fold, file. With each crease, Jenna's words warmed me a little more. I made one thing right. Confidence surged in me. Maybe I could handle Xander, too.

I snuck a glance in his direction. Right now, his hair fell over his face as a girl with black curly hair and a tiny waist leaned across the ticket table to touch his arm. He was smiling at her like she was a piece of candy tossed at him from a parade, which I guess was kind of accurate. My stomach sank, but I should have expected it. Typical Xander. I don't know why I thought anything was different between us.

As if he could sense my thoughts, his head turned. I met his gaze head on. I wasn't spying. He was flirting in public for anyone to see. I raised my hands in a *Well?* gesture.

He leaned back in his chair, frowning like he was confused. Of course he wouldn't see the issue. Flirting was as natural as breathing to him.

As the crowd thickened, I kept myself busy handing out programs. There was a constant line because the show was almost sold out. When the lights lowered, I folded more programs for the next night until the intro music blared through the doors. Then I snuck into the theater and sat in the back row to watch the show.

Jenna was fantastic. When she sang the duet "I'll Know" with a junior whose name escaped me, the chemistry was so hot, I was surprised they didn't make out right then and there. She'd transformed herself into her character so completely, her crazy-white teeth and huge doe-eyes amplified perfectly onstage. She was made for the theater. I felt even worse for the way I'd taken the lead part last year. But then I took a look at the stage, at all the signs and walls that I'd helped put up, and it kind of made me proud, too. It was a small, worthy contribution, and I really had liked it better than being up there under the lights.

Then Xander came to sit down beside me, and just like that, my focus on the stage disappeared. His hand rested on the narrow armrest only millimeters from mine. His leg was so close I could feel the warmth of his body through his jeans. Why didn't he sit next to the girl he was flirting with instead of me? My hands shook as I pulled them into my lap. I could hear every breath he took, could smell the splash of woodsy cologne he was wearing.

Nothing had changed in the past three years. I was still just as affected by him as I was as a freshman. More so, now that we'd… That he'd… My breath quickened as I remembered the way I arched against him on my bed, trying to take from him something that maybe I wasn't willing to give up yet myself.

"You're really into it," he said quietly, making me jump about a mile out of my seat.

He flashed me another one of those trademark Xander smiles, his teeth white and gleaming in the low light. Was this one as fake as the one he'd just shown to the parents at the ticket counter? And what if it wasn't?

As soon as the lights raised for intermission, he turned to face me. "We should talk." He moved his hand over mine.

I sprang up from my seat, my fingers burning where he touched me. "I have to go to the bathroom!" I practically yelled as I pushed through the crowd without looking back. Once I was inside the crowded restroom, I looked at the stupid, scared girl in the mirror. *What am I doing? Xander is out there right now. He's not avoiding me. He's... He's...*

I took my time washing my hands, blasting every speck of water off them with the painfully loud hand-dryer. It was gut reaction to avoid him, but it was more than that. Acknowledging what happened in my room would start something. Something that would mean more to me than it ever had freshman year.

I took a deep breath and exited the bathroom. But when I returned to my seat, Xander was nowhere to be found.

I collapsed into the padded chair. It wasn't like I knew what to say, anyway. Wasn't like I knew what I wanted *him* to say, either.

The rest of the play was amazing. Jenna shone like the sun, stealing every scene. Her talent was far above high school level, and though her co-stars tried to match her energy, her raw talent pushed the show to a whole other level. In the end, I surged to my feet with everyone else in the audience to give a standing ovation, grateful to have been a part of something so smartly done. The production would run the next two nights, but I was no longer needed since I'd already folded all the programs. A crew member would pass them out.

For me, it was over. I didn't think Jenna was the graffiti artist. Hadn't, actually, for some time. Even if she was, she said we were good. It was nice to make at least one thing right.

11

SOMETHING BAD

WHEN XANDER SAT NEXT to me in History the next afternoon, everyone noticed. Whispers crescendoed around us as I straightened the pencils on my desk until they were in a perfectly even line. What was he *doing?* We never hung out in public. Maybe he was trying to create gossip about us so someone would slip and say something about the graffiti.

I strained to hear what they were saying, but after a minute, I tuned them all out. It was all speculation about what we were to each other. Nothing about graffiti. Tamara was specifically annoying. I did *not* pant after Xander like a dog.

Stop it, I mouthed at him when the teacher wasn't looking.

His expression was innocent, like he had no idea what I was talking about. I watched him write in that sloppy scrawl of his while the teacher talked. He folded the paper once, twice, then slid it onto the corner of my desk, never looking away from the front of the classroom.

I stared at it as nervously as I would a pop quiz. Who wrote notes by hand anymore? And what did it have in it? Would he say our kiss was a mistake? Tell me he didn't want to help me anymore? Ask me out? None of those sounded right.

He glanced at me, then tapped his pencil against his desk impatiently.

Ugh, fine. I unfolded it behind my binder as quietly as I could. Were those O's or U's...or A's? He needed a handwriting class, for God's sake.

When I finally managed to make out his message, it wasn't what I expected.

Heard a rumor of something bad going down today. Be careful.

My heart stuttered. I scribbled back a response. When the teacher squatted down to help a student on the other side of the silent classroom, I slipped the paper under his binder.

What rumor? Bad how?

Seconds later, the paper re-appeared on my desk, and I practically ripped it as I unfolded it.

No idea. Just talk, and you're at the center of it.

So frustrating...and scary. Was it Trent? Did I rip open a wound when I tried to talk to him, and now he wanted revenge in a more direct way than the graffiti?

I tucked the paper into a pocket in my binder. What more could I write to Xander? *Stay with me, I'm scared? Come live in my dorm room with me until the bad guys leave me alone?* For all I knew, it was a jealous girl who wanted in Xander's pants, and now she was annoyed he was spending too much time with me. Him sitting next to me now was probably making whoever it was angrier.

As soon as the bell sounded, I dragged him into the hallway. "Who did you hear that from?" I demanded.

His gaze dropped to where my hand touched his arm. We were standing very close, and our kiss flashed through my head. I let go of his sleeve and stepped back.

He gave me a knowing smile. Smug jerk. "Chad Brunswick," he said.

"Chad Brunswick," I repeated. Chad who asked if he could staple the broken bus window back together after he had a temper tantrum in the back seat, Chad? He was built like a MAC truck and his favorite words were *Oops* and *My bad*. Still…

"Did you ask him about me?" Students slid past us as the hall emptied. I didn't need to whisper, but I did anyway.

"Nah, he just thought I'd like to know." Xander matched my volume. I craned my neck to hear him.

"Well, how does he know?" What connection did Chad have to me?

"How should I know?"

God, Xander was in a frustrating mood today. "Where is he now?"

"You don't wanna know." He cocked his head to the side, watching my facial expressions as my anger rose. This was fun for him! He was enjoying this!

A couple of girls walked by. When they saw Xander, they started whispering and giggling.

"Ladies," he said smoothly.

"Xander!" I hissed.

His attention shifted to my mouth. My breath caught in my throat. How could he do that, seconds after flirting with someone else? More importantly, was he going to kiss me right now? Our mouths were inches from each other, and his breath was hot on my cheek.

"It's after school, Virgin. Where do you think he is?"

Why would I know…? Ugh. Chad was a linebacker on the

football team. He'd be in the boys' locker room getting ready for practice. I almost groaned aloud. There was no way I could go back to the scene of the crime to confront him. Not to mention all those guys with their shirts off, making me feel all kinds of uncomfortable as they put on knee pads or whatever was needed for the coach's year-round craziness. Ew, what if I saw more than I wanted to?

"What are you thinking?" Xander pulled away to study my face.

"Nothing." I needed to know. More than ever, I needed to know what Chad knew. How he knew. Who he'd heard it from. And if there was a time crunch, I didn't have time to wait. Xander hadn't been there for the brunt of my parents' visit, so he didn't understand how I couldn't disappoint them. I didn't... I didn't know how.

I headed for my locker to stow my backpack, a plan already forming in my head. If I made quick work of it, I'd be in and out before their practice even started. Obviously, Xander had done a poor job interrogating Chad.

Xander's stride matched mine as I practically ran down the freshman hall.

I dumped all of my stuff in my locker and slammed it shut before hurrying back to the front of the building where the locker rooms were.

"You can't be serious," Xander said.

"I need to hear it from Chad myself."

He sighed. "At least let me go with you."

"Fine."

"Fine."

He almost slammed into my back when I jerked to a stop in front of the locker room door. I'd only been in there once, and it had been a disaster. *Woman up,* I thought before shoving through the door.

Just like last time, I was kind of let down by the scene that unfolded before me. I tried to ignore the smell of new paint that meant the graffiti had been covered up as I strode through the common area. I don't know what shows I was watching or books I was reading that made me believe I'd see guys in white towels, their chests bare and glistening with water from their showers. It wasn't like you'd take a shower before practice. And why was I fantasizing about that, anyway? Man, that kiss Xander landed on me must have brought up some weird feelings.

The guys in the locker rooms were in running shorts, and most had their shirts on. I resisted the urge to cover my eyes like a prude and stepped forward until I was in front of the lockers. "Chad?" I called out. Xander sat down on a wooden bench a few yards behind me. I yelled louder. "Chad!"

"What?" A belligerent voice rang out. An annoyed Chad stepped in front of me, all two hundred and fifty pounds of football jock in a cut-off T shirt that sported some serious pit stains.

"Virginia?" he asked. He looked around and I could see the wheels turning in his brain. Was he sure he was in the guys' locker room? Then why was I here?

"What did you hear about me?"

Chad glanced behind me to Xander, who put his hands in the air in surrender.

"I can't tell you," Chad's expression was still baffled. "You're not as scary." As if that made any sense.

"Oh, I don't think you know how scary she can be," Xander said.

I was going to kill them both. "Chad, I need to know—"

And that's when the coach walked into the room. Chad turned like a soldier at attention, ready to listen to whatever it was he needed to get done.

"Alright, guys, we have a lot to do today," the coach said as he began to pace around the locker room. He was coming straight for me!

Crap, crap, crap! He couldn't see me here. No one could see me here! All Dean Alton needed was one more thing against me, and I was history. I couldn't leave without passing in front of the coach's line of vision, but I couldn't stay where I was.

Xander grabbed my arm, motioning to the janitor's closet at the side of the room. We sprinted to it and slid through the opening, pulling the door closed one inch at a time until it clicked shut.

The closet was tiny, and it was filled to the brim with smelly cleaning agents, brooms, buckets, and whatever else was jammed up against us. Our bodies pressed together in the small space. Xander's hip dug into my side and, after a second, I could feel him shaking with laughter. I elbowed him in the gut.

"It's not funny," I hissed. I pressed my ear to the door, trying to make out the sounds in the locker room. Was the coach still talking?

"It's pretty funny," Xander whispered against my hair. "Half the guys in this school were dying to get seven minutes in heaven with you freshman year. Remember?"

A mop jammed into my back, and I shifted away from it. No. I didn't remember. I'd gone to exactly two parties, and I never participated in that side of them. All I'd wanted then was… Xander.

"Shut up," I shoved him back. A box stacked in the corner of the closet shifted and pushed him even closer to me.

Our time smooshed together in the closet seemed to stretch into oblivion. Xander's shirt was scrunched up, and his partially bare stomach pressed against me in the dark. My breathing quickened. Intense heat radiated from his skin, and I reached out to touch it before I realized what I was doing and pulled my hand back.

Xander shifted his feet until our bodies were no longer at an angle. It was more comfortable, but it created a new problem of my chest against his. His heart thudded against my ear, strong and reassuring. In the darkness, I thought I felt him move his neck until he was looking down at me.

"Virginia." His hand lowered to touch my hair. His face was less than an inch away. I licked my lips. This time I was sure he was going to kiss me.

The coach blew his whistle, loud and long, and we heard the shuffling of feet. The locker room was emptying. When we could no longer hear anything, I let out a breath.

"Um," I said. "We should probably get out of here."

Xander's arm reached over me and turned the knob of the door. We tumbled out of the closet together, the buckets and mops crashing into a heap behind us as we fell. At the last moment, Xander twisted his body so that he went down first, and I fell on top of him.

For a moment, my hair covered both of us in a long, dark cocoon.

"You okay?" he asked hoarsely.

"I—" Holy crap, what was I doing? I scrambled off of him and sprang to my feet.

He got up more slowly, his expression cautious. "Virgin, we should—"

"I have to go." I whirled around to leave the room.

He followed behind me, not saying anything else as we stepped through the door and began our trek down the long, empty hallway.

When we parted ways to go to our separate dorms, Xander clicked his tongue and winked as if nothing happened. As if almost kissing me was no big deal. To him, it probably wasn't. And in the end, I guess nothing did happen. We got nothing from Chad. I was going to have to fend for myself.

When I went running that afternoon, I took a different route and didn't realize until I was halfway through that my return would be entirely uphill. It was horrible on my calves, but when I got back to my room, I was feeling pretty proud of myself for sticking it out. It was a nice distraction.

The only thing more relaxing than a shower would have been a bath, but there weren't any tubs at the school. Sticky and hot, I shucked my clothes as quickly as I could behind the curtain of my favorite shower stall and stepped into the unforgiving overhead spray. God, what would it be like to wash away problems the way I washed off my sweat? I was tempted to stay here forever, despite the ugly green tiling.

I took my time shampooing my hair, massaging my scalp as I rinsed away the suds. Sometimes showering felt like a chore. Today, it felt like therapy. The hot water pelted my shoulders as I snapped open my conditioner, working it into the ends of my hair and twisting it to pile it high on my head to soak in as I shaved. I braced myself against the shower wall, reveling in the steam and heat.

It was then that I noticed a faint, familiar scent mixed with the lavender smell of my conditioner. Like the closet from today, or a salon...

Oh my God. I un-twisted my hair and let out a bloodcurdling scream.

Bleach. In my hair!

How long had it been on my head? Five minutes? Ten? Was it even bleach, or something else? I pulled apart the sopping strands with shaking fingers, barely registering what I was seeing. Orange and yellow threaded through my dark brown. *Get it out. Get it out now!*

I scrubbed violently until huge chunk of hair broke off in my hand. *Oh my God.* I didn't even turn off the shower as I flung open the door, groping for the sink. Wiping aside the fog on the mirror, I could see clearly all the splotches that covered my once-beautiful hair. Huge, uneven pale blobs on the top, and the ends were absolutely ruined. They were going to break off any second.

Everyone who knew anything about me knew how proud I was of my hair. I never cut it, except to trim the ends. Never colored it because my parents forbid it. Sometimes it felt like the only thing I had going for me was my naturally thick, beautiful hair. And now... I gently lifted a limp chunk and tried to cover a spot, my lip trembling. It didn't work. Tears streamed down my cheeks as my dripping body became colder by the minute.

My hair.

Eventually, I forced myself to calm down. A plan would make me feel better. I needed to get to my hair salon and let my stylist sort it out. But I didn't have a hat because I never wanted to cover my head before. Even in the winter, I preferred headbands. How could I get there without everyone noticing?

I gently twisted my hair into a towel and threw on my clothes. Then I crept into the hallway and dashed into my room before anyone could witness the total meltdown that threatened to consume me at any second. There had to be a scarf somewhere in my room. I rifled through my drawers until I found one, groaning when I could see my hand right through it. Maybe if I double-layered?

Ten minutes later, my head was covered, and I looked incredibly stupid. Still, it was better than people knowing the truth about what happened. I just had to get to my car as quickly as possible and not look at the broken strands of orange and yellow bleached hair that now littered the floor of my dorm room.

Halfway across the parking lot, I was beginning to think I'd make it without anyone seeing me.

"Nice scarf!" an underclassman to my left called. He elbowed his friend in the ribs and chuckled.

My vision blurred and I lengthened my stride into a speed walk. Only when I got to my car did I draw in a shuddering breath. It could have been worse.

I jammed my foot onto the brake and pressed the ignition button and... Nothing. I jabbed at it again and again, and all I heard was the click of the button. I had no idea what that meant. It was a brand-new car. My dad got it for me only two years ago! How could it already be broken?

My stomach dropped. This was part of the plan. Whoever put the bleach in my shampoo knew I'd find a way to fix it. But not without my car. Smart. Horrifyingly smart and well-planned.

I needed Agnes, but we hadn't been seeing eye to eye lately. And I had no one else. No one, except...

With a shuddering sigh, I scrolled all the way down my contacts in my phone.

"What happened?" Not even a hello when Xander's deep voice answered. Like he'd predicted, I'd been screwed over. His cryptic warning had done nothing to prevent this disaster.

"I'm in my car. It won't start. I have to get to town." I worked to keep my tone even. He didn't need to know everything. No one did.

"Oh, is that it? I thought you were in trouble."

Okay, maybe I'd made myself sound too casual. I needed him to help me. My knuckles were white against my phone.

"Xander," I ground out.

"Yeah?"

"I have to get to town." This time I was a little more forceful than before.

"Well, I'm not giving you my keys. I've seen the way you drive."

What? When did he see me drive? I shrank back into my seat. What was I going to do?

"But I'm standing right in front of you. I can drive you, and you can tell me why you look like you're about to board a covered wagon." He jingled the keys at me through the windshield.

I pushed through the door and sprinted through the parking lot to his car, one hand on my scarf to keep it in place.

He adapted his speed to match mine. "Jeez, you're in a rush."

I slammed the passenger side of his car shut and tapped my fingers rapidly against the center console as he drove down the long driveway of the school. "I need to get to my hair salon," I bit out. "On Pearl."

He made the turn. "Are you going to tell me what happened?"

I could feel his eyes on me as I stared straight ahead. "Bleach," I said through gritted teeth. "In my conditioner." I panicked as I imagined my hairdresser's face. Would he cut it all off? How damaged was it?

"That sucks. Good thing it's just hair," Xander said. "Could have been way worse." What a guy thing to say.

I was silent. He couldn't understand, but I just...really loved my hair. Loved. Past tense.

Xander was silent the rest of the way, but when I got out of the car, he followed me through the swinging door of the salon.

I marched up to the main desk with him two steps behind me. "I don't have an appointment, but I need Vincent," I said through my tears to the receptionist. "Please."

She glanced up, annoyed. "Honey," she said, "he's booked through July, and he only takes appointments." She stared at my stupid bonnet-looking scarf pointedly.

"I know. I'm here every month. Benson. Virginia," I choked out. I was trying not to take offense. I knew how it looked. How I looked.

"Oh my God, are you going to cry?" Her voice had now gone quiet and concerned, but it didn't help my rising panic. I couldn't deal with this right now!

"No one can see my hair but Vincent." I struggled to keep my voice level.

She tapped her French-tipped manicure on the wood of the desk while we locked eyes. Whatever she saw in my face, her expression softened. "I'll see what I can do," she said and pressed a button on her phone. "Vincent, I know you're booked." She paused. "Right, well, there appears to be some sort of hair emergency out here, and she's a regular." After a moment, she replaced the phone. "He's coming out to talk to you."

Vincent rounded the corner, a comb in his left hand. He looked pissed. "What is the—Virginia Benson." A smile immediately spread over his thin face. "What are you doing here, girl? You're clockwork." Then he spied the scarf. "Oh my God, what did you do to our hair?" He screeched so loudly that everyone in the shop paused in what they were doing. One lady almost spilled the coffee she'd just poured herself from the table in the corner.

"I…" But it was too late. Vincent ripped off my scarf, and my hair was on display for all to see, including the five people waiting in the plush chairs in reception. Vincent sucked in a breath. He looked like he was about to faint.

"It's not that bad," Xander offered.

I almost forgot he was with me. When I turned to him, his eyes were wide as he tried to reassure me. Even he was shocked. I wanted to sink into the floor and disappear.

"You poor thing," an old lady in the waiting room said, rising from her perch. "You can have my spot. I'm only getting my curls re-set. I'm sure someone else can do that." She didn't even blink as she took in my hair. "You need Vincent more than I do."

The receptionist nodded mutely.

"Thank you," I choked out as Vincent led me to a chair in the back.

Xander followed like some sort of bodyguard, his mouth set

into a firm line. I wasn't sure why. He couldn't protect me from what had already happened.

"I'm fine," I told him.

He just shook his head at me, his expression stern and unreadable.

Vincent was almost in tears as he finger-combed through the mess that was once my beautiful hair, finding new bleach spots everywhere, strands of it sticking to his fingers like spiderwebs. "What could possibly... How did you..." He wasn't going to form real sentences anytime soon.

"Someone put bleach in her shampoo," Xander said in a murderous tone.

Tears streamed down my face. I couldn't hold them back anymore. "Conditioner," I whispered, as if it mattered.

"Who would—why would anyone do this? Are you sure it was only bleach? Well, we'll just have to do our best to... Let me think." Vincent let go of my hair and rinsed his hands. He sat down on the chair next to me, studying my head. The plastic of his comb clacked against the arm of the chair as he thought. *Click, click, click, click.*

After a minute, he tossed his comb in a tube with blue sanitizer. He stood over me as he waited the long minutes it took me to get myself under control.

"You already know what we have to do," he finally said, all traces of his normal chipper voice gone.

I nodded. I could hear the buzzer already.

"I can make you a fierce pixie cut. You'll rock the hell out of it with your face shape, and the bleach didn't make it all the way to the roots, so you'll still have your natural hair."

"Oh my God," I whispered. Short hair looked great on some girls, but I didn't have that kind of confidence. Every time I looked in the mirror, all I'd see was a boy with a swollen balloon for a face. It would be a far cry from the image my mom had carefully crafted for me.

Vincent stood back up and snapped a black plastic cape into place around my neck. "I'm sorry, baby doll. It's just…" He lifted a piece and dropped it. "It's way too damaged to dye back. It won't survive. There's no way this was only bleach."

"Can I have a second?" I whispered.

"I'll go get some tools." He disappeared into the back room.

Liar. All his tools were right here. Still, I appreciated that he gave me a second to say goodbye to the only thing that ever made me feel beautiful. I don't know how long I stared dully at my ruined hair before Vincent returned, light glinting off the edge of his silver scissors.

"Ready?"

I nodded, not trusting myself to speak. Crying wasn't going to fix this.

"I'm going to make you look so badass. Then you better show that bitch who's boss."

"How do you know it was a girl?"

Both Vincent and I jerked. I'd completely forgotten Xander was there. Again.

"Guys wouldn't have access to the girls' showers," I said. It sure would be nice to be as relaxed as Xander appeared in the reflection of the mirror.

"And a guy would never think of something like this," Vincent added.

I couldn't rip my eyes from the limp mass of ruined hair that hung over my shoulders. "I'm going to look like…"

Xander regarded me carefully. "Don't take this the wrong way, Virgin," he said. "But it would take a hell of a lot more than a bad hair day to make you anything less than drop dead gorgeous." He flopped into the chair Vincent had vacated. "At least we can take Trent off the list for good, if you're so sure it's a girl."

"Yes," I said flatly. I couldn't even muster up annoyance at the fact that Xander had yet again called me a virgin. "At least that." I swallowed, then looked to Vincent. "Okay. Cut it off."

12

CINNAMON TURKEY

VINCENT SPUN me around in the chair so I didn't have to see what he was doing. He continued to reassure me as his scissors and comb worked. *Snick. Snick. Snick.* Every chunk of hair that fell made my head lighter and my heart heavier. Xander stopped trying to console me after the first "It's gonna be great" when I pinned him with a death glare and banished him to the reception area. I didn't want him to see me go from hot to not, and I definitely didn't want his lies about how it was fine.

After an hour, a shampoo and conditioner—that smelled like fruit instead of bleach—and a ton of products and muttering from Vincent, he twirled me back around.

"See? You're a knockout!"

I stared at the girl in the mirror. The one with a splotchy face and shorn hair. It was *short*. Too short. Way too short.

"I was able to keep more than I thought. Magic hands," Vincent gloated.

My fingers threaded through the back of my hair, where it had been hacked to less than two inches. The front was a longer swoop of side bangs that I might be able to put behind my ear after a little bit of growth.

I couldn't be objective about it. I collapsed back into the chair. "Thank you," I muttered brokenly.

He unsnapped the cape. "Give me a hug."

Bensons didn't really hug. Not for more than a second, anyway. It got awkward fast. Despite that, I basically collapsed into Vincent's slender arms, breathing in his smell, a mix of cologne and the scent of hair spray.

"Come back in four weeks and we'll reevaluate." He guided me by my arm to the front of the salon. "We'll make room in the schedule," he said to the receptionist.

She smacked her gum at him. Then she saw me and did a literal double take. "Wow."

"Virginia Benson." Vincent ignored her to flip through the pages of the appointment book.

She penciled in my name where he pointed. He muttered something in her ear, and she grinned.

Vincent kissed me on the forehead. "Go kick some bully booty." I blinked back tears again as he disappeared around the corner.

"How much do I owe?" I whispered, placing my credit card on the counter.

She slid it back to me. "Nothing. Vincent is a fixer."

I nodded and pulled out a wad of cash for a tip. He'd been so nice to me. I loved Vincent. I just didn't love…

My hand fluttered to my head, and my throat clogged. I was going to have to wear a scarf for the rest of my life.

When I turned toward the exit, Xander glanced up from his phone. "You ready to g— Oh."

I touched my very short hair. "I know. Don't make a big deal out of it."

"What?" His eyes remained glued to my haircut, his jaw slack. Like I didn't feel like enough of a freak already.

I waved him off as I passed him on the way out the door. If his reaction was any indication, I looked as terrible as I thought

I did. Everyone would know by tomorrow, and then the rumors would start. My stomach clenched. God, what a mess.

When I climbed back in Xander's car, the clock flashed the time. It was much later than I had thought. My stomach rumbled uncomfortably. I flattened out my scarf to put back on my head. "I'm sorry this took so long."

"What are you doing?" His hand stilled my efforts.

"What?"

"You're apologizing? And covering up your hair?"

I waved the scarf at him. "Obviously."

"Why?"

What did he mean, why? "Have you seen it?"

He stared at me. "You have no idea, do you?"

I leaned back on the seat. I was exhausted. "I can't play games with you right now."

"Benson, you're *stunning*."

My mouth dropped open. "What?"

He cleared his throat. "My mom wants me home for dinner. Want to come?"

My hands clenched the scarf, but I didn't put it on my head. I almost considered saying yes before I remembered the last time I saw his mom. I could never live down mistaking her for the cook. "I don't want to impose. You can just drop me back at the dorms." The words tumbled out of my mouth. *Stunning?* He thought I was stunning?

"The dining hall is closed now. What are you going to eat?" He paused. "You need to eat."

"I have food in my dorm," I lied.

"You have half a sleeve of crackers. You could just say you don't want to eat with me," he snapped. His hands tightened on the steering wheel.

Great, now I'd offended him. "That's not it."

"Then what's the big deal?" He stared straight ahead, apparently unwilling to let it go.

"Fine!"

He chuckled.

So frustrating! Why did everything with him have to be a fight? Then a calm settled over me. How many guys would stay for hours while a sobbing girl got her hair done? That couldn't have been a comfortable situation for him. "Thank you for driving me."

"You're welcome," he said cheerily as we pulled into the driveway of his house. "Now let's eat."

Dread coiled in my gut as I let Xander pull me through the door to meet his mom. We found her in the kitchen again.

Mrs. Hearst grinned when she saw us and pulled her apron over her head to hang on a hook. "Virginia! What a wonderful surprise!" She wrapped Xander in a hug and held her arms open for me, too. Shock didn't begin to cover my reaction. She wasn't mad at me for saying what I did about Xander last time? Had he told her I thought she was the cook? Wait, had I ever told him my mistake? This night might be salvageable after all. Absently, I tried to hug her back.

Xander's mom set another place for me at the table, and I sank into my seat, my face flushed hot at what an intrusion this must be. She waved me off, completely comfortable. We ate at a table large enough for ten, but we crowded together on one end so we could talk. It was very different from dinner with my parents at home, where we all shuffled to our designated seats, equally spaced away from each other.

"I love your haircut!" Mrs. Hearst beamed. "It's so pretty! I want you to try the turkey and tell me your honest opinion, okay?"

She served me way too much of everything on the table: turkey, green beans, some sort of casserole, and sweet potatoes. "I'm doing some experimenting, and I'm only keeping the good recipes," she said.

Well, now I felt the need to try everything. She expected it. I cut a tiny piece of turkey and popped it in my mouth.

It almost melted on my tongue, it was so delicious. There was no way turkey tasted like that. I cut a slightly bigger piece and ate it, slowly again, trying to figure out what she could have possibly put in the meat to make it taste that way.

"It's amazing." Something about the rich food made my brain settle after the intensity of this day. I took another bite.

"Yeah, Mom." Xander's voice was muffled as he chewed. "Better than last night's, anyway."

My mouth dropped open in horror. That was so rude. What would she say to him? Would he get in trouble?

But his mom took it in stride. "I thought so, too. Believe it or not," she confided in me, "the secret ingredient is cinnamon. Who knew?"

Xander snorted. "Ma, the secret ingredient is always cinnamon." He turned to me. "She puts cinnamon in everything. She's a cinnamon freak."

She ignored him. "Chew your food, honey. There's a lady present."

"Meh, it's just Virgin...ia." He tacked on the last part of my name a little too late, and his mom gave him a stern look.

"I'm sorry for my son's manners, Virginia. He's the youngest of five boys, and a little wilder than they were, I'm afraid."

I knew that Xander had older brothers, but four? Xander told me freshman year that his brother Chris graduated right before we entered high school. What were each of them doing now?

I went to push my hair back from my face, my hand stilling when it met the air. *Don't let it affect you in front of his mom.* "It's okay, Mrs. Hearst. I know what he's like." I smiled and she grinned back.

"Mrs. Hearst. You're so polite! But please call me Peg, okay?"

"Sure," I said. I had no intention of ever doing that. It was way too informal for an authority figure.

Xander caught my gaze and raised his eyebrows like he knew exactly what I was thinking. Then he turned to his mom and changed the subject. "You know," he said with his mouth full of food, "Rodney was way worse than me."

His mom's eyes crinkled as she laughed. Every reaction she had was so honest. So open. So genuine. He was exactly like her.

"Remember when he jumped into a rushing river when we were hiking with Dad?"

She grimaced, as if recalling the incident caused her real physical pain. "Don't remind me."

"Or when he—"

His mom pointed her fork at him. "Don't pretend that you've asked permission for all of your dangerous stunts, Mister. Or I might just embarrass you in front of Virginia by telling her about when you were at your grandma's house last summer, and—"

"You wouldn't dare."

She took a sip of water, her lips curled into a devilish smile.

I was curious about what he'd done that was so embarrassing that he didn't want me to hear, but more than that, I was watching their exchange with extreme interest. It was like when Agnes's family came to visit. Xander and his mom had a language of their own, built on shared memories of fun events. It was kind of hard to follow, but I didn't need to know what they were talking about to know they loved each other. It seeped into their stories, the way her eyes twinkled with pride when she looked at her son.

That wasn't what puzzled me. It was the way she included me in conversation, encouraging me to talk about myself and tease Xander, the way she patted my hand and offered me more food. I knew now where Xander got his big toothy grin from, and why he used it so often. His mom shone like the sun.

My parents loved me too, but we weren't like that. We didn't talk much unless it had something to do with a test or a concept I hadn't understood. Then it was more like a lecture. I found myself out of place in this kind of conversation, murmuring lame responses and watching them talk more than anything else.

I could have basked in their happiness forever.

My shoulders relaxed, the stress of the day beginning to seep out of me. The third time I covered a yawn, Xander said, "I think that's it for us, Ma."

She walked us to the door, and he kissed her on the cheek.

As I started to follow him out, she grabbed my hand and squeezed it. "I loved seeing you again, Virginia. Let me give you my number, in case you need to tell on this brat." She jabbed a teasing finger in Xander's direction. "My son tells me your parents live across the country. It's always good to have another adult in your corner."

"Really?"

She held out her hand for my phone. "Really."

I pulled my phone out and she put in her information. She actually meant that. Of course, I'd never use the number, but…

"And you come by anytime, with or without this one," she said. "It's nice to have another woman in the house. Anything you need. I bet I could fatten you up in no time." She laughed.

I didn't doubt that one bit. For once, the thought didn't fill me with dread. "That's so nice. Thank you," I said quietly. My voice might have wobbled on the last word, but thankfully we all pretended it didn't.

She hugged me again, her arms at once foreign and warm. When we said goodbye and she told me she couldn't wait to see me again, I could almost believe it was true.

On the way back to the dorms, I asked Xander, "Why do you live on campus again?"

"Virgin, I'm shocked. You're actually taking an interest in

me?" A streetlight illuminated his face for a moment. It was twisted into one of his obnoxious smirks.

"Just wondering." I didn't meet his eyes. If his mom reprimanding him didn't stop him from using that rude nickname, it was unlikely anything I said would. That's what I got for trying to care about him. The light turned, and we inched forward in traffic.

"I stay in the dorms," he said finally, "because I want to get the full experience. You know?"

I was silent. No. I didn't know. If I had a mom like his, I'd never want to leave.

"Where's your dad?"

"Away on business. He makes it back for a lot of stuff, though. He loves fencing. He's been at a bunch of our matches."

I hadn't noticed. Wasn't that the theme this year? That I never noticed anything? I traced the seam of my pants with my fingernail.

"You're quiet."

"Yeah." I didn't explain myself, and he didn't make me. After everything that had happened today—my hair, his reaction, his mom… I didn't have anything to say. Maybe we weren't *always* at each other's throats.

Streetlights lit our way back to campus. "So… Not Jenna then. Or Trent. We're back to square one on the Asshat mystery," he said.

I laid my head on the window and sighed. And then there was that.

As soon as Xander dropped me off, I snapped back into mystery-solving mode. With Jenna and Trent off the suspect list, the mystery of who was trying to frame me—and who caused half my hair to break off in bleached clumps—had hit a dead end. I needed to enlist Agnes. My hair was the last straw. Xander and I were in way over our heads.

"Do you know anyone who's mad at me right now?" I said with zero preamble the second the dorm room door snicked shut.

Agnes was sitting on the couch in her fuzzy socks reading a smutty novel and hadn't even looked up with I came in. "Where have you been?"

I pointed to my hair as I kicked off my shoes.

Her book fell to the floor. "What *happened?*"

This was the proper reaction.

"The investigation isn't going well." Understatement of the century. I collapsed next to her. She reached out to touch my hair, then pulled back her hand.

"Someone put bleach in my conditioner and broke my car." I'd have to call the nearest garage tomorrow to get someone to look at it. "But we don't think it's anyone we talked to."

"We. You and Xander?" she asked in a sharp tone.

I nodded.

"Vincent did a great job," she said. I thought I detected a little envy in that statement. "Well, who have you talked to? I mean, Jenna, obviously. You got paint all over the good shower."

I thought I had already told her about Jenna. My cleaning was meticulous, too. I guess I must've missed a spot. "Sorry."

Agnes waved me off. "Don't look at me like that. I'm your friend, not your mom."

"I know."

"Mmhm." She bounced off the couch and started pacing, casting worried looks at my hair when she thought I wasn't looking. God, I must be hideous, despite what Xander said.

She snapped her fingers. "Did you talk to Trent?"

"I tried to." The fact that she was able to come up with his name made me think that our sleuthing at the party was stupid.

We could've just asked Agnes. I leaned back on the couch in defeat. All that work for nothing.

"And Gabriella?" she threw out.

I flinched in surprise. "What about her?" Gabriella was a nice girl, and I was always polite to her. Agnes sighed, grabbing her comforter from the floor and throwing it back on her bed. As she smoothed down the corners, she said, "I appreciated you making me your VP this year for Student Council, campaigning for me and everything. But I think everyone assumed you'd be pulling for Gabriella."

"Why is that my responsibility?" Gabriella could have run a campaign for Vice President. She was definitely smart enough.

"It isn't," Agnes said flatly. She was avoiding looking at me. My hair must really be as awful as I thought it was. "Maybe she just thought that when she ran the blood drive for you when you were sick, you would've appreciated it."

I opened my mouth to protest. I'd been coughing all week, and the blood drive was on a Sunday. I still would've done it, but she volunteered!

"Or that when she organized the Stuff-the-Bus for the local shelter in the middle of that windstorm, you might notice."

I closed my mouth. There it was again. Something I missed. I thought of my plan to go to Yale. To get a law degree like my mom. Almost every job I could imagine myself doing with it involved dealing with people, but apparently, I couldn't deal with anyone.

My vision blurred as I stared at my hands in my lap. Every time I thought I made something right, fixed something I did wrong, someone else showed up that I somehow screwed over without meaning to.

"You okay?" Agnes sat beside me.

"I... I don't know if I can do this anymore," I whispered.

"Do what?"

Thinking about Gabriella broke something inside me. She

had a lot to do with her own animal charity commitments, but she'd gone out of her way to help me, and I didn't even thank her. How did she feel when I passed my support onto Agnes? Did she go back to her dorm and cuss me out? Cry? Everyone at this school was fighting for an Ivy League education. What if, by denying her my support for an officer position, I ruined that for her? And I didn't even notice she was mad at me.

Xander. Jenna. Trent. Gabriella. *Yale.*

Oh my God. How had it gotten to this? I didn't know what I was doing anymore. This whole process had thrown me so far sideways that... Why had I ever wanted to go to Yale? Weren't there other schools, like Agnes had said, that would be just as great? And why law? Why any of this?

Even though I'd already cried more today than I had in years, I was already choking on a new round of tears.

Agnes put her arm around my shoulders, which shuddered with each jagged breath I took. I wished I could talk to her. Really talk to her and not avoid her questions. It just didn't come naturally to me with anyone. Except...Xander.

I remembered the way his lips tasted as they pressed against mine. I couldn't talk to him about this. Not when I'd spent so much time forcing him to help me with an all-important goal that might not mean anything to me anymore.

"I'll make it right," I eventually hiccupped. That was what really mattered.

Agnes didn't say anything. She just stroked my ruined hair as my guilt consumed me.

The next morning, I was a girl on a mission. I ripped the mangled Yale sticker off my laptop and went in search of Gabriella. She wasn't an easy person to find because she was involved in so many activities. It was like trying to track the schedule of the President himself. Eventually, I was able to confront her at her locker between classes.

"Gabriella, I know we don't have much time, but I realized I didn't nominate you for the position you wanted this year, and I'm sorry." I managed to get it all out in one breath and followed it up by giving her a winning smile. She didn't smile back at me. She didn't so much as look at me as she shifted her papers and her laptop to her left arm. Her bracelets jingled as she grabbed the materials for her next class.

"You feel better now?" she asked. "Your conscience suddenly, magically cleared?" This wasn't the same girl who helped me with the blood drive. She was definitely mad.

"No?"

"I shouldn't have been surprised when you passed me over. You're so entitled. You don't notice us peons."

I swallowed, and the words I wanted to say got stuck in my throat. It wasn't true. Not exactly.

"I heard what you're doing, okay?"

She did? Was my cover blown? Did Xander tell someone about the case?

"You're trying to impress Xander so he'll date you again," she said. "You're worried about your image after the 'Asshat' thing. We all get it."

"What?" I croaked. It was so far from the truth that it threw me off. "That's not—"

"Well, save it. I don't forgive you and I don't like you. Your new haircut and innocent smile might fool some people, but they aren't going to change my mind." She slammed her locker. "*No me importa tu vida amorosa,*" she muttered before shouldering past me.

I knew enough Spanish to understand her meaning. When did this become about my love life? She was taking everything the wrong way. That's not why I was doing this at all. But actually, it might have been more noble than why I was, in fact, apologizing. I folded my arms tightly around myself, suddenly more aware of the people around us. Had we made a scene? Gabriella was the first person bold enough to mention the graffiti.

She needed to understand that I was different now. That I was sorry. I hurried after her. "Excuse me." I kept things polite, as I'd been raised to do. "But—"

"Yes." She used one braceleted hand to push me aside. "Excuse you."

I stood frozen in the hallway as she stormed away. She completely rejected my apology. In public. This was the kind of hatred I'd been looking for. Gabriella wanted to ruin Yale for me because I ruined Student Council for her. It was obvious.

Then... Why didn't I feel victorious? Why wasn't I relieved?

"Harsh," a nearby sophomore said under his breath.

I couldn't stay here. I needed Xander.

Air whooshed out of my lungs. Holy... When did that happen? When did *he* become the person I went to for comfort? The person I most wanted to see?

Oh my God. I liked Xander.

It was more than a kiss, more than freshman year. I had fallen for him. Again.

In a daze, I walked to class and sat in my normal seat. *Breathe. You don't know it was Gabriella. You want Xander because you're not in your right mind. You're upset. Apologize, and be better, just like Xander... Stop it.* Gabriella had to be the one who framed me. Maybe now I could find a way to prove it. With... Xander. Everything came back to him.

As if I had summoned him with my confusion, he walked into class and sat down next to me. God, he was so close. I couldn't even have space to think! Why did no teachers believe in assigned seats this year?

He leaned over his desk. "Heard you talked to Gabriella in

the hall." He raised his eyebrows, waiting for me to spill my guts.

"Uh, yeah." I reached to pull my hair between us before realizing it wasn't there anymore. What was I supposed to do now when I was feeling suddenly shy?

If he looked closely, would he see what I finally figured out? What if he didn't feel the same way? What if this whole thing was just a "teach the virgin a lesson" thing?

"That bad?" he whispered as the teacher walked into the room.

It would be easy to play it off that Gabriella was what was wrecking my mood, but I couldn't do it. I tried to concentrate when the teacher began the lesson, but it was impossible. As soon as I understood the instructions for the assignment, I pulled the bathroom pass off the hook on the wall and headed to the safety of the nearest girls' restroom.

I sat there for at least ten minutes, shredding the cheap toilet paper one square at a time as I tried to think, but only fragments came to me. Xander shimmying up a rickety ladder to spy on Jenna. The way his eyes softened when he looked at his mom. How his arms surrounded me at the party, protecting me. Us arguing all the time. The way he kept trying to feed me.

I liked him. Maybe I always had. We picked on each other because we were both mad about freshman year, but in different ways. He hated that I dumped him, and I hated… I swallowed. I hated that I'd dumped him, too. I'd never wanted to. And now… he might like me. He probably didn't. I couldn't fix it with Gabriella. And there were probably about a billion other people who hated me.

Eventually, my breathing slowed, and so did my toilet paper shredding. I didn't need to decide anything today. I could deal with it all, one piece at a time. Today, knowing everything was enough.

I went to unlock the stall but stopped when I heard

footsteps. Two girls entered the bathroom, chatting a mile a minute. I didn't need anyone to see me having a mental breakdown. Talk about a way to start rumors.

"Oh my God, what is that on your neck? Is that a…" The girl broke off in an obnoxious squeal.

From my position in the stall, I could see through the crack that one of them was blonde and the other had dark hair, but I didn't recognize them from their backs alone. They must not be seniors.

"Hickey." Even from behind the stall door, I could hear the smug tone of the brunette.

"You let one of the guys mark you?" the blonde asked.

My thoughts exactly. I could plug my ears and wait for them to leave, or I could push through the door and go before they said any more, but I was frozen where I stood.

"It's not like I meant for it to happen. Sometimes, you just get into it." The brunette's voice was muffled as she applied lip gloss in the mirror. Maybe that meant they were almost done?

"Are you going to tell me who it was? Oh, no. Was it Brett? You said you were done with him!"

"I—of course not. Why would I ever… That's not even—"

"Uh huh," the blonde replied smugly. "Just remember what happened last time."

"It wasn't Brett."

I needed to get out of here. I shouldn't be listening to this.

"Then who was it?"

There were whispers before a distinct voice said, "Xander."

I sat back down hard on the toilet. It's not like I could pretend it was a different Xander. All the other Alexanders went by Alex or their full name.

"Oh my God, no one gets with Xander anymore," the blonde gushed.

Obviously, that wasn't true.

Throaty laughter from the brunette. The door clanged shut

on their way out, but I couldn't make myself get up and unlock my stall for a long minute. When I did, I walked calmly to the sink and washed my hands. I fixed my own lip gloss in the mirror with a steady hand. It was hard to believe the girl I saw reflected was me, because she looked so composed.

I walked slowly back to class. Hadn't I known that was what she was about to say? I mean, I hadn't really thought all he was doing was flirting with all those girls who fluttered around him. Why I assumed I was the only person he was kissing in their dorm room was beyond me. So stupid to fall for someone like that. So naive. I should've known better.

When I entered the classroom, everyone was reading silently, and I received a stern look from the teacher because I'd been gone too long. I pretended not to notice as I settled back into my desk. Stiffly, I opened my book to the right chapter.

"You okay?" Xander whispered.

I nodded but didn't make eye contact with him. I couldn't. Was I okay?

Of course not.

13

CAN'T KEEP UP

BY THE TIME the school day ended, my jaw hurt from clenching it whenever someone asked me about my hair. What else could I do but nod and smile when another person complimented me on how "brave" I was? I didn't need anyone to tell me how brave I was. What I needed was a friend.

Agnes and I hadn't spoken since I cried all over her like a selfish baby. I needed to apologize for that. She was my person, and I'd been so caught up with the stupid case. People were bound to hate me, and no matter how hard I tried, I couldn't be perfect. I didn't regret trying to fix it with Jenna, Trent, or even Gabriella, but I couldn't go on this way anymore. Especially with Xander.

Back in my dorm room, I collapsed on the couch and waited for Agnes to get back from class, checking the time on my phone every three minutes. When she didn't show, I changed a little later than I normally did for my nightly run. I'd catch up with her after.

It was weird trying to get used to the fact that I didn't have to use a ponytail holder, and completely ironic that my head was so physically light with such heavy thoughts dragging me down right now. It also didn't help much to clear my mind when, on the corner at the start of my second loop around campus, Xander sprang up from out of nowhere in his running shoes and shorts, his chest bare and slick with sweat. When he saw me, he turned and kept pace with me, his hair flopping up and down as he ran.

We didn't talk at first. Even with the distraction of my music streaming from my earbuds, I could hear his faint breathing as our feet slapped against the pavement. It screwed up my pacing as I felt myself accelerate past where I was comfortable to keep up with his long stride. I was hyper-aware of his arm inches from mine as we raced forward. Concentrating on my training was almost impossible when my eyes kept drifting to his powerful legs. Could those running shorts be any more low-slung? God, what a butt. He barely had any clothes on at all.

"You run?" Duh. Of course he did. What were we doing right now? It was a little hard to think because I wasn't sure what to do with my body when he was this close to me. He had invaded every space in my life. How did I let that happen?

Our feet pounded around the next curve in perfect sync.

"Yeah, but usually I wait until you're finished to go."

Wait, what? He watched me run? And he didn't want to run with me?

"You know, because you ripped my heart out freshman year." He picked up the pace.

"You seriously have been avoiding running at the same time as me for two and a half years?" I puffed as I tried to catch up.

He didn't answer, pointing to his earbud like he couldn't hear me over his music. What a bunch of crap. How dare he make me feel bad when he was sucking on necks left and right like some horny vampire?

My calves burned and I backed off, abandoning my effort to match his longer stride.

"What's wrong, Virgin? Can't keep up?" he said over his shoulder.

I slid to a stop, rested my hands on my hips, and watched him grin as he jogged backwards on my route, taunting me.

You know what? No. I turned and crossed the street. Guess I was taking the long way back, because I couldn't be whatever it was he wanted me to be right now. And I couldn't keep up with his sexual exploits, so there was nothing left to say. He came out here all sweaty and looking like he did and called *me* out? He was always calling me out.

I needed Agnes.

When I got back to the dorm, it was still as empty as I left it, though.

"Agnes?" I called, pushing the door open to her room. Nothing but silence answered me.

Seriously? Whatever.

I grabbed my shower caddy and trekked down the hall. In the bathroom, I took a slow shower, sniffing both the shampoo and conditioner before applying them. God, it had been stupid to just keep my stuff in the communal showers. Never again.

After a while, I switched the cold water to hot, no longer needing to stop my sweat. I massaged coconut body wash into my skin, willing my muscles to relax after the events of the day. Unfortunately, even a good shower wasn't magical.

When I got back to the room and Agnes still wasn't home, I texted her. Was she okay? I pulled out my homework and started in on it, but I was done by the time she finally walked through the door close to nine.

"Where were you?" I asked from my bed. "I was getting worried."

"With friends," she said casually as she dug through her drawers for pajamas.

"I texted you." I tried not to be annoyed. It was just Agnes being Agnes.

"Yeah, I was driving." She slammed her dresser drawer shut. "You know, I—" She shook her head at the floor.

I sat up straight. "You what?" Was she mad at me?

"Nothing. Just forget it. Sorry I worried you."

"Okay." What was going on here?

"I'm tired," she said. "Going to take a shower and go to bed."

"You—" My throat caught mid-sentence as I watched her walk away carrying her towel. Why was she being like this? Maybe she was having a really bad day too. I bit my lip. Now was obviously not the best time to talk.

I curled up on my bed, and when Agnes got back, she lay down on hers. She messed around on her phone for at least an hour before nodding off, which was plenty of time to have a short conversation with me. She just didn't want to.

I hugged myself tighter. With all that had happened today, this made me saddest of all.

The next day, I got ready for school in a daze, barely aware of shoving my body into a school shirt and black pants before heading out of the dorm. I might look like crap, but at least I wasn't holed up in my room. That would've made things worse. It might've been easier if Agnes was anywhere to be found, but she was gone again. And she hated waking up early, so she must be pissed at me for something. My chest tightened at the thought of losing her. I couldn't keep track of what I'd done wrong anymore.

It somehow wasn't a surprise when, as I was rifling through my locker, the intercom crackled, and the announcement I'd been dreading since that horrible confrontation about the graffiti finally came. "Virginia Benson to the dean's office. Virginia Benson to the dean's office."

I turned to the long hallway, concentrating on putting one

foot in front of the other as whispers followed me. I threw my shoulders back and smiled as I passed other students on their way to class. They might raise their eyebrows, but I would dare any of them to talk about me while I made eye contact with them. My stomach clenched as I refused to allow a single person to think I had done something else wrong as I pushed through the office doors. I was innocent.

"Hi, Ms. Anderson."

She looked up, startled, as if she hadn't just announced my need to come down here to the whole school. "He's waiting for you." She gestured to the door with her pointed nails—dark red this time. Like blood.

I didn't know what to expect. It occurred to me that just because I was having a mental breakdown, it didn't stop the clock on my two weeks. How many days did I have left now? Five? I rubbed my sweaty palms on my pants and pushed through the door.

Dean Alton looked up from the book he was studying at his desk. Today his black coat hung on the back of his chair, and he'd rolled back his sleeves. "Ah, Virginia," he said as I lowered myself into the chair across from him. He straightened a pen that had been slightly crooked on his desk and picked up a single folder. "Glad to see you're keeping to the straight and narrow."

I didn't answer. He might seem like he was in a good mood, treating me the way he'd done before the whole graffiti mess, but I wasn't fooled. The countdown was still on. Even though I was completely innocent, he was making me feel like I had to prove myself. I hated people like that. I might have to shut up and take it at home, but this school was supposed to be my safe space. Still, like at home, I knew when silence was the best policy.

"I'm sure you're wondering why I've called you down here," he continued.

Yes, I was. But these extended pauses were super helpful, thanks. Adults who wanted to feel like they had power over kids always did that. Told stories with lengthy morals, or paused every time they spoke and gave self-important chuckles, waiting for other people to acknowledge their superiority. Maybe a month ago, I would have humored Dean Alton. Now, I wasn't sure if I even wanted a letter of recommendation from him. It was almost unforgivable that he accused me of what he did.

The silence between us stretched, and the only sound in the room was the *tick tick tick* of his ridiculous pocket watch from the corner of his desk. Finally, when I wouldn't play, the man continued speaking.

"We've read all the essay submissions from—"

Just then, Ms. Anderson walked in the door carrying a batch of papers. She slapped them on the desk and glared at the dean. "Your wife is here to see you." She swung around and left as quickly as she came, slamming the door behind her.

For a moment, we both stared after her.

Then Dean Alton cleared his throat, shaking his head slightly. "As I was saying, we've reviewed the submissions from the essay contest last term, and I'm sure you're not surprised to hear yours was excellent." He moved to the stack of papers Ms. Anderson had brought and straightened them out on his desk. "Very moving. The concept was truly original. Would you like me to wire your father's secretary the monetary prize?"

I swallowed. Original concept. That's what won it for me. Trent's face flashed in front of me. Here was my chance to make it better, to come clean, but...

"Have you announced the winner to anyone?" My voice was thin, even to my own ears.

"The winner?" He raised an eyebrow. "You're the winner. I was hoping to get your statement first to publish in this month's parent newsletter." He walked over to one of the tables heaped high with organized stacks of paper, distracted by whatever it was he was trying to find.

My heart skipped a beat, then kicked back into gear as I debated. I could take the money and award. I'd earned it. Had Trent gone and interviewed twenty seniors in various nursing homes? Had he pored over every comma, every conjunction in his paper until three a.m.? Had he sent it to his parents, even though they were super intimidating, hoping that even if they tore it apart, that would make it better? I'd worked really hard on my finished product. Confessing that we'd brainstormed together would take all of that away from me.

But would whispering an apology at his back mean anything if I didn't give credit where it was due? Would "sorry" matter if I still screwed him over by accepting the award? My hands shook. What I was about to do could ruin me.

"I can't accept the money," I whispered to the floor.

"Beg pardon?" The dean turned back to me.

"I can't accept the money," I said louder. "I worked with someone on the essay, and I didn't know, but..." I exhaled. "He submitted the same idea."

There was a giant pause as he stared at me, but I couldn't hold his gaze. I couldn't bear to see his reaction.

His tone was formal. "What are you saying?"

"It was Trent Rosenthaal's idea," I said to my shoes. "I can't be the winner."

The room was quiet again for a long minute. God, he was good at that. No wonder so few people got in trouble at this school. I felt about as low and disgusting as a cockroach. Guilt crushed my lungs and made it hard to breathe.

"Well. Thank you for your honesty. We'll disqualify your essay, then." He crossed his arms, looking down his nose at me.

I nodded once.

"You may go back to class," he said.

I nodded again and stood to leave. I paused as I was about to touch the door handle and looked back at him. He was flipping through papers on his desk.

"Dean Alton?"

"Yes, Virginia?" He asked in his famous I'm-Disappointed-In-You voice.

"I'm sorry."

"Indeed."

And that's all I'd get out of him. I was lucky there wasn't going to be a more severe punishment than the loss of the essay scholarship. Academic integrity was everything. My vision blurred as I rushed past Ms. Anderson and the dean's wife.

A new crackle in the speaker brought me up short as I was about to re-enter class. "Trent Roosenthaal to the dean's office. Trent Roosenthaal to the dean's office."

Through my tears, I smiled.

Class was painful, and I put my head down for most of it. I'd have to steal Agnes's notes later—if she was even talking to me. Not taking notes gave me some time to think, which wasn't exactly great, either. The person I really needed was Xander. When our class spilled into the hall, I sought him out in the senior hallway.

As I was searching, a giggle sounded behind me, long and loud and totally fake. I turned. Two girls had their arms threaded through Xander's. He was bending down to hear what one of them whispered, her perfectly colored lips millimeters from his ear. He chuckled and flipped back his hair.

Giggles was holding his bicep like a cavewoman claiming ownership of a caveman. Her eyes were big and doe-like, and her curves pressed against every inch of him. How would he even walk? Hearing about what he was doing was different than seeing it in a live show like this. It was disgusting. My hands curled into fists, even though I had no actual claim on him. But he'd made out with me, hadn't he? I should've known it meant less than zero to someone like Xander.

Talking to him in the first place had been a stupid idea. Best to cut ties with him altogether. Just because he kissed me the way he did, showed up for me when he was afraid for me to be alone with my parents... We were friends, and nothing else. It was obvious that's how he felt. Otherwise, why would he flirt with those girls in the middle of the hallway for everyone to see?

I clutched my books close to my chest and looked away as I tried to sweep past him, but of course luck wasn't with me.

"Hey!" Xander's voice rang out through the hallway. He was trying to flag me down.

I sped up and rounded the corner of the hall. He wouldn't follow me with his bachelorettes attached to him. It would ruin his image.

That night, I chose the flattest route to run. I needed to think. Music pumped into my brain to help me keep my rhythm, and I gave myself over to the problems that twisted me up in knots.

I couldn't make things right with Gabriella. Why did I think it was going to end like a fairytale, with everyone forgiving me and all of us friends? That wasn't going to happen.

The dean's opinion of me was worse than ever, I was sure. He could have just expelled me on the spot. Wasn't stealing another student's idea something going "awry"?

Why wasn't I upset about Yale right now? Was it because I was burned out on everything, or was it because I really didn't care anymore? Did I ever want it for myself, or did my mom and dad force me to want it? How could I even exist without it pushing me forward?

And Xander... I picked up the pace, pulling my body along through the next loop a little quicker. What about Xander? He was so strange. Painting and laughing with me one moment, helping me with my problems, taking me to fix my hair. It was almost as if he really liked me, might even want to date me again.

Then he acted the way he did in the hallway, girls draped all over him and sporting his hickeys like badges of slutty honor. The two versions of Xander didn't go together. Unless... I stopped at an intersection and waited for the light to switch to WALK. Unless the kiss was a fluke, and Xander really did just want to be friends.

I pressed my fingers into my neck to check my heart rate as I waited for the light to change. I was almost back to campus, which was a record time for me. Xander hadn't showed up to run with me. I guess that answered that. It was over. Whatever we'd revisited from freshman year was a mistake. I swallowed the lump in my throat.

I wanted Agnes so bad, but yet again, she wasn't there when I got back to the dorm room. I took a shower and sat in the silence for a long minute, flipping my phone over and over in my hands. I really needed to talk to someone safe. Someone supportive.

I couldn't believe I was even considering the thought that came to me, but it was like my fingers had a life of their own when I pulled up the contact information and pressed the call button. Maybe it would go to voicemail. This was a terrible idea, anyway.

"Hello?" a kind voice answered.

I swallowed. "Hey, Mrs. Hearst."

Xander's mom was already in town, so we met at the coffee shop right next to the school. It was one of those mom-and-pop places with overstuffed armchairs and poetry readings at night. I walked there since my car was still at the shop waiting to be fixed.

When I sat across from her, my heart was in my throat. She'd already ordered for both of us. How she knew that I loved Chai tea, I wasn't sure. Maybe she didn't. Maybe Xander told her.

"I'm surprised to hear from you, Virginia," she said, her smile so like Xander's that it hurt me to look at it.

"Yeah, I… Wait, why?"

She hummed a little. "Xander describes you as self-sufficient. Fierce. Independent."

I nodded. That was true. What else did he say about me? But that wasn't the point here. "I guess I just… I needed someone outside the situation to provide perspective." There. That sounded professional. Still an independent person, but someone looking for input.

She raised her eyebrows. "Is this about the graffiti?"

I sighed. "Yes. And…other things." Of course, I wouldn't talk to her about her son, but slowly, with heated cheeks, I confessed everything happening with the case. Jenna and Trent and Gabriella. Then Agnes and her mysterious anger. Mrs. Hearst sat and listened, sipping her own tea. When I was done, I leaned back into the comfort of the chair.

"And where is Xander in this?"

"Everywhere. He's in everything. He's been helping me so much, but I…" I couldn't tell him what I was about to say. "I feel like a horrible person, and I'm scared that I can't change that," I whispered. What I didn't say was that her son knew I didn't deserve him. Why else would he flirt with other girls?

Mrs. Hearst was silent a long moment. Then she reached over and touched my hand. "Whoever told you that you had to be perfect was wrong, Virginia. This is the time to make mistakes. You are learning. That is your job right now."

I nodded, my eyes blurry. I wished I could believe that.

"I know this has been painful to deal with, but you are doing everything you can to make things right. That's life. You're allowed to be human. You're allowed to fail."

I let go a shuddering breath. Allowed to fail—that was a thing?

"Can I hug you?" she asked in a kind voice.

When I stood to hug Xander's mom, I understood how people could come to love hugs. We stayed in the embrace for longer than was probably normal, my wet face pressed against her small shoulder, breathing in the same fabric softener that matched her son's. And it wasn't horrible. It was actually kind of…nice.

Xander didn't text me the next morning, even though I half-expected him to, if only to check on the case or ask why I had been called to the dean's office. When I went to class, he turned his head away from me when I sat next to him. We both reverted to the way things had been before the whole graffiti thing and my stupid attempt to involve him in it.

I took perfect notes that I re-wrote during free period, color-coding them the way I used to before Xander stole most of my brain.

Lunch went by the way it always did, though Agnes was cooler to me than usual. By the end of the day, I was feeling like maybe I could handle this new version of normal. Eventually, I'd get to a healthier place where my face didn't flush red and my heart didn't want to beat out of my chest every time I saw Xander. Agnes would tell me what was wrong sooner or later. Maybe not before graduation, but eventually.

Then, as I was headed to fencing that night, Xander fell into step with me in the hall. "What's wrong with you?"

No preamble whatsoever, but then, we never really did the small-talk thing.

I shrugged, avoiding eye contact. Once I was at practice, I'd be safe from the way he saw through me.

"Hey," he said. "Talk to me. Is it your parents? Gabriella?"

See, and this was the trap. He would be this fantastic person, and I'd want to kiss him, want to be near him. But it wasn't real. What *was* real was the way girls were all over him, knowing they'd be the ones he'd touch, that they could give him what "Virgin" never could.

I stopped short in the hallway and turned to face him. It was better to get it over with.

The freshman girl Amy walked by us, and we traded polite smiles. I couldn't do this here. It wasn't private enough.

I pulled Xander by his sleeve into an unused Chemistry classroom. It was partially dark because the lights were off, though natural light streamed in through the windows facing the courtyard.

Just say it. "I can't do this anymore."

"The investigation? Are you going to tell me what happened with Gabriella? Maybe I can help." He adjusted the strap of his duffel on his shoulder and peered down at me.

The room smelled like burnt chemicals. That was probably why I was tearing up. "No. I mean yes. I can't do the investigation anymore because it's too much. There are too many suspects, and I think... The best way to fix it is to just be nicer to everyone in general." That part, I'd been mulling over since Xander said it when we were fencing. What good was apologizing if I wasn't going to change? I needed to change.

Xander nodded, but he didn't say "I told you so" the way I thought he would.

"But I'm not talking about the case." If I could give myself points for being brave, I'd have a million right now.

That got his attention. "What?"

Air escaped my lungs in a rush. "I can't... I can't be around you anymore, Xander. Not without it meaning what I want it to, and we'd be terrible together, really, so that's okay." I wasn't even sure if what I was saying made any sense. I started for the door. He had the out he needed. I could try to move on for real now.

"Wait." Xander grabbed my arm as I moved past him.

Just like in the diner, I stared at his hand, and he dropped it.

"Sorry. I'm trying to process. Can you give me a second before you walk away?"

I didn't want to, but I did anyway, and I watched as the wheels spun in his head for a long minute.

A slow smile spread across his face, his straight white teeth gleaming in the low light. Xander dropped his duffel on the ground. His hot stare pinned me in place. "You *like* me."

"I—what?" God, was he making fun of me?

He took a step toward me, still smiling. I managed to stumble back.

"You're not actually ignoring me. You *like* me, and it's freaking you out," he said gently.

"I am *not* freaking out."

He made a frustrated sound in the back of his throat. "Yes, you are."

I shook my head. He couldn't have this. Couldn't have me and every other girl in the school. I broke his heart? He was breaking mine!

"Then prove it," he said.

"Prove it?" I parroted, stumbling back as he stalked me across the room. My back bumped against the door.

He braced his arm above me and leaned in. "Tell me you don't like me. Tell me everything ended freshman year. That I'm crazy to believe we were never over. Not for one minute."

"I..." I could lie. I could tell him exactly that, but he'd know it was a lie. He always knew when I was lying. "I can't," I whispered brokenly.

His head descended, but I pressed my hand to his chest. "Wait. Have you...um..."

"Have I um, what?" He grinned, his mouth mere inches from mine.

"Have you been hanging out with anyone else lately?" *And giving them hickeys...*

He cocked his head to the side. "There's no one but you, Virginia. There never was."

A lie. He'd dated tons of girls. But I was powerless to stop the dark, dangerous heat between us. His lips brushed mine, his hand dropping to my hip. I met him halfway, smashing my body against his, my skin tingling in all the places we touched. Fire licked through my veins, blinding me to anything outside of us and the pressure of my need for everything Xander. He was right. We were never over. Not for one minute.

Too soon, he broke it off. I laid my head against his chest to keep from throwing myself at him. If it were up to me, we'd never ever stop. Maybe I *could* do this. Maybe it didn't have to mean anything bigger, be a whole relationship.

When Xander snapped back to reality and saw where his hands had drifted, he pulled back, a boyish smile dancing on his lips. "We're going to be late." He shouldered his duffel and pushed through the door behind me as I stood there in shock. What the—?

Fencing that day was electric. I kept sneaking glances at Xander when he wasn't looking, but he caught me a few times and held my gaze until I looked away, blushing. One time, as he effortlessly parried against his opponent, his head tilted toward me, and I could tell he was barely watching for their next attack. I tried not to think about how terribly sexy that was. What was happening here? I didn't even know.

I, on the other hand, was disarmed in ten seconds flat, and my foil clattered to the ground. I scrambled for it and tried to refocus, but time and time again, no matter who I squared off against, my attention drifted to Xander. The point of my opponent's sword smacked against my padding moments later. I lost every match, and the exertion from sucking so much made the sweat cling to my eyelashes and sting my eyes.

Amy, the freshman girl I'd helped a few practices ago, sat down next to me after my last match. She picked up my unused water bottle and passed it to me.

My mouth was suddenly the Sahara, and I nodded gratefully at her, forcing myself to take small sips rather than the huge gulps I needed. Xander was watching me. I couldn't see it because he was just outside my line of vision, but I felt his eyes on me. Even though I was sweltering, I shuddered. It took a while to notice Amy was talking to me. She was that quiet.

"—without you," she finished. "Thanks."

"I'm sorry," I said. "I couldn't quite…" *Pay attention to you.* She was right next to me. I could hear her fine.

She smiled thinly. It was the type of smile that said this happened a lot, which made me feel bad. "The day you helped me. I just wanted to say thanks."

"Of course." It had kind of been the highlight of my day. She was so quick to pick it up, so eager to learn.

She picked at the wooden bench beneath us. "I was wondering… Would you do that again today? When the instructor talks, I just don't…" Her hand fluttered in front of her like a frantic bird.

"Sure." I hopped off the bench. We made our way to an unused space in the gym, and I got right down to business, correcting her form, her grip, her lunges. She had great questions, ones I remembered having and being embarrassed about when I started. So much of fencing was touchy and specific. It was easier one-on-one, and slowly her steps became surer, her attacks quicker, her grip tighter until, at the end of the session, she pulled her mask off, smiling huge. "Thank you," she mouthed as the instructor dismissed us. Practice was over.

I was beaming with pride as I set my mask on the bench. To go from as painfully shy as she was to this…

Xander was headed my way, smiling in a proud sort of way. In helping Amy, I'd forgotten all about him. How was that even possible?

My heart banged a desperate rhythm as I adjusted my gear. He closed the distance between us, and I almost gagged as I tried to swallow.

By the time he reached me, my body was vibrating with energy. When he tucked a stray piece of short, sweaty hair behind my ear, I almost jumped out of my skin. "Meet me outside the dorms in ten, Coach?"

Coach? I didn't trust myself to speak, so I nodded.

He winked at me, and I shamelessly watched his butt as he walked out the door.

"Benson? Any day now." The instructor gestured to the door. Geez, calm down.

I ran back to my room for clothes, not even looking at what I grabbed. The shower I took was quick and freezing, because I didn't bother to adjust the water temperature. As soon as I was sure I didn't smell that bad and the conditioner was mostly rinsed from my hair, I slammed out of the stall and ran for my clothes. All I had with me was a pair of faded yoga pants and a threadbare school T shirt. It would have to do.

I flipped my phone over as I slipped my shoes back on. Nine minutes. It was now or never. I stared at my scrubbed pink skin in the mirror.

"You can do this." My reflection glared back at me, incredulous. I wasn't wearing makeup. I sweated through the whole shower. My hair was short and jagged and un-styled. Not exactly the sexy impression I wanted to give.

I gripped the edge of the sink tightly. It didn't even matter how I looked. My problems were deeper than that. Maybe my outside was finally reflecting my inside, and it was ugly. I screwed up so many things. It hadn't escaped me that Xander hadn't really answered my question about him seeing other girls. I mean he had, but it was a lie.

And the worst question was, did it matter? Xander and I felt inevitable. What if all he wanted was kissing? Could I do that? Be that girl? People had friends with benefits all the time. It wasn't a new thing. We were leaving for college next year, anyway. It was unrealistic to hope that we'd get together and stay together. Right?

I shook my head. I wanted him, whatever that looked like now. I didn't care if it was selfish and too late. I could be mature about this.

I sucked in a breath and swung the bathroom door open.

Xander leaned against the wall, waiting for me. His lips curled into a sinful smile that made my blood simmer in my veins. "Ready, Virgin?"

14

DIGGITY DOGS

XANDER'S GAZE slid over my clothes. "I like this look on you," he said as he pushed off the wall to walk with me. "Almost as good as the jammies."

The floor suddenly became interesting as I remembered how indecent I'd been that day. And how I wouldn't mind doing it again.

"Come on." He took my hand and pulled me along behind him. "I'm hungry, and I know a dive we're perfectly dressed for."

My mouth stretched into a smile he couldn't see as he dragged me down the hall. Of course he did.

It didn't take much to convince my monitor to give me a break on curfew. A combination of the fact that I never asked and about two grins from Xander, and that woman was toast. Was this how he was getting into the girls' dorms, or was he sneaking in a different way? She couldn't be giving him a free pass all the time, could she? What side deal he had going with his own hall monitor, I didn't even want to know.

I rolled my window down in Xander's car as he drove too fast to get to our late-night food run. It wasn't like I could ruin my hair at this point, and in the dark, the wind whipping at my clothes made me feel grounded. This wasn't real. We weren't on a date because I wasn't his girlfriend. He was just hungry and I... I was convenient. He liked me and I liked him and that's all this was right now.

And so what? I didn't need labels. I didn't.

When we reached downtown, I had to laugh when I saw the sign for Diggity Dogs. This guy had a thing for alliteration. It was basically a hallway with two booths and the best hot dogs in the history of forever—or at least that's what everyone in the dorms said. Well, he hadn't been kidding about me being perfectly dressed.

Xander made a big deal of opening the door for me to enter, like this was some fancy restaurant instead of a grease joint, which was so him. I couldn't help the giggle that bubbled out of me.

I opened my mouth to complain when he started to order for both of us, but when I saw the menu, I realized that I would've ordered the exact same thing for myself: a turkey dog on whole grain with veggies piled high.

I waited with him at the counter, shifting from foot to foot without speaking. When our food was ready, he grabbed both the containers with one hand and placed the other on the small of my back, guiding me to the farthest booth. I stumbled along until we were seated across from each other, trying not to make a big deal about the fact that he touched me.

He took a big sloppy bite of his hot dog and closed his eyes briefly in joy. The look on his face almost made me drop my fork.

I sawed on my hot dog with my knife. He watched me for a painful few seconds before finally breaking our silence. "That is not how you eat a hot dog, Virgin. Come on."

"Can you not?" I said. "You're ruining this." I raised a defiant forkful to my mouth and popped it in. God, it was amazing. What was in this food, crack? I went back for more.

He shook his head, laughing, and we both ate in silence for a few minutes. When about half my hot dog was gone, I set down my knife and fork. Wow, that was satisfying.

Of course, Xander had already polished his off. "You know, that's the most I've seen you eat in a while."

For some reason, his words didn't bother me. Practice was rough today. It was probably enough to offset the extra meal.

"Maybe being around you makes me hungry," I said before I had a chance to think about how that sounded.

Xander picked up my discarded food and set it on top of his container. His eyes blazed as he bent toward me. "That might be the best compliment I've ever gotten," he said, his breath tickling my ear.

I sucked in a breath, but before I could respond, my phone buzzed in my pocket. Agnes! She was talking to me again! I didn't care if I was being rude as I yanked it out.

It wasn't Agnes, but I still grinned as I swiped into the call. "Hello, Mrs. Hearst."

Xander's eyebrows rose.

"Virginia, you can call me Peg, you know. I just wanted to check on you. See how you're doing."

I stared across the table to where Xander was pretending to be interested in cleaning up. He was so listening to this right now.

"So much better. Thanks for coffee. I really needed that."

Coffee? Xander mouthed.

I held up a finger for him to wait.

"I'm so glad. You know you can call me anytime. Is my son treating you well? You let me know if he's not."

Xander bit my finger. I almost dropped the phone in shock. "Well, he's right here if you want to talk to him," I said.

Xander gave me a dirty look. I stuck my tongue out at him.

"Oh no, you two have a good night. Just make sure you're not a stranger. Come over for dinner anytime, okay?"

"Thanks, Mrs. Hearst... Er...Peg."

After I ended the call, Xander waited silently for an explanation. I gave him my best, most innocent expression. "What?"

"You hang out with my mom now?"

"No. She was in town. We had coffee. She likes me," I bragged.

"Of course she does." The way he said it made it sound like it was a foregone conclusion. The back of my neck warmed. "So did you talk about me?" he wheedled.

I scoffed. "Like there aren't more important things to worry about."

His teasing smile faded. "We're going to find the Asshat. I promise."

"You can't promise that," I snapped.

"Come on, Virgin. We've already eliminated a lot of heavy hitters. How many more could there be?"

That was the question, wasn't it? I twisted my napkin in my hands as I thought. "I honestly don't know. I've never meant... I know you won't believe me, but I haven't been trying to offend people."

"I believe you," he said quietly. He kissed me on the cheek on his way to the trash. "Come on, Virgin. Let's get you back to the dorms."

<hr>

That night, I had trouble falling asleep. All I could think about were the small ways he'd touched me. For some reason, that teasing little finger bite, the way his hand pressed against my back, that quick peck goodnight on the cheek—they meant more to me than the kiss in the Chemistry room. Why was that?

1 5

LIVING IN LIMBO

THE NEXT DAY, I woke up feeling like a live wire. I couldn't even sit. Staying in my dorm wasn't an option. When I glanced out my window and saw Xander in the parking lot, it was like fate. I didn't think. I opened my door, looked around to make sure no one saw me, then ran outside. As soon as I caught up to him, I grabbed his shirt and pulled him around the corner of the building, out of eyesight of the cars.

He didn't say anything when I did it, and he didn't even seem that surprised.

My plan stalled when I looked up into his stupidly attractive face. I wanted to be alone with him, but I wasn't good at living in limbo like this. My body was basically vibrating with excitement, but what was supposed to happen now?

He raised one eyebrow in a silent challenge.

I could never resist a challenge.

I yanked his head down to meet mine, kissing him hard. But he was letting me do all the work. He stood there, his hands at his side, his lips curled in that ridiculous smile of his even though I was trying to kiss him through it. It was so frustrating! I stood on my tiptoes and pressed my chest against him. When I wiggled a bit, he groaned, the sound vibrating through his body into mine.

Then his mouth parted and suddenly, I was playing defense, trying to keep up with the feverish way he kissed me. His chocolate eyes melted me from the inside out. All that arguing, all that sleuthing, all for nothing. This was what I really needed. I pushed my hands under his shirt that was never tucked in and found the warmth of his back. I could do this. It was okay if we didn't define it.

His fingers drifted over me, pausing at the small of my back, stroking, teasing, mirroring the swirl of his tongue in my mouth. I moaned impatiently and he chuckled, finally cupping my butt. He pulled as I jumped and wrapped my legs around his waist. My fingers twisted into his shaggy brown hair. I wanted to crawl inside his clothes and stay there. *Then I won't lose him.* How far would we make it before—

"Dude!"

I untangled myself from Xander just in time to see a group of sophomore guys headed our way. One had already seen us.

"Gotta go," I said. I couldn't help skipping a little on my way back inside, feeling excited and powerful. I knew if I looked back, he'd be standing there, hair all messy-sexy. How could he make out with other girls if I kissed him all the time? He couldn't.

For the rest of the day, the clock numbers on my phone changed so slowly, I could've gouged my eyes out. No texts. Why wasn't he texting me? I wanted to see him tonight, but I didn't want to make the first move again. What if I scared him off? I didn't have Yale anymore, or even Agnes. Xander was it.

I was about to go over my History notes for the twelve millionth time when my phone finally chimed.

Football stands in 10?

It wasn't exactly romantic, but that's not what we were doing, right? Right. Why did he always give me ten minutes? Ten minutes wasn't enough time to do anything!

I was rifling through my drawers when Agnes walked into the room.

We needed to talk. It was weird between us, and I hated it. I was also going to be late to meet Xander if we did. Silence stretched as we both waited for the other to start.

"What are you doing?" She nodded to the mess I'd made of my dresser. I remembered the scrunched clothing I was holding and dropped it back into the drawer. All I had were dress clothes and school shirts. I'd never needed anything sexy before. Maybe she could help.

"Can I borrow—" I looked up and her face was so smug that I rethought asking her for anything. The moment was gone. "Never mind. I've got it." I grabbed one of my tighter school T-shirts.

"I doubt you're going to tell me what's going on."

I was already ducking into the bathroom. "I'll update you when I get back!"

When I emerged three minutes later in a fresh outfit and makeup, she was gone.

I raced to the football stands. I knew it was stupid, but it was like if I wasn't exactly on time, he'd disappear in a poof, and I'd never get another chance.

When I got close, I slowed to a walk. He didn't need to know how desperately I wanted this.

"Benson," he drawled from halfway up the stands as I rounded the corner. He'd changed too and was now in a pair of basketball shorts and a black T-shirt. It was casual, but he still looked delicious.

Goosebumps spread over my shoulders, and I hugged myself, even though the air was still and hot. "Xander."

"Get up here." He smacked the seat next to him.

I sprinted up the steps two at a time, making sure I looked where I was going so I didn't fall flat on my face. When I got to his row, I slowed down. We'd kissed a few times now, but this was different. Planned. I didn't like it. I wasn't nervous, but... Okay, I was nervous. I gingerly lowered myself to the space next to him and folded my hands in my lap, not touching him.

He looked out over the field as he held out a package of Starburst candies to me. "Your favorite, right? Like freshman year."

I plucked the package out of his hand. "Share with me?"

We unwrapped candies, his orange, mine pink, and sat chewing on them. The scoreboard wasn't lit up and there were no players. We weren't formally dressed, but freshman year was exactly what it was like...and wasn't.

He wanted me, but not like freshman year. He knew better now than to want the virgin who ruined other people's lives to be his girlfriend. "Is that why you brought me here?"

He turned his head to me, mouth already open as if he was going to say something. Then he frowned. "Are you cold?"

I realized I was hugging myself, trying to keep it together again.

He lifted his arm. "Come here."

I scooted over and leaned into his side. The contact made me shudder. A low weight settled in my stomach.

He pulled me closer. I felt his lips press against my short hair.

"Benson?"

"Mmm." My eyes were closed now. I squeezed him tighter.

"Virginia."

I tilted my head back to look at him, desperate not to give anything away that I couldn't get back. I was ninety-nine percent sure he'd see through me.

He took his time, searching my face carefully, seeming to be okay with what he found. His lips brushed mine once, so agonizingly soft. Then again.

I angled toward him so my chest pressed against his and wound my arms around his neck. I might only get this, but it was everything. His mouth was gentle, searching.

I wanted more.

I leaned into him, and his thumbs came down to thread through my belt loops. I was going to pass out from pleasure, from the warm shock of orange candy and pure happiness that was Xander Hearst.

The shrill sound of a whistle pierced through my fog. Xander continued kissing me as football players sprinted onto the field.

I pulled back. "Xander."

His eyes were still closed. "Virgin," he mumbled.

The word was a bucket of cold water over me.

"The team is here," I pointed out.

"So?"

So I couldn't be the dirty girl who made out in the stands and got in trouble for it?

He straightened, letting go of my pants. "Tomorrow?"

I nodded, standing up with shaky knees.

"Alexander Hearst!" the coach's voice boomed over the field. "Does this mean you're finally joining the team?"

Xander laughed. "Nope," he said. "Just hanging out."

"Looks like you're doing more than that!" one of the guys called. Chad. It had to be Chad.

Just hanging out. Of course that's what we were doing.

Backing away from Xander, I shook my head.

He frowned, reaching for my hand.

I almost bowled over one of the wide receivers as I pulled away and ran back to the dorms.

At nine a.m. the next day, my phone chimed a calendar reminder at me: TWO DAYS.

I sat up and stared out the window into dark, foreboding clouds. Two days until the dean was going to throw a fit, and… What? Throw me out of school? I brushed my teeth so hard that when I spit, there was pink in it.

It was going to be fine. Everything was fine. Except… Except I'd given up the search. Given up Yale. Given up everything. Letting everything fall where it was going to wasn't any kind of plan. What was I thinking?

I shouldered my bag and started for the library. Agnes had left the dorm without me. Everything was going to be fine. I was fine. I had Xander. Kind of.

A dark, skinny guy darted out in front of me when I rounded the corner. Trent.

"Trent! Hey, Trent!" I tightened my grip on my backpack and sprinted down the hallway. If I could just talk to him, I could tell him that I'd made it right. The essay contest. Maybe we'd be okay for real.

But just as quickly as he'd come, he disappeared into one of the many classrooms in the hall.

I stood there frozen for a long moment until, as if he'd been summoned, Xander rounded the corner, talking to Claire's boobs. I blinked, then resumed my trek to the library. *We're not dating. We're casual. It doesn't matter.*

But seeing them with their heads so close, his wry smile playing at the edge of his lips like that, the way it did when he was amused by something I said, pushed an uncomfortable thought into my brain. One I couldn't get rid of, no matter how hard I tried.

I didn't like it.

I turned and strode back down the hall with no plan whatsoever. He didn't notice me until I was right next to him. Was he ignoring me? Or was his conversation that interesting?

I placed my hand in his and yanked him away. "I need to talk to you."

He let me pull him down the next hall.

"That's a scary phrase," he said after we'd walked in silence for a minute.

"What?"

"We need to talk. *I* need to talk," he air quoted with the hand I hadn't captured. "What did I do?"

Please. Like he didn't know. I glared at him.

He barked out a laugh. "You're... Are you jealous? Of who, Claire?" He craned his head around like he was searching for the answer in the hallway. Like he didn't remember her literally hanging off of him two seconds ago.

We stopped outside the big double doors of the library. This was a bad idea. "You know what? Forget it."

"Absolutely not." He chuckled again. Awkward silence stretched between us until Xander smiled wide. "But if you want to leave, you might have to let me go."

Both our gazes dropped to where I was holding his hand so hard my knuckles were white. I dropped it like a hot poker.

"Right." I gave him a weak wave and practically flew to the farthest table. I put my head down as my face blazed.

He didn't text me for the rest of the day, and I knew it was because he was laughing at me. He probably viewed our situationship as done now. That's how it worked, right? Someone got weird, and it was over. At least, that's what Agnes always said. Obviously, I had zero practice with any of this.

I dove into my homework, getting ahead in the syllabus, trying to get back that academic swing that was so hard to find lately. It didn't work. All it did was stain the tips of my fingers neon from the highlighters Agnes had given me for my birthday. I tried to block everything out and really dig into my studies during classes, sitting right in the front row when I didn't have an assigned seat. It almost worked, but I still found myself slumping back to my dorm room, feeling defeated. Xander hadn't talked to me. I didn't even see Agnes. She was probably skipping. Gabriella glared at me a handful of times, so she might be the graffiti artist, but I had no way of proving it.

I had just put my pajamas on when there was a knock at the door. Did Agnes forget her key? I hadn't seen her after school. Maybe *she* had a new boyfriend. I'd have to ask later.

"Coming," I said.

I opened the door, and there stood Xander.

I was wearing plaid pajama pants, and my hair was a wreck from running my hands through it. I had no makeup on! It didn't matter that he'd seen me like this before, kissed me when I'd been like this before. This time I had the presence of mind to be embarrassed about it. What on earth was he thinking, sneaking into the girls' dorm at night? There was no way we could tempt fate again.

"What are you doing?" I hissed. I crossed my arms over my boobs, because of course I wasn't wearing a bra. I'd been about to go to sleep.

"I wanted to see you. Maybe hold your hand again if you promise not to break mine," he teased.

"We're going to get caught!" I whipped my head back and forth, looking up and down the hall, to see if anyone had already noticed him. A snarky part of my brain wanted to point out that Claire's door was two down from mine. Did he have a hard time choosing who to visit tonight?

"If you leave me standing in the hallway, definitely."

"You're not coming in." It sounded like a question, but it wasn't. I blocked the small door opening with my body. We couldn't be alone in my room again. I wanted him too much.

"Then I guess you better throw on a sweatshirt and come with me." He grinned.

Adrenaline flooded my body. He wanted to spend time with me. Me, not Claire. And I could do casual. I could.

Whatever my reservations were, I was already grabbing the closest sweatshirt and sneaking back down the hall with him.

We spent the next hour walking the mostly deserted campus. The clouds hung low now, even darker than they were this morning. It was almost like they were framing my stolen moment with Xander.

It should've been lame, but having the full, undivided attention from someone like him was like sitting near a fire in the dead of winter. He was that compelling. When he listened, he did so with his whole body, like there was nothing more important than what I was saying. He asked me about class, my new highlighters that he actually noticed me using, what I'd thought about the food they'd served in the cafeteria today. He listened to me telling him about how I had no idea how to style my hair now, like it actually mattered what I felt about how I looked. When I told him I was googling guy styling tips online, his laugh echoed loudly across the outskirts of campus. I actually forgot for half a second that I was in public with pajama pants on. It was so unlike me. My mom would die. But Xander had never cared what I wore.

"I feel like we haven't talked like this in forever," he said as we rounded campus the third time. "I don't know enough about you anymore."

My heart soared. He wanted to do more than tease me. He wanted to know more than the feel of my lips against his. But wait. How did that fit into the casual relationship we'd started? Maybe it was normal.

"What do you want to know?" I reached up to push my hair back when the wind kicked up, but my hand only met heavy air. Would I ever get used to this haircut?

"I don't know. What do you do on holidays? Do you have a big family? Like, I know you're an only child, but do you hang out with cousins, maybe?"

It was crazy how much we'd never said to each other

freshman year. How much we still didn't know. "No. My parents are only children, too," I said. "They work a lot."

He waited. What else was I supposed to say?

"Um. We have a cook. Her name is Betty. She makes the most delicious food. Most of it goes to her church, but the kitchen always smells amazing." I smiled. "I used to sit outside the door when I was a kid just to smell the cinnamon rolls and cakes. Of course, I'd rarely eat that kind of thing." He knew that, though.

He frowned. "You didn't go in there and taste test? It's your house."

I looked at him blankly. "She was working. No one needs a kid underfoot when they're working." My dad told me that about a thousand times as a child.

He kicked a chunk of sidewalk that had broken off in our path. "That's sad, Benson."

I shrugged. It was normal for me. "Are your brothers around a lot?"

His face transformed. If I thought he was hot before, this was blinding. He talked about how funny his brothers were, telling stories from his childhood that always ended with him as an innocent victim getting blamed for everything, which I was sure was a stretch. He explained how his mom was his biggest role model. How, despite the way everyone said he was so easygoing, fencing and boxing were the only places he ever felt completely calm.

"But it's fighting!" I protested. "How can you feel calm while trying to stab or hit someone? And there are more pauses than actual matches in fencing."

"It makes me feel confident," he said lightly. "Fencing is about being fast, precise," he said. "And boxing is the only thing that helps me when I'm frustrated."

I smiled. He was still trying to be a ninja, like freshman year. Kind of.

"It doesn't have to be in a book to be worthwhile, Benson." He nudged me as we walked over the uneven sidewalk. Then, as if it were the most natural thing in the world, his hand closed over mine like we were dating, instead of being whatever we were. Warmth radiated from him as he threaded his fingers through mine. It was like the wind forgot to blow after that. Or maybe I just didn't feel it.

All too soon, our loop brought us back to where we could see my dorm again. He paused, pulling me back gently by my hand.

"I think we need to talk for real."

This wasn't real? I scratched the back of my neck. "Aren't those the worst words ever or something?" He was going to end this. What Gabriella said came back to haunt me. I was hurting his popularity because everyone hated me, and now we were going to be over. It didn't matter that we never made it official. I didn't want it to end.

"I just…" He let go of my hand to run it through his hair. His eyes were a more shadowed brown in the dark of night.

I stood frozen in front of him, waiting for him to finish his sentence and wreck my heart. "I just…" was as bad as "We need to talk," and we both knew it. I flexed my hand, already missing the presence of his fingers between mine.

Then the sky opened up. One second, he was being adorable and sexy and nervous about breaking my heart, even though we weren't supposed to care since we were casual. The next, we were both running for shelter like we were going to melt. The rain came down hard and fast, drenching us in seconds. It couldn't have been timed better.

I waved to him as I escaped into my dorm. If I didn't let him finish, would he forget about wanting to get rid of me?

When I shut the door to my room and turned, Agnes was there, tapping her foot.

"I was searching everywhere for that hoodie!" she accused.

I winced as I peeled off the soggy sweatshirt. "Sorry." I hadn't even looked to see if it was mine or not. "You've been gone a lot lately."

She put her hands on her hips. "I'm surprised you even noticed."

"What?"

"Nothing." She stared at me.

What was I supposed to say? I noticed things. I noticed how she barely talked to me anymore, how she was always gone when I tried to find her. But I couldn't say that. I couldn't lose Agnes on top of maybe losing Xander. Then I'd have no one.

"You know what? It's not nothing. You're never around. You're always with Xander. And you don't talk to me anymore. I didn't think that when we moved in together, I'd see you less."

"*I'm* gone?" She was literally never here anymore.

"You're becoming one of those girls who ditches everyone when they have a boyfriend. It's a bad look, V."

"He's not my boyfriend," I said automatically.

"That's even worse! You know what? I can't with you right now. Just no." She snatched the wet sweatshirt out of my arms and stomped back to her room, slamming the door.

I flopped into my bed, shivers running up and down my arms that had nothing to do with the rain. Agnes was mad at me, and I was mad at her too. Xander was… I didn't know. He didn't even kiss me today. I didn't know how to fix anything. Maybe I didn't deserve either of them.

16

SOMETHING MORE

IT TOOK ALL my self-control not to rip out what hair I had left by the roots before class the next day. No matter what I did, it fell like wilted grass. I'd woken up with a scratchy throat, and my face looked more swollen than normal. I'd never been any good at contouring my make up, and it seemed pointless to try now that this haircut would make my face look puffy no matter what I did. I sat down on the toilet and blew my nose with toilet paper. I better not be getting a cold.

Agnes was waiting for me by the door, and we walked together, but it'd been a while since we did it and I didn't know what to say after last night. I guess she didn't either, because all she did was take dainty sips from her cup as we wound through hallways to get to class. I didn't even remember to make myself any coffee, and I really could've used it today.

"Okay, spill. What's wrong with you?" she finally said.

I tilted my head. It could be that she was never around anymore, and I needed her help. It could be that I didn't know what I wanted with Xander. Or it could be that my time was almost out, and I was going to get kicked out of school, of Yale

—not that I'd even gotten accepted there yet. But I didn't say any of those things. "I don't know. Bad mood."

"I'd think you'd be in a *great* mood if the rumors are true."

I collapsed into my seat and braced my elbows on my desk, rubbing my temples. Was I getting a headache now, too? "What rumors?"

"About you and Xander basically having sex in the football stands."

"If I were having sex, I hope I'd be in a better mood than this, yes," I replied before I could censor myself.

"Ha!" Her eyes flashed like the old Agnes. The one who wasn't mad at me. "That's what I said. I told Chad that—"

"You talked to Chad about me?" I paused in pulling my laptop out of my bag.

"Don't be a snob. He's kind of nice." Her eyes glazed over. Oh, Lord. I recognized that look. "If you're hanging out with Xander all the time, maybe we can all chill together."

"You, me, and Xander?" I asked as I booted up my computer.

"And Chad. They're roommates, you know."

I did not know. I tried to picture sexy, funny, athletic Xander with big, bumbling Chad. It was enough to break my mood. I started to laugh.

Then Xander walked into class.

I stopped laughing and stared at the home screen on my laptop. He said I was "sad." That was code for pathetic, right?

Agnes frowned, but whether it was at me for laughing about Chad or the appearance of Xander, I had no idea.

It was a tense hour.

On the way out, like some kind of unfunny repeat of the first day I'd asked him for help, Xander was waiting for me in the hall in the exact same position. "Come with me."

"I have class," I said breezily. Or at least, I thought it was breezy. Who could tell the difference between that and breathless, anyway?

"Lunch, then."

I nodded at my books. *Stop it! You're being stupid!* But I couldn't stop. He knew too much about me now. What was I thinking last night? I'd be safe in my next class without him. *Go,* I ordered my feet.

They obeyed.

When lunch came, I fought the urge to sneak back to my dorm and lock the door. I wouldn't, though. I'd stick with my promise to see him. He texted me to meet him at his car, and I turned in that direction. Even if everything I'd said last night made him want to be done, I owed it to both of us to power through that conversation.

As soon as I opened his car door, the smell of greasy cheese and salt assaulted my nose.

Tension oozed out of me as I sank into the passenger seat. One thing I could always count on was that Xander wanted to feed me. No matter what happened, at least I'd have some carbs.

"Nachos," he said.

I lowered my voice. "But like, *nachos.*" My voice broke because of the scratch in my throat. It was the worst impression in the world. I scooped up a paper boat and lifted a chip to my mouth.

"You getting sick?"

"It's probably a cold." *Or nerves. Just say what you're going to say.*

He looked away from me, even as he got in the car and grabbed the other greasy Nile Pile. Why wasn't he looking at me?

"Did you skip class to go get these or something?" I teased.

"Don't worry about it."

I wanted to tell him not to skip class for me, but that would be assuming he was getting the nachos for me only and not for himself. Maybe he really wanted these specific nachos. I shoved a chip in my mouth, savoring the flavor as I chewed.

Xander's eyes flared. He cleared his throat. "What are… What are you doing?"

I swallowed. "Eating?"

He sighed. "Okay, eat."

"Thank you for your permission? You don't get to tell me what to do, Alexander Hearst." I reached for another chip. I wasn't letting them get cold. The cheese would get rubbery, and these weren't just any old nachos.

We ate in silence for a few minutes. When I couldn't hold any more, I placed my half-full container on top of his empty one. I fully expected him to grab it and chow down on my leftovers, but he didn't. The second my hands left the chips, his were on me. His lips captured mine, salty and sweet and full of fire.

Wow, I was really terrible at reading signs. I thought this was a sendoff, but he wanted to make out? I drove my hands through his hair as he trailed kisses down my jaw. I wasn't complaining.

"I've never seen you laugh like that," he mumbled against me.

"What?" I couldn't concentrate as his lips migrated to my neck. I guess he didn't care about my possible cold.

"What were you and Agnes talking about?" His teeth pulled at my earlobe.

Agnes? Why were we talking about Agnes?

"Chad," I whispered absently.

He sat back, and every cell in my body screamed in protest. "You were talking about Chad? Chad is who makes you laugh?" His face contorted into a look of confusion so comical, he could have been a meme.

"Would you rather this," I gestured to the air between us, "make me laugh?"

He growled and reached for me.

"Oh Xander, your touch is *hilarious*," I teased.

His mouth came down on mine and I tasted his smile. His fingers toyed with the bottom of my shirt.

My breath hitched.

"That wasn't a laugh," he mocked.

"Sure it was."

His hand moved to the waistband of my pants. Was he going to undo them?

The bell rang and we sprang apart like the dean himself was tapping on the window. But I'd gotten my answer. He wasn't done with me. We were just getting started. And God, did I want him. So much that I wanted to skip class and see where this took us right now, right here in his car. Maybe.

A truck pulled in right beside us. Maybe that was a good thing.

He groaned in protest as I tried to finger-comb my hair back into submission. "Don't leave."

"We have class," I said.

He dropped his head back against the headrest. "I know."

"We have to go."

He turned his head to look at me, his expression unreadable. "Go ahead. I'll catch up to you."

Smart. We didn't need to start rumors by coming in together. I nodded and got out of his car.

But Xander didn't show up to our next class. Maybe he needed a minute. Maybe something else had happened. I tried not to stare at his empty desk every three seconds, but it was a constant distraction. I needed a second to recover, too, but I didn't skip class. Maybe I'd find him waiting for me in the hall after, like he so often did. But when I exited the classroom, he wasn't there.

I slipped back out to the student parking lot. His car was still here, but he wasn't. Weird. I'd text him later. Just to make sure he didn't need the notes from class. That was friendly enough. Then he could tell me where he was. If he wanted to. I leaned against the passenger's side for a moment and let the heat from the sun sink into my skin. Somehow, I missed running more than once this week. I needed to go again, if for no other reason than to enjoy this.

"So slutty," a girl said from a few cars over. She didn't bother to talk quietly.

Shamelessly, I tuned in. Who was slutty?

"The way she hangs on Xander, then acts so high and mighty the rest of the time? Like she's above the rest of us when she's doing him in his car?" another girl said.

"Right?"

They were talking about me. Did they know I was right here? Their voices sounded familiar. Too familiar.

They were the same girls in the bathroom who were talking about Xander giving one of them a hickey. My blood chilled in my veins. Could they be so jealous that they would want to frame me for graffiti? Wait, no. That didn't make any sense. Xander and I hadn't spoken in years when that happened.

Still, maybe it was better to be safe and find out. They didn't sound like seniors, but… I craned my neck around the corner of Xander's car, only to see the backs of their heads as they retreated into the building. One blonde, one brunette, but that didn't help. I didn't recognize either of them.

I ground my teeth together in frustration. My headache was returning, and now all I could think about was the case. I needed to run.

When Xander's text came, I ignored it. I'd see him later.

But running didn't help anything. With every footfall, it was like I was stomping a clear line to my doom. I tried to push it out of my head, but then all I could think about was Xander's mouth, his hands. It was like he was a drug, and I was an addict. It wasn't healthy, but I was far beyond caring.

And something was building. Soon we'd go farther, and would there be any turning back from that? I wasn't stupid. I already knew that no matter what happened now, there was only one outcome for me. When I got back to the room, I took aspirin for my head and crawled into bed.

I made it through another whole day until I caved and met Xander after fencing. It had been too long between fixes. One second we were shucking sweaty padding, and the next we were making out in the back of his car, the windows fogging up quickly. I straddled his lap, leaning down to kiss his neck. When he groaned, I used the opportunity to press harder against him. I wanted something. Something more. This wasn't enough now.

He worked my shirt free from my skirt and his hands reached up to my bra. In a practiced gesture, this time he undid the clasp, his warm fingers caressing the skin where the band had been. The entire atmosphere of the car changed. His smile turned feral as his hands migrated.

I was out of my mind at this new development. If we were going to do big things, concentrating on undoing his shirt button by button seemed like a good move. Of course, I'd seen him shirtless before. He went running without one. It was a little different when he was below me, his fingers inches from touching places on my body no one had ever touched before.

Though it still didn't seem quite equal to what he'd done, I placed my hands on his bare chest, and his heat radiated through me.

"Virgin," he rasped.

I flinched, but recovered quickly, nuzzling his neck. I couldn't get comfortable. There was a low, burning heat in my stomach that kept me up at night now, and I knew it was because of Xander. I knew it meant I was turned on, that I wanted him.

My hands reached for his belt.

"Wait," he said. "Wait, stop."

I froze. Did I do something wrong? I was the inexperienced one here, and Xander... He had a lot more practice than I did. I slid off his lap, my bra hanging loose. What was wrong with me? Was I that un-sexy to him? I tried to reach back to re-hook the stupid clasp, but it was too hard to do this way. I struggled for a minute, my fingers shaking as I jammed the two pieces of fabric together, but they wouldn't latch.

Xander's hands brushed mine away. "Stop," he said. "Calm down."

I breathed deeply, forgetting the clasp as I struggled against the wave of emotion that threatened to let those stupid tears fall.

"Let me." A second later, he'd fixed it.

I couldn't look at him. I considered opening the car door and running all the way back to the dorm.

He started buttoning his shirt. "We need to talk."

A cold bubble of laughter escaped my lips. "So talk."

"We... I..." He let his shirt go. "Let me start that again."

I threw my hand out in a go-ahead gesture.

"I like you." His mouth barely moved as he said it, as if talking about it was some kind of torture. No one was making him say anything right now.

I snorted. "No kidding. What were we just doing, playing chess?"

"No, Virgin. I like you. Like, I think I'm... I think I'm in love with you, and I don't... I don't want to do anything you don't want to..." He stared at the fogged-up windshield. "I don't know how to do this."

My heart slammed against my ribs. "Is this some kind of joke?" I whispered.

With his thumb and forefinger, he turned my face to meet his. "Not a joke. I want... This is stupid. Why am I so nervous?" He chuckled. "Will you go out with me?"

He was saying all the right words, all the things I'd wanted him to tell me before all our kissing started, but I couldn't. I swallowed. I needed... I needed to let him go.

"No," I said quietly. I was already regretting his words for him. He'd just ruined everything. "Xander, no. Why are you doing this?"

"If it's because your parents told you not to date, then screw them, Virgin. It's not like they visit enough to know, anyway." His face was inches from mine. "You haven't cared about the Great Graffiti Mystery in days, and I know why." He gave a small smile.

I shook my head and pushed him back. "It's not because of my parents. Wow, could you be any more full of yourself? I can't believe you're serious right now."

He sat back. "What?"

"You don't like me, Xander. You flirt with anything that moves. I've seen you in the hallway with your groupies." I spat out the last word.

"I was keeping up appearances for the investigation, Virgin. If it bothers you, I won't let another girl touch me." He smiled. "Nice to know you're jealous."

"Did I ever ask you to 'keep up appearances'? Did I ever tell you I want to be like the girl whose neck you bruised with your suction cup lips?"

He frowned. "What?"

"Don't act so innocent! I know what happened. I know I'm not the only girl you—"

"The only girl I what? Spend every spare second with? The only girl I've been completely obsessed with since I was fourteen years old? I've never given anyone a hickey in my *life*, let alone last week." He dragged his hands over his face. "I can't believe I have to tell you that!"

"Please. Don't try to act like I'm the only girl you've ever been with."

"Everyone has been a place keeper for *you!*" He hit his thigh with his hand. "No one can even touch you! Stop acting like a jealous brat."

"*Jealous?* I am *not* jealous! And you're going to tell me that you're okay stopping, with not doing more when you can get it from half the girls in our class whenever you want it? Why don't you just have sex with me and get it over with?"

Wait. I didn't mean to say that, and now that the words were out of my mouth, I knew I didn't want that. I wasn't ready to have sex with anyone...even Xander. At least, not in a car. Not like this.

"Having sex isn't something you just get over with." He shook his head. "It should be special."

"You don't know everything," I snapped, though I'd come to the same conclusion.

"And you don't know anything! I tell you stuff. Important stuff, and I—"

I reached for the door handle.

"No, wait. I didn't—can you just stop for a second?" He gripped the steering wheel tightly and looked through the windshield. "This isn't how it's supposed to go," he muttered.

My fingers clenched into fists as we both stared at the bumper of the black Accord in front of us.

"You're not ready." His tone was gentle when he finally spoke. "It's okay. It's not something to be ashamed of." He turned to me with eyes blazing, serious and stupid. How dare he tell me what I was and wasn't ready for, even if he was right? "I don't want to do something we can't take back. I don't want us to do this big thing and then have you disappear again. What are we even doing, Virgin? I thought you wanted to date me."

Until this moment, I thought I wanted to date him, too. "I'm sorry, you call this dating?" I gestured to the inside of his car.

"You—I—"

"Did you ask me out and I just missed it? You've never even

said the word 'date' before today. We were hiding in a booth at a hot dog dive or eating chips in your car. You don't sit with me at lunch just so you can keep me your dirty little secret!"

He glared at me. "That's bullshit and you know it. You're not the kind of girl who messes around."

"Then what are we doing? What are we *doing*, Xander? Because that's what it looks like to me. That's what it looks like to everyone else. I guess I'm just lucky you haven't given me a hickey like you have other girls this week." He was right. I wasn't the girl who messed around. I wasn't the girl who let herself be distracted in class and ate junk food and went on walks in pajamas with a boy around campus. He'd completely ruined me.

"And who did I give this mysterious hickey to?" he said.

I waved my hand in front of me because I didn't know her name, and it didn't matter anyway. That wasn't even the worst part. It was time to finally confront the real problem.

"You call me Virgin," I whispered. "As if that's the most important thing about me. Do you have any idea how that feels?" My words hung in the air between us, thick and emotional.

His face morphed from scrunched and angry to open and sad, but there was something else there, too. Guilt. "We were... We had a thing. I thought you knew I was joking."

I wasn't going to fall for that gorgeous face. Not again.

"Virginia, I'm sor—"

I covered his mouth with my hand. "Xander, stop. Just stop." I opened the door and exited his car with whatever dignity I had left. I wanted to believe it was nice while it lasted, but I couldn't. I thought I'd be able to kiss him and be okay, even though I wanted more. I never realized that if he offered a relationship, it would tear me in two. I wouldn't be with someone who didn't respect me.

Trying to hold back until I got to my room was useless. My tears exploded out of me after about five steps.

17

THE DEAN'S LOOKING FOR YOU

I SPRINTED BACK to the dorm and slammed the door behind me. My chest heaved and my hands shook as I balled them into fists and pressed them hard against my sides. *Stop crying.*

"The dean's looking for you," Agnes said.

My head was so full of Xander that I didn't hear her at first. "What?"

"He's looking for you. You're supposed to go directly to the main office when you get in," Agnes repeated. She looked up from a textbook at her desk. "You should wash your face. Your makeup is everywhere."

"Thanks." I didn't have to look in the mirror to know I was a hot mess right now.

She thrust her hand through her already frazzled hair. "Look, I have something I want to..." She paused when she finally looked closely at me. "Are you crying?"

God, I could not handle anyone else right now. Not today.

"Agnes, can we do this later? I promise I'll listen. I just can't right now." I was on the verge of hysterics. I had to go see the dean *now?*

"Okay." She deflated, flopping on the sofa as I hunted around for anything that might make me look semi-presentable. "Are you crying because of Xander?"

I paused, one leg in a pair of pants. "Why would you think that?"

She picked a piece of lint off our sofa. "Because he's the only one you hang out with anymore."

I struggled to zip up my pants as her words sank in. I knew the weirdness between us was just as much my fault as hers, if not more, but she wanted to do this *now*?

"It's not like that."

"Then what's it like?" To her credit, her tone was only half-bitchy.

"Over," I whispered as I stripped off my shirt, trading it for one less wrinkled. I smoothed my hands over my hair, knowing I was probably just making it worse. A makeup remover pad got rid of my tear streaks, but it didn't do anything for my splotchy face. My mouth got the most attention, as my lip gloss had smeared while making out with Xander. I probably was a little too rough, but I didn't have time to care. I didn't even re-apply my makeup. The dean didn't like to be kept waiting.

"I—" My brain clogged with thoughts of Agnes, Xander, and the dean.

"Just go," Agnes said in a disgusted voice. She was giving me an out.

I took it, sprinting down the hall and out the door. I arrived breathless at the office, where Ms. Anderson asked me to take a seat and wait. I sank down into a chair across from her, listening to the click of her fake nails against her keyboard. Her clothes today were more conservative, and she was wearing less makeup than normal. She almost looked tired. The minutes ticked by on the clock on the wall, and then it hit me.

This was The Meeting.

Oh my God. I was out of time. And that meant...

My mom strode into the office in her perfectly pressed shirt and dress pants, looking every bit the put-together professional. She was the type of person whose personality took up all the air in a room when she was in lawyer mode. No four walls were large enough to contain her. She scowled at the waiting chairs with disgust.

"Is he here?"

Ms. Anderson nodded, shrinking back in her chair. I almost felt sorry for her, but it's not like she had to live up to anyone's expectations.

My mom's eyes flashed to me and zeroed in on my head.

My hand flew to my hair.

"What did you *do?*" I could tell she was struggling to keep it together in front of a stranger. We were not a family who aired our dirty laundry in public.

I didn't have an answer that could be spoken in a sentence or two.

She blinked once. I could almost see her compartmentalizing, prioritizing. She crooked a finger at me, her eyes only lingering a second longer on my hair before she swept us both into the dean's office.

Dean Alton looked up from a file as my mom entered, every bit the conductor in the most formal black suit I'd seen him in to date, the chain from his pocket watch hanging in a perfect arc from the vest under his suit coat.

"I'll make this short," my mom said, with no preamble whatsoever. "You have no hard evidence that my daughter has done anything, and you'll be wasting the board's time, because they'll tell you the exact same thing."

The dean's face turned a deep shade of red as he faced her down with all the wrath of a man who'd been done wrong. "Your daughter has been implicated in a string of vicious graffiti strikes on school grounds," he said in a quiet voice.

My head snapped up. A string? As in, more than one?

"First, that slanderous incident in the boys' bathroom."

"Libel," I corrected before I could stop myself. "Slander is spoken." I felt the warning in my mom's gaze, so I closed my mouth.

"And your timing today couldn't be more appropriate, Mrs. Benson," he said. "An offensive attack on the west lockers occurred just a few minutes ago."

The west lockers were in the freshman hallway, right where... I would've groaned aloud if the fear of my mom didn't keep me silent. That was right where my new locker was.

Mom's eyes snapped to me.

I knew what she was waiting for. An alibi. Where had I been when this new "strike" had gone down?

There was no way I could tell her. *I couldn't have possibly done it, Mom. Xander was helping me re-fasten my bra?* I shook my head slowly.

She frowned.

Dean Alton did not miss our exchange. He raised an eyebrow in challenge.

"Did you find paint in her locker this time?" my mom interrogated. She wasn't going to give him time to get smug.

"No, but—"

"And where are the cameras in this institution? Did you check the film?"

"Our system is undergoing maintenance while we update to digital. None of the cameras are scheduled to be back online until tonight."

"Convenient." Mom folded her arms.

"Indeed." He mirrored her position.

"Do you have any evidence whatsoever that my daughter was involved in this most recent incident?"

He didn't have much of a case, even without my mom's impressive cross-examination. Maybe I was just a teenager, but his evidence sounded like crap. Just because new graffiti showed up, it didn't mean that I was the person who did it. Even if I had been the person to paint the Asshat thing, it could easily have been someone trying to copy-cat that crime.

The dean mentioned they'd searched my dorm room, but they hadn't found anything. Did they do that while I was waiting with Ms. Anderson? Agnes must have been mortified. It was a total violation. But I was with my mom on this. They could do whatever they wanted if it would prove I didn't do it.

"And then there's the matter of the essay she submitted for last term's contest," he inserted during the millisecond my mom took to inhale.

Oh, God. I sank down into the nearest seat, willing myself to disappear.

My mom pursed her lips. Life was tough when you couldn't review the evidence before a case. "The essay you sent me to proofread?" she finally asked me.

What could I do? I nodded.

"Seemed fine to me. What happened?"

It was good parenting, I knew, that this question was addressed to me. She was going to let me explain first. Unfortunately, there weren't two sides to this issue the way there was for the graffiti.

"I cheated," I whispered. I glanced at Dean Alton, who was leaning against his desk, pulling that face that was supposed to make me think he was disappointed in my choices. "But I didn't mean to, and when I realized it, I gave up the award." I tried to keep the defiant tone from my voice but failed.

"How is that possible?" she asked softly.

In halting words, I explained the situation. I couldn't decide whether to focus on my mom or the dean, bouncing back and forth like a game of ping pong as I spoke. When I was done, I dropped my head to stare at my shoes. There was a long pause as Mom digested this new information.

"There's been no intellectual copyright infringement, and you have little to no evidence that my daughter has had anything to do with this paint fiasco. If you're not careful, Mr. Alton, you're going to have a lawsuit on your hands for slander." Mom's words were calm, measured, a lot like the dean normally was, but no one in the room was fooled.

Dean Alton pinched the bridge of his nose, closing his eyes.

My mom waited him out.

"Mrs. Benson," he said in a low tone. "While we appreciate the generous donations you and your husband have—"

My mom held up a hand. Her eyes were so cold I almost shivered. He'd crossed a line. We didn't talk about money. Or at least, my parents didn't discuss it in front of me. It was rude.

Guilt flowered inside me, but I couldn't place it. I hadn't done anything wrong, but for some reason my parents' "donations" made me feel dirty.

"Virginia, I'd like to speak to your dean in private."

She didn't have to tell me twice. I pushed through the door and sank into one of the chairs outside the dean's office. My mom's voice was an indistinct murmur from behind the door, and the dean's... Well, not so much.

As their conversation escalated, Ms. Anderson got up from her desk and sat down beside me. "Are you okay?" Her hands reached out to touch my mine, but it seemed like she thought better of it, and her pointy pink fingernails fluttered to her hair instead.

I shook my head. Blood pounded in my ears, because I knew what was coming. Mom was going to get mad and threaten to take me home. To Boston. She wouldn't mean it, of course, but if Dean Alton called her on it...

Minutes later, my mom held my arm tightly as we left the dean's office. Students stopped to watch when they saw us. The term "walk of shame" didn't begin to cover it. I struggled to keep up with her pace, trying to look like things were at least semi-normal. I wasn't fooling anyone.

The janitor walked by with a can of paint remover in one

hand and a bunch of rags in the other. He shook his head when he saw me, and I almost screamed in frustration. Why wouldn't anyone believe me? Why was everyone so quick to think that it was me who defaced public property? Was I that horrible? I'd always had a ton of respect for authority. Why wouldn't anyone let me talk?

And then, like a scene straight out of a horrible movie, the sea of students parted, and there was Xander. His eyes studied us, lingering on the way my mom held my arm as she pushed me forward.

I looked at him helplessly, horrified. Through a gap in the crowd, I spied what everyone was gathered around. The reason my mom was pulling me from school while the board reviewed my case. The lockers spelled out my doom as we headed to the exit through the freshman hallway.

DEAN ALTON IS A SHIT LICKER

One brown letter marred each light blue locker, stretching toward the exit like individual slaps in the face. And my mom's grip on me shouted the one thing I never wanted anyone to think: *Virginia did it.*

It was like I could smell the sour breath behind the whispers that coated the halls through the paint fumes. I wanted to wrench my arm from my mom's grasp and scream until my throat bled. Because even as this new fresh hell faced me, all I could wonder was whether Xander thought I was guilty too?

Regret churned inside me. I'd been so scared. Scared he'd drop me flat when he finally got tired of my inexperience. Scared he wouldn't stop with his many girls. I was mad at him for calling me Virgin, but what if he really did think it was a joke? It was horrible, but... My chest tightened into a hard knot as we brushed past him. At the last second, I yanked my head around.

I'm sorry, I mouthed. For what happened in the car. For freshman year. For so many things I didn't mean.

He stared at me, his eyes wide with an expression I couldn't identify.

Only later did it occur to me that maybe that made me look guilty of the crime I didn't commit. That he'd have no idea what I was talking about. That he wouldn't understand what I was trying to say. It was too late. Everything was too late.

The flight home was long and tense. I wasn't even allowed to tell Agnes goodbye or gather any of my things. Boston in the winter was much colder than California, but my mom just handed me her coat.

"You have plenty of clothes at home," she said quietly. All she did for the first hour was stare at the top of my head, her lips compressed. Then finally, "What possessed you to ruin your hair?"

I explained the situation to her in a shaky voice. Just remembering it made me want to cry.

She blew out a breath, her face finally losing some of her attorney look. "Why didn't you contact me or your dad? We could have helped you."

What could she have done? The damage was instant. "I handled it." It's what she'd taught me to do. Did she want me to change that now? Trying to live up to her expectations was exhausting, especially lately.

She reached out and touched the side of my head, briefly making contact with the longer part of my bangs.

I flinched.

"We can get you a wig until it grows back if you want," she said in a soothing voice.

"I'm okay." I frowned.

"Do you know who did it?"

"I said I handled it," I reminded her.

"The negligence at your school is astounding."

I didn't respond, because what could I say? I hadn't reported it. It didn't even occur to me, but it should have. It would have made the case for someone framing me for the graffiti stronger. I blew out a sigh. I couldn't fix that now.

Thankfully, Mom didn't care to continue the conversation. Eventually, I fell asleep on the six-hour flight, the weight of the day too overwhelming to stay conscious. When I woke up, the plane was landing in Boston. Mom was as unruffled as ever. She grabbed her small carry-on, and in no time at all, we were in the car and speeding through the snow to our house.

When we didn't speak during the ride, my shame had time to fester and morph into an anger that couldn't be expressed through words. I didn't even feel the cold in the ten steps that it took for me to crunch over the dirty snow and enter the brownstone house we called home. Silently, Mom gestured to the winding staircase that would take me to my room. No dinner, then. I wasn't hungry anyway.

That night, I stared up at the ceiling of my room in the darkness with gritted teeth.

The whole thing was unfair. And my mom's reaction? Not once in the eight-hour trip did she ever ask me for my side of the story. She believed me about my hair, but she didn't care if I was guilty or not when it really mattered. She only cared about winning.

The next day, it was as if someone pressed rewind on my life. Everything was as it had been when I was homeschooled. A schedule arrived, detailing my "required activities" and mealtimes. The quiet rhythm of my pre-teen years didn't exist anymore, though. It was like trying to wear a sweater that didn't quite fit. I kept studying the wrong thing at the wrong time, and

I itched to return to the routine I'd established at school. One that wasn't so strict, so minute-by-minute.

I was sure Mom talked to Dad at some point based on his complete silence at the rare dinners we shared, but they didn't let me in on the conversation. Maybe that was for the best. How many times could I hear I was a disappointment before I started to actually believe I'd been the one to paint the graffiti?

Surely only a few more.

A tutor came during the day to help me keep up with my schoolwork while the school board reviewed my case. My mom would fly back to the academy during the final proceedings to present our side. She didn't tell me if she was optimistic about it or not.

I didn't concentrate on much with the tutor. I couldn't care about the complicated concepts she was trying to teach. I wondered if the thinning of her blonde hair was from dealing with brats like me. Mostly, I just wanted to hide in my room and rage, though there wasn't anyone to hide from during the day since my parents were always at work. And I mean, always.

At night I lay in the dark, watching my phone. It was like a game. How long could I go with it turned face down? How long before I flipped it over for what had to be the millionth time? No new texts. No new calls. Not even any new emails. Everyone had written me off. Agnes... Xander. I hadn't left things right with either of them.

Maybe *I* should text them. Call them. I even thought about texting Xander's mom. But what would I say? My finger hovered over the screen until it developed a cramp.

Then I'd turn my phone off. Restart it. Maybe I had crappy service. My phone showed a solid connection, but someone must be trying to contact me. Right?

The house was still and silent and empty as I refreshed my screen over and over and over again.

A week passed before a piece of mail came for me. It wasn't from school. The Yale blue return address glared up at me from a thin, legal-sized envelope. Even though it seemed less important after everything that happened this year, I still wanted to get in. To have choices.

An acceptance would mean that my parents were right, though. My life spent under pressure would continue, would probably get worse at Yale. A rejection, though…

To be honest, all I wanted now was to clear my name. To be a better person. Not for Xander, like Gabriella so nicely accused. For me. It wasn't like it was before when, if I couldn't get Yale, I was nothing. I loved California. Maybe I should apply to UCLA. There was still time. My grades had dropped a bit, and I hadn't picked up any new contests to continue my quest for my dream life after graduation. Still, I probably would be okay no matter where I landed. No parents. No drama. Just learning something I might be able to enjoy doing for the rest of my life.

I sat down at the table where my grilled chicken salad waited for me. No cheese. Dressing on the side. I pushed the plate away. How could I eat right now? Tapping my fingers on the table, I watched the letter, willing a great hole to magically appear and swallow me up so I wouldn't have to see how much of a failure I was in black and white.

I used my fingernail to rip it open and unfolded it fast. I scanned the first few lines before setting it down, my hand shaking.

My shoulders relaxed and I looked up at the dining room ceiling. "I did it." I began to shudder, violent laughter bubbling up through my lungs and out a scratchy throat. "I did it!" I cackled. "Yale, here I come!" It was so funny! At the cost of my body, my love life, my childhood, I'd done it. It was all worth it, right?

…Right?

Wrong.

I wasn't going to be a lawyer. It was the worst possible career choice for someone like me. I wasn't going to read legal briefs for the rest of my life, chewing on highlighters until my jaw ached. In fact, the only things I enjoyed other than Xander were running and teaching Amy how to fence.

God, this was so wrong. All of it was wrong. I never got to play as a kid, have fun family vacations every year like Agnes did. I didn't have stories where I'd gotten up to the kinds of things Xander did with his brothers because I was either alone or being constantly grilled about my learning.

I'd been forced to give up my boyfriend because my mom and dad were so laser-focused on me getting into Yale. But plenty of people dated in high school and ended up in an Ivy League school. Why didn't I figure out something was wrong right then?

Because I trusted my parents. I thought they were normal, that I was normal. The truth was that none of this was normal. I'd be better suited to something physical, like coaching or maybe even physical therapy. I didn't need Yale for that.

Laughter clawed its way out of my body in big wheezing peals that echoed off the high ceiling. Even though nobody else might care, it didn't matter. I finally knew what I wanted to do. I knew who I wanted to be.

18

WHY ARE YOU HERE?

I PROBABLY SHOULD'VE TOLD my parents about Yale right away. We'd planned on it for so long. All the lectures, every sacrifice was for this moment. But for some reason, I hesitated. It was almost as if, by telling them, it took something from me. Took some of my joy and gave it to them. It was stupid, but that's how it felt. So I waited. They weren't around anyway.

Still, my mood was better the next day, and I actually attempted to smile at my tutor. This prompted her to be a little nicer to me, and that cheered me up even more. By the time lunch came, I was hungry for the first time since I'd been home. Even the bland diet of egg whites, salads, unseasoned fish, and vegetables my mom had me on was better than nothing.

I was straightening my already clean room when the doorbell rang.

My chair clattered to the ground as I flew down the stairs. With my hand on the banister, my feet skipped every other step on my way to the door. This was the most excitement I'd had in days. Someone was here! At this point I wouldn't have cared if it were the dean himself. Anyone would be a welcome interruption. I swung the door open.

Xander.

"Hey, Virginia." His breath puffed out and he smiled that half smile of his as he pulled his hands out of the pockets of his dark jeans.

I wanted to fling myself into his arms and sob. I wanted him to look at me that way he always did where he saw right through me. I wanted to hide my clothes that were a little too loose on me now, knowing he noticed. Instead, my excitement morphed into nerves. I silently let him in.

He shook the snow out of his hair. When he opened his arms, I melted into them. Neither one of us spoke for a moment.

Then, "You shouldn't be here. My parents…"

"I don't care. Let them see me here. I have to tell you something."

I squeezed him harder. "Xander, I'm grounded. Probably until I die."

"Not when they hear what I have to say." His voice was so sure, so confident. I'd missed that.

I pulled back, smiling through unshed tears. "That's sweet of you, but I don't think standing up to them is going to work. I'm… I'm going to be expelled."

"No, you're not." He smiled gently. One hand reached out to brush away a traitorous tear that dared fall without my permission.

"What?" His touch was more than a little distracting.

"They probably already got a call from the school board, but no, you're not going to be expelled. The real graffiti artist came forward and confessed."

It was the last thing I expected. Why would they, when I was already taking the fall? "They… What? Who was it?" *Gabriella.* It had to be.

"The office lady. Ms. Anderson."

"Wait… *What?*"

"We were looking at it the wrong way the whole time. It wasn't someone out to get you. It was someone who was mad at Dean Alton."

And with the viewpoint switched 180 degrees like that, it made perfect sense. "The rumors were true?"

Xander nodded. "Yeah, they were involved. Then he dropped her flat and went back to his ex-wife."

I remembered the cold way he talked to Ms. Anderson when he called me out of math.

"But graffiti? Isn't that a little childish?" It didn't quite fit with the image I had of an adult. *Asshat? Shit licker?* Hilarious, but kind of immature.

"The heart wants what it wants." Xander shrugged, shoving his hands in the pockets of his jeans. "She's been drinking a lot lately, I guess."

If she was drunk, it made more sense. I remembered the way I pressed against Xander at Nikki's party. What did I call it? Hug dancing?

"But why put the paint in my locker?" That was pretty low.

"She panicked. A janitor was coming down the hall and she needed to get rid of the evidence. Yours was just the closest locker. You know she has the master key."

"And the second time?"

Xander lifted one shoulder and let it drop, his hands still stuck in his pockets. "I think she was just mad. Or couldn't handle it. I don't know. She's fired now, though."

I nodded, still a little confused. "Well, aren't I lucky?"

"I just thought I'd come tell you in person. It seemed right," he said lamely.

"Xander," I said.

"I'm sure you're really busy." He eyed my obviously empty house. "So I can get going. But we solved it." He smiled slightly. "Maybe just in the nick of time, but it happened."

"What do you mean? Who's we?"

"Jenna. Trent. Me. And Agnes, too. You really need to talk to her, actually."

The conversation was switching gears quickly, and I struggled to keep up. "I do?"

"Your hair," he said.

I was suddenly self-conscious. It was in an awkward stage of regrowth. How bad did it look to Xander right now?

"Your hair wasn't Ms. Anderson. It was Agnes."

I stumbled backward and sat at the bottom of the stairs.

Agnes. Well, that made horrifying sense. She was mad at me, but I kept putting her off, only caring about Xander and the case, and…and I hadn't learned anything. The whole time I was trying to fix the selfish moves I'd made, I was making another one. I was shutting her out to the point where she wanted to see me hurt.

On the other hand, she ruined my freaking hair.

"Wow," I said.

Agnes had never been good at confrontation, despite her loud family. Not when it really mattered. I replayed some of our conversations in my head. Had she wanted to help with Jenna at set construction? Hang out at Nikki's? She'd asked about Xander several times, and I'd blown her off.

Every flash of memory made me feel lower and lower until I could have sworn I was about a millimeter tall. How could I even begin to fix it? My hand reached for my once-beautiful hair, and I remembered the horrible scene at the hairdresser's with Vincent. Did I even want Agnes's friendship back?

My skin went cold. She tried to tell me before I left school. What a mess. Every time I was near someone, I made a mess.

"I can't believe she broke my car," I whispered. The wheels in my mind couldn't turn fast enough to keep up with the information flooding my brain. Agnes didn't even know anything about cars.

"Eh, I think your car just died," Xander said. "It happens."

So many coincidences. Two culprits. I never would have been able to figure that out, but Xander... Xander did. And he'd had help. Why would Trent and Jenna help me?

"Did Agnes tell you about my hair?" I asked.

"When I rounded up Jenna and Trent, she did. She was feeling pretty guilty about everything after you left. I guess some freshman named Amy went to your dorm when you didn't show up to fencing. Not sure what that has to do with anything, but the next day, Agnes hunted me down. Wanted to help with the case."

Amy. I never expected her to notice when I went missing.

And Agnes... Her helping made me feel slightly better about what she'd done to my hair. But I was still missing pieces. Ms. Anderson coming forward still made no sense. "And then you..."

"And then Trent volunteered to help Ms. Anderson in the office during free period so he could try to overhear what went down between you and the dean, but he ended up finding out a lot more. Her guilt was killing her, and she called her best friend to talk about it during school hours." Xander shrugged. "When Jenna confronted her about it later, she just about sobbed to death and promised to confess. The next day, she was gone."

"Thank you," I said simply. It was incredible. Me leaving the school made it possible to solve the case. I had to be gone to be proven innocent. And Trent, Jenna, Xander, even Agnes... They didn't have to do what they did, but they did. Even after what I'd done, they stepped up and helped me.

I felt a little sorry for Ms. Anderson. It couldn't be easy to see the guy who brutally dismissed you every day and even have to do what he said because he was your boss. I was tempted to cry when Jenna was mad at me too, so I could relate. But...

"Xander, why are you here?" And why did he go to all the trouble of traveling across the country after what happened in his car?

He caught my hand. "I told you, I—"

I cut him off. "That's not what I mean. None of you texted me, called me, or even emailed me. Why are you here?"

"We didn't know how strict your grounding was. What your parents would do. We didn't know if you'd have access to your phone." He scuffed his shoe against the floor, staring at the mark it made before erasing it with his toe. "I didn't know if you'd want to talk to me."

Okay, that was fair. "But you jumped on a plane and flew...hours."

"I did."

I waited for his explanation. *Virginia, come back with me. Virginia, I love you.* It didn't come. Silence hung thick between us. There was the low growl of a snowblower starting outside.

"Why?" We hadn't ended things in a place where this conversation would be comfortable, but we needed to have it.

He shrugged.

I waited for him to say something. He didn't. My heart accelerated. That was it? He flew all this way, and that was it? Did this clear his conscience, then? It was okay to call me Virgin as long as he cleared my name?

I raised my eyebrows. *Come on. Give me something.* He shook his head.

I swallowed back my disappointment. My anger. What was all of this even for? "Okay, then. Thanks for...everything. I owe you." I turned to walk back up the stairs, my fists clenched, my heart pounding in my ears.

After the first step, he grabbed my hand and turned me back toward him. Our faces were almost level. "You're kind of sexy when you're mad."

Then he kissed me.

I wrapped my arms around his shoulders and leaned into it, every nerve in my body attuned to how close his chest was to mine, how tender his lips were, how warm. God, I'd missed him.

He cradled my face in his hands like I was made of glass. It was different than the heavy make out sessions I was used to with us. It was so much more, like fireworks and sunsets and everything sexy and meaningful at once.

After a moment, he pulled back. "I need to tell you something."

"Me too. I feel it too." Why were we talking? I wanted to keep kissing him.

"Not that." His voice turned serious. "I wanted to apologize. For calling you Virgin. I—"

"Shh, it's fine." I put my finger to his lips. I didn't want to ruin the mood.

He grabbed my hand and lowered it. "No, it's not. I was mad you broke up with me, and then you wouldn't give me the time of day. I was immature, trying to get your attention when I said it, because even if you looked at me like you wanted to kill me, at least you were still looking at me." Xander blinked, and I realized he was trying not to cry.

"It became this stupid habit. I didn't realize what it meant to you when I said it, and I should have. You've always... You've always been able to take anything I dish out and give it right back. I don't think I knew when I really crossed that line, but I'm sorry. I'm so sorry. It wasn't okay. It's not okay. And I don't expect sex from you. I need you to know that. Okay?"

It was obvious he'd rehearsed that speech, and what he said made my heart just about fly out of my chest. "Okay."

But he wasn't done yet. "I never really got over you freshman year. I don't think I ever will. Maybe somewhere in the back of my mind it was because I was mad and hurt. I'm sorry."

I rocked back. This grand romantic gesture, his heartfelt words, I didn't get it. I'd done nothing to deserve this kind of attention. "Why do you even like me?"

"Why do I—are you serious?"

I should say no. I wasn't trying to fish for compliments. It was just...

"Virginia, you're the most passionate, dedicated person I've ever met. I couldn't believe you paid attention to me freshman year. When you looked at me—look at me—it's like I'm the only person worth seeing. You're like the sun. I lived in terror that you'd quit shining on me. When you did..." He threw his hands up. "No one is like you. No one will ever be like you."

Tears streamed down my face. How could someone like Xander feel less than anyone? He was everything: gorgeous, thoughtful, tender, funny. And all the parts of myself I hated he loved. Even my darn hair. I pulled him down to kiss me, tears and all.

"How soon do you think you'll be coming back to school?" he asked when we finally took a break from making out.

"We should probably talk about that," I said as I smoothed my hair. A plan was forming in my head, and he wasn't going to like it.

"They're reinstating you immediately, you know." His hand slid over mine and pulled it from my hair.

I knew I must look a mess, but this was a conversation that couldn't wait. "Xander." A dull pain throbbed in my chest.

Don't do it.

But I had to. It was the right thing to do. He deserved so much better.

He kissed one of my cheeks softly. "You could probably jump on a plane with me on the way back. You could call your parents, and I'm sure it would be fine."

"I'm sure it would." My parents would no doubt love to be free of me. "But..." I sucked in a breath. I was about to ruin everything. I pictured Agnes's face the last time I saw her. I was about to fix everything, too.

I forced myself to say the words. "I don't think I can go back."

"I'm sorry, what?"

"I got a letter in the mail yesterday. It was from Yale, and—"

He grabbed my hands, bringing them to his chest. "Whatever it is, the school will retract it. You know they will. They'll probably call Yale themselves, and your dad went there—"

"Xander, stop." I smiled. "It's okay. I got in."

A huge smile spread across his face. "That's so awesome! I'm so proud of you." Then he paused, frowning. "So, what…"

"And maybe what I need is a fresh start." I refused to pause and absorb the fact that Xander had just uttered the one phrase I'd never heard from my parents. "I have a tutor here, and…"

I thought of the mess I'd made of my relationships, the horrible things I'd done to people in the last three years. The letter from Yale was a wake-up call. Last night as I lay flat on my back in my sensible bedroom, staring at the ceiling, I imagined a world free from my mistakes and my parents. And now, hearing how I had ruined things with Agnes, too… I was ready. Ready to take whatever hit I had to in order to protect myself. To protect them. This decision was right for everyone.

"Maybe I need a little distance to become a better person and stop hurting people. There are only a few months left of school. I can finish my education here. Then I'll get on with my life, and everything will be different." I stared at him. *Please understand.*

"You can't be serious. What about Agnes? What about… No." He broke away from me and started pacing, his movements filled with anger. "I'm not going to be the guy who says, 'What about me." He paused. "But what about fencing? And finishing what you start?"

He was reaching. Fencing was the least of my problems.

"I don't want to be the person I was, Xander. The person I am. I've thought a lot about this." It was painful to admit, but really, how many people would have a better high school experience without me? My face burned as I remembered

Gabriella's angry brushoff in the hall. Maybe this was the way I could make that right.

Xander squared his shoulders. "No one else is going to tell you the truth, Virginia, so I have to do it."

I flinched. I didn't know how much more truth I could handle this year.

"This is a coward's way out. Face your mistakes. Fix them. What have we been doing this whole time? You're already a better person. You were never a bad one."

"Xander, I can't." I had to look away, because watching his face crumple in pain was tearing my heart out.

"Then there's nothing left to say." I tried not to hear the tears in his voice, or the firm click of the door shutting a moment later.

After a long moment staring after him, I turned and dragged myself back up to my room. Each step was heavier than the one before.

Staring blankly at the ceiling of my bedroom, I replayed his apology over and over, willing myself not to feel anything at all.

It didn't work.

19

SOME REAL FOOD

For the rest of the week, I went about my life the way my parents expected. Though I didn't see them, there was a sticky note on the fridge on Wednesday saying my mom had "taken care of it" with the school.

No, she didn't. Xander and Agnes and a whole bunch of other people had. People who liked me.

I tried to catch my mom or even my dad on their way to work a couple of times before I gave up and relayed my decision to stay home to study through a sticky note of my own. Instead of them praising me for making a mature choice, there was no reaction. Not even a note back.

I ate what Mom told Betty to make me. Even though our cook was nice enough to try to talk to me when she gave me my meals, I wasn't able to do much more than lift a shoulder or nod.

I took a special interest in everything my tutor said, throwing myself into studying even when I didn't have to, but it was hard to concentrate. I spent a lot of time tapping my pencil against the pages of books, staring into space, and missing the highlighters Agnes gave me. That was, before she made me hack all my hair off.

I started running again because I missed it, but also because I didn't have fencing and I couldn't handle another lecture like the one my mom had given me in the dorms. The music was loud in my ears as my feet pounded over the snow and pavement, and none of the tracks seemed to sync up with my footsteps.

It wasn't like when Xander ran with me.

A beautiful trail wound through a forest and over a river only a mile away, but I couldn't find motivation in the beauty of the still air or the perfect white snow that blanketed everything. The air cut like razor blades, and I shivered the second my feet hit the ground. I could feel myself slimming down though I never stepped on a scale. It wasn't for me, after all.

Of course, my parents helped me, too. The refrigerator notes from my mom reminded me to stick to my diet and not get "too comfortable."

I thought hard about those sticky notes while I stared at my hard-boiled egg one morning, sitting at the too-large table in the insanely big dining room. We never entertained. Why did we even have this big of a table? All the chairs were empty except mine. I tried to picture every seat filled with friends and relatives but quickly gave up. It would never happen. The trio of us would never jam together on one end like I had with Xander and his mom. My chest constricted with pain.

Xander.

My fork scraped against a plate in the quiet. No noise. My life was a colosseum of silence, broken only by education.

Could I really live this way?

My stomach growled, uncomfortable with this breakfast delay. I pushed back from the table. Today, for the first time since I'd been home, I wanted company. I opened the kitchen door. Betty paused, a bagel halfway to her mouth.

"Sweetheart, are you okay?" Her concerned words poured over me like a salve. Would she actually help me, or would she keep to my mom's very strict diet instructions? I'd never asked before.

I slid into my stool across from her at the breakfast bar in the kitchen. "Betty, may I please have some real food?" I asked nicely.

She blinked at me, silent.

"I can get it myself, I swear, if you just point me in the right direction," I started to get up. "I just... I can't eat eggs today. I'm sorry."

Betty snapped out of whatever trance she was in when she saw me getting out of my chair. "You sit right back down. I'll get you whatever you want. Pancakes? Waffles? Here." She set her bagel on a plate in front of me. "Eat this while I make you something. Lord knows you look like a strong breeze would knock you over."

And she got to work. I munched slowly on my bagel and smiled at her back as she pulled frying pans down and began to mix batter with arms muscular from years of kneading bread. I don't think she was aware of it, but she was muttering things like, "Thank the Lord," and "Skinny as a twig," under her breath. I'd always liked Betty.

When she finally stopped making food, there was a huge buffet of bacon, pancakes, hash browns, toast, and biscuits in front of me. I laughed when she started putting dish after dish on the bar.

"I can't eat all of this!" I protested, even as I pulled a sampling of each food onto a plate in front of me.

She pointed her spatula at me. "You can try!"

She sat beside me, and for a few minutes we ate in silence. Then she said something I wasn't expecting. "Your mom and dad love you, honey. You know that, right?"

I set down my fork and picked up my glass, sipping my

orange juice. "No. I'm not sure I do," I replied quietly. It was the first time I said it aloud, but it was true. Mom said she did, but it was clear I was a burden. I felt it when I was younger, but since I'd left for the academy, this... Whatever this was, it wasn't any kind of a family life. Not like Xander's.

"They love you," Betty said confidently.

"How do you know?" I pushed the plate away from me. It was my second plate, anyway.

She pushed the plate back toward me. "I've known your mom a long time."

I nodded. She'd been here as long as I could remember.

Betty smoothed a stray hair back into her iron-gray bun. "When you were a baby, she lost her job. Did she ever tell you that?"

I shook my head.

"And your dad made some bad financial moves. The business..." She waved her muscular arm in front of her face. "Subjective."

I nodded. He talked all the time about how selective his clients were, how much was built on reputation, how hard it was to break into what he did for the people he did it for. Financial consulting was a career that brought in a lot of money, but it was also risky.

I tried to read between the lines of what Betty was saying. There were a lot of pictures of me at my gran's house before she died. Had they lost it all? Did we live there for a while? Mom always played it off as an extended vacation. But my dad's parents, though I rarely saw them, had loads of money.

"How could my grandparents let that happen?" I knew the answer even as I asked it. That relationship was strained because they hadn't wanted him to marry my mom.

She scooted off her stool and started washing the dishes. "They want you to be brave, strong, financially independent. They never want to see you go through what they did."

That much was certain. It made more sense now. But it still wasn't right. There was a line.

"It's too much right now." I swirled the juice around in my cup.

Betty nodded as I took a bite of bacon. "It's gone a little far the other way," she agreed.

She rolled her sleeves up over her elbows and began to wash the pans. As with everything she did, she was efficient and calm. The rushing water and her gentle humming was soothing, homey. Why hadn't I talked to Betty before this? Why hadn't I stood up to my parents' eating rules? I overlooked her the same way I overlooked people at school, but this was worse. She was more family than even Agnes. And now…

"Aren't you afraid they'll fire you for helping me—for feeding me different stuff?"

There was a pause. "No. I've been holding on until you go to college. I could have left years ago, and your mom knows that."

I nodded and brought my empty plate to the sink to rinse, trying to process that she was here for *me*. I turned and hugged Betty tightly.

I had a lot of thinking to do.

It's amazing what a few pieces of bacon and some toast can do to build courage. Knowing what I did about my parents didn't make me want to forgive them, but it helped me see their lives the way they did. In their own way, they loved me. By the time I got to my room, I was reaching for my phone.

I was going to talk to them, whether they wanted to hear me or not.

***

My dad got back to me first. He didn't answer my text, of course. Betty relayed that he had talked to my mom, and they'd both be home tonight to discuss my education, given the new developments. It was just like my dad to take control of the conversation, to assume that's what I wanted to speak to him about. And it was, I guess. Kind of. And that was...good. Yes, it was good.

When I sat down to dinner, I watched as Betty brought out grilled fish and brussels sprouts for each of my parents. Dad winced as he glanced down at his food, but Mom gave him a quelling look.

But Betty, per my request, had doubled my portions and added a roll and butter to my meal. When it arrived, Mom noticed immediately. She opened her mouth to call Betty back, but I shook my head at her, picking up the roll and taking a big bite. It might have been stupid to anyone else looking on, but to me, it was a roll of revolution.

"I want to talk," I announced when I was done chewing.

My dad folded his newspaper and set it aside. "So you said," he replied. "And so do we."

Okay, maybe it was better to let them go first. I nodded once, and he wasted no time.

"We think it would be best for you to go back to the Academy," he said. "Holed up in this house all by yourself while we work isn't a healthy atmosphere in which to finish your studies. If you still have a hope of getting into Yale, it would be best to look to them as if you were able to finish what you started."

"Your health benefits from the structure that the Academy provides, if you can stick to the plan this time." Mom looked pointedly at my plate. "Fencing, running, balanced meals."

They wanted me out from underfoot, just as I predicted. Why did it hurt so much to hear it out loud? They didn't even acknowledge the fact that I had been innocent all along, just as I told them multiple times. Why I was surprised by that, I didn't know. They'd been pretty clear about how that didn't matter to them. It ignited a dangerous rage inside me.

"Being alone in this house isn't... I can't..." Mom readjusted the cloth napkin in her lap. "I can't be home the way I used to be when you were younger."

"Why did you even have me?" The words erupted from my mouth before I could think them through. This wasn't part of the plan, but I couldn't help what I said next. "You obviously don't want me." How were these even the same people who threw everything away for love? Had one financial scare made them the way they were with me? Or was I just that stressful to parent?

"Don't be ridiculous." My dad wasn't even slightly ruffled by my outburst. "We're doing the best we can to get you the education you deserve."

"To get you everything you deserve," Mom said quietly.

I gripped my fork until my knuckles turned white. "I got a letter from Yale this week," I reminded them.

Both sets of eyes zeroed in on me. They hadn't read my sticky note. So much for our system.

"I got in."

A smile stretched across my dad's face for the first time this school year. "Well that's just fine," he said. "Now we need to make sure you keep that status."

Oh, for the love of God. Nothing. Nothing I did was good enough. Suddenly, I didn't care what had happened to turn them from who they'd been into who they were today. I was ready to be done.

"Do you know what a BMI is?"

Mom blinked, caught off-guard by the change in subject. "Yes, of course."

"So you're aware that I'm almost underweight?" It hadn't taken long to throw my height, weight, and gender into an online calculator. Hadn't taken long to confirm what I already knew—that I was fine the way I was. The weight of working out but having greasy food once in a while with Xander? That was normal.

Mother stared at her fish, at a loss for words. Could she see the sick irony in all of this? First they couldn't feed me, and now they wouldn't. Silence blanketed the room for the millionth time since I got home, and I wanted to scream. Wanted to shake her. Maybe I just wanted her to tell me I was enough. God, that was pathetic.

I looked up at my dad. He'd already reopened whatever important email he'd been reading on his phone, completely dismissing this part of our conversation. Well, then.

"I don't know what to say. I thought…" She pressed her lips together.

I threw my hands out in question. What did she think?

"I'm just trying to give you the best shot, Virginia. The very best one. The world may seem body positive now on the outside, but I know what gaining a few pounds does to your body, your chances of success. I know how hard you have to work to stay on top. Appearances matter more than they should. I was trying to help." Her last sentence was little more than a whisper, but it echoed in the otherwise silent dining room.

Maybe now she was starting to get it, but I wasn't willing to take the chance that she didn't. "Your diet is hurting me." *You're hurting me.*

Tears filled her eyes as she stared at me across the table. "I don't know what to say."

"I don't need you to say anything, but I will be eating what I want to from now on," I said firmly. "I want to be healthy."

Silence as she looked to my dad, who hadn't tuned into the conversation at all. He was still immersed in whatever he was reading on his phone.

"Okay," she said in a frail voice, so very unlike my mom.

At her tone of voice, Dad finally looked up, his eyes darting from me to Mom. He set down his phone and covered her hand with his. "Virginia, everything your mom and I have done has been to help you lead a successful life."

"You've said that." My heart hammered. Dad fully tuning into a conversation was so rare.

"The reason I work the way I do, the reason your mom guides you the way she does... You've never lived without the money our careers provide. You don't know what it's like to struggle."

"We don't want you to struggle," Mom added, wiping her eyes with the corner of her napkin.

"I understand. I get it, I do," I said. "But I'm struggling now in a different way. You have to let me..." I sucked in a deep breath. "You have to let me go."

I couldn't live like this. Maybe I decided to live at home so I wouldn't keep offending other people, but I'd never survive in this toxic environment. My mom should know that she wasn't helping me by controlling my every breath. She should be taking care of me, not driving me to an insane level of perfectionism that made me scared to eat more than two bites. I knew she loved me, that they both did, in their own way. But now I didn't trust her, and I couldn't stay.

I set my fork down. "I think you're right. Please book me a ticket back to the Academy. I do better there." My hand didn't even shake as I reached for my water glass.

Mom was frozen, watching me for a long moment, her eyes brimming with tears.

My anger faded, and I looked away. There was too much to unpack between us. The matter was resolved. And though there was no talking to them about the why of anything, at least we could agree on the things themselves. They loved me. It was the wrong way, sometimes. But it was okay. I loved them too. It was just time to leave.

I excused myself from dinner early to pack and say goodbye to Betty.

2 0

I CAN START

MY DAD DROVE me to the airport the next morning and told me he loved me before I crossed the security barrier. I stared blankly back at him. He had nothing more to say, and I had nothing more to give. My mom wasn't able to accompany us. Whether it was because she was still upset over our conversation or because she had a work commitment, my dad didn't clarify. I didn't ask him to.

It was a relief when I boarded the plane and found my seat. With every passing minute in the air, the press of anxiety on my chest lessened. My parents were a Boston problem. I'd taken charge of my destiny, had finally made a decision by myself. It was time to live it.

But the moment I stepped off the plane into the dry California air, reality came crashing down. Now what?

The answer was obvious: I needed to talk to Agnes. I dreaded my confrontation with her, but I knew that was the first thing I needed to do. Before Xander, before anything else. I was too mad to try to text her before I got on the plane, and now that I was off... Xander was right. It was time to stop being a coward.

There was no way he'd come back to school without running into her and telling her what happened, right? Yet my phone hadn't so much as vibrated since then.

I was required to check in to the dean's office first, where the words "deeply regrettable circumstances" were thrown around more than once. I guessed that was as close to an apology as I'd ever get. I almost felt sorry for the guy as I watched him sputter at me. They hadn't found a replacement for Ms. Anderson yet. From the dean's loosened tie to his rolled-up sleeves, as well as all the paperwork scattered over his desk, it looked like he was trying to field it all himself. I didn't enjoy my moment of victory over him the way I thought I would a couple weeks ago. I might've gotten the short end of the stick, but he had, too.

I didn't hesitate when I walked into our dorm during the end of last period, because I knew Agnes wouldn't be there. I took my time rearranging the stuff I'd brought with me. My fingers brushed the golden highlighters that sat in a perfect line, exactly as I'd left them when I'd been forced to go back to Boston.

That was where Agnes found me. When she entered our room, she dropped her backpack and sat down hard on the edge of the couch. "I don't even know where to start," she mumbled to the floor.

"I can start."

She nodded. I recognized the set of her shoulders, the tense way she clasped her hands in her lap. It was the same thing I did whenever my parents yelled at me. I wasn't them. I'd never be them.

"Agnes, I am so sorry." I'd rehearsed what to say before leaving Boston. Now, I was grateful for the time to prepare because my voice broke, and I was already a mess.

Her head snapped up in surprise.

"I've been the worst friend this year. I was so obsessed with finding the person trying to frame me, so involved with whatever was happening with Xander, that I completely ignored us." I sat next to her.

"But you... I..." She stopped, then restarted. "I'm sorry about your hair," she said softly. "I was so mad, but I didn't know they'd have to cut it off."

"You definitely knew how to hurt me." This was the part I didn't want to talk about, the part I wished we could ignore. "Why didn't you just talk to me?"

She blew out a breath and collapsed into the couch. "I tried."

I nodded, trying to pull back the wave of frustration that threatened to make me yell at her. "Okay."

"It was horrible. I was horrible." She covered her face with her hands and started to shake with sobs.

I leaned back against the couch until our shoulders touched. "Yeah," I agreed. Definitely. I knew this was what she was waiting for. We could leave it here. Our friendship. I should, honestly. My *hair*.

But it was Agnes.

I nudged her softly. "So was I."

Through her tears, she nodded.

And just like that, we were okay again. Ish.

When I finally got her calmed down, the interrogation started. "What are you going to do about Xander?"

I sighed, rubbing my face with my hands. All my makeup had melted off on the plane, anyway. "I don't know," I said. "We blow hot and cold all the time. It feels like it will never be right, you know?"

Agnes pursed her lips as she thought. "You guys are total opposites."

That was an understatement.

"But I heard he was pretty pissed when he came back from the airport," Agnes said. "Went down and let Dean Alton have it for letting you go."

I swallowed. Xander truly angry was a rare and intimidating thing. "Was it bad?"

"Yeah," she said. "He got detention for a week. Guess the swearing was pretty imaginative." She smirked.

I picked at my cuticles. "Is that where he is now?"

Agnes wiggled her eyebrows at me. She wasn't fooled by my casual act. "Yeah, they've got him shelving books in the library."

"Okay." I stood.

"What are you going to say to him?"

"I have no idea. I never do with Xander." My palms itched just thinking about it. He was still mad. Otherwise, he would have texted me after that night in Boston.

"Well, tell me about it when you get back, whenever that might be?" Her voice wavered.

I nodded. It's all she really wanted—to be on the inside track, to be my friend. I needed to be better about asking her about her life, too. Number one on my list was, what the heck was going on between her and Chad? "Want to do a girls' night tonight? I'll go get junk food and you can pick the movie," I offered.

"You're going to get junk food?" Her mouth twitched as she fought a smile.

"Oh, shut up." I could find things that were bad for us...if I tried.

"I'll hold my breath for my two crackers."

I barked out a laugh.

I wasn't laughing when I stood outside the heavy doors of the library. Should I even be here? Was there anything I could say to Xander that could begin to fix us at this point?

"She looks like she's about to chicken out," a voice behind me said.

"You give her too little credit," a lower voice replied.

I whirled around, and there stood Jenna and Trent. It was like worlds clashing, but maybe they'd become friends when they were trying to... I swallowed. When they were trying to help me.

"So?" Jenna asked, her unblinking owl-eyes fastening on the indecision written all over my face.

I eyed the door again as they came to stand with me. "Xander's in there," I said softly.

"And he knows you're back," Trent guessed.

I nodded. "Probably."

"Definitely," Jenna said.

She was right. The speed gossip traveled with in this school was frightening. The fact that Jenna was being nice after she'd already done so much for me didn't escape me.

I turned to both of them. "Thank you for defending me to the dean," I said. "You didn't have to do that."

Trent shrugged. He was the real MVP in the plan they'd devised. "You weren't guilty." To him it was simple, but he'd had more faith in me than most.

I stared at him, tears shining in my eyes.

"You think I don't know what you said that day in the dean's office?" he asked in a quieter voice, his eyes intense behind his glasses. "It was you who was called down first, then me. We're okay, Virginia."

I nodded, blinking quickly. "I'm sorry."

"I know."

A weight lifted from my chest, but it wasn't enough. "I am innocent," I whispered to the library door. Xander had always known that. "But it doesn't matter."

"What are you talking about? Of course it matters. It always matters," Jenna said sharply. "Are you going in there or not?"

It looked like avoidance wasn't going to work. "I..." My hand reached for the door, but I couldn't make myself push it open.

"Oh, for the love of…" She shoved me through the swinging doors. I struggled to keep my balance as she yelled, "You're welcome," loud enough to gather the attention of everyone in the library. Which was…just Xander.

He looked up briefly, then placed a book on the shelf, as if me bursting through the doors and almost falling on my face was an everyday occurrence.

I stepped toward him. "Xander."

"Virginia." He stared at me, waiting.

"I'm back." For some reason it sounded more like a question than anything else.

"So I heard," he said.

"So…" I blew out a breath. God, I couldn't even form a coherent sentence around him. What was he expecting? *Please take me back? I'm sorry, I was wrong about everything?* I wasn't sure I could force that out.

"So," he replied.

"You're not going to make this easy for me, are you?" I ventured a smile. Maybe we could joke our way through it?

Xander turned back to the book cart, grabbing another volume. "Sure I am." He was dismissing me. After all we'd been through.

Anger boiled up inside me, even though he was completely justified in his reaction. I'd told him no. Told him I wasn't coming back. Rejected him again. He deserved to move on, but I couldn't let that happen. Not when I finally knew that what I'd always wanted was him.

I stormed over to him and yanked at his shirt. "Do you want to date me or not?"

Xander's expression was cold as he glanced down at me. "Not."

The bottom fell out of my world. I'd really done it this time. Completely killed whatever it was that had ever made him like me. God, would I never learn?

I sank down into the nearest chair. "Well, shit." *Don't cry. Don't do it. Get up and leave.* But I couldn't. It was like all the energy had leaked out of my body.

He sat next to me. "Did you just swear?"

"Yeah." I stared straight ahead. The hysterics would come later, but right now... Right now, the weight of what I'd lost threatened to crush me.

Xander's hand covered mine. "Virginia. Look at me."

I did as he asked, but I couldn't see him clearly. My eyes were swimming with tears I couldn't let fall.

"You just swore."

I used my sleeve to wipe at my eyes. "Well..." I threw my other hand out in front of me helplessly. If swearing wasn't warranted right now, I didn't know when it would be.

He caught my hand mid-air. "I accept," he said.

"You... What?"

He threaded his fingers between mine. "I accept your apology, and we're dating now."

My mouth gaped open in shock. Wait a minute... "Because I said 'shit'?" Of all the...

His mouth twitched. "Pretty much."

"You are so ridiculous." I laughed, but I was crying, too. I probably looked like a maniac.

"You love it." He scooted his chair closer to mine and pulled me into a hug.

"This isn't a joke? We're really dating?" My voice was muffled against his shirt.

He pulled away and kissed me on my nose. "It's not a joke."

Relief flooded my body. "Oh, thank God. I thought I was going to have to kick your butt." I was still sniffing back tears like a complete dork.

"Ass, Virginia," he corrected. "Kick my ass."

"I don't swear," I told him as he pulled me out of the chair.

"Mmhmm." He didn't let my hand go as we started walking.

"Shut up."

Agnes practically had a heart attack when I re-entered our dorm room bearing two pints of ice cream, chips, and Coke.

"What?" I asked innocently.

"There's no way you picked all that out on your own," she said. Her gaze was drawn to the peanut butter swirl, so I forked it over, saving the Oreo one for myself.

"I might have had some help," I admitted.

"Xander?"

I couldn't hide the slow smile that spread across my face.

"I knew it! Tell me everything, and then we can watch the movie." She grabbed spoons for us and sat cross-legged on the couch, picking up the remote to scroll through the channels.

"No," I said, sinking down next to her.

"Seriously, Virginia?" I could almost see the wheels behind her eyes turning. She thought I was shutting her out again.

"No, I mean... I'll tell you about Xander, but I want to hear about what's been going on with you first."

Agnes relaxed, sinking back against the side of the couch and peeling the foil off the top of the ice cream. "I thought you'd never ask."

Then girls' night started for real.

The speaker crackled right after the pledge of allegiance the next day.

"May I have Virginia Benson in the dean's office please?" a man's voice asked.

I sighed as I scooted out from behind my desk. *Now what?* I didn't waste any time getting there because seriously, what else could go wrong this year?

When I arrived, the new office assistant greeted me. "Ms. Benson, the dean is waiting for you." He was an older, potbellied man, maybe in his forties. That was a switch.

When I pushed through the doors, I got another shock. Dean Alton wasn't the one who greeted me. It was a woman with a cloud of greying hair pulling files from a filing cabinet in the corner.

"Hello?" I asked. "I'm supposed to see Dean Alton?"

"Oh, I'm sorry." She turned to me. "I'm the interim dean. Mr. Alton made the decision to retire quite unexpectedly this year, and we wish him all the best. The announcement will go out to your parents in the newsletter tonight. I'm Ms. Walsh."

"Nice to meet you." I shook her hand before I sat. Dean Alton was really gone? I just saw him yesterday. Was this because of me? Or because of Ms. Anderson? Maybe he planned to retire and just hadn't told anyone. I flashed back to Xander telling me about how he was up for review this year. *Yeah, that's likely.*

Ms. Walsh smiled pleasantly at me, and I couldn't help but feel completely out of place. What did she need from me?

"Am I in trouble?" God, that was all I needed right now.

"Should you be?" The look on my face must have been alarming. "Sorry, just a little joke. I know you've had a rough year, Virginia, but I just wanted to tell you that your academics are stellar, and we're very excited to support you as you work toward Yale for the last few months of your education."

"Okay..." The school was still attempting to make amends. God, this was awkward.

"That's it." She stood. "Oh, wait. Your parents sent you a package, but it was too large for your mailbox. I'll grab it."

They what? My stomach constricted at the way we'd left things. My mom's face...

Ms. Walsh walked back into the office with a package slightly larger than a shoebox and handed it to me. She was right. That was my mom's handwriting on the return address. I frowned as I took it.

"And that should be it," she said. "I hope you have a great rest of your year, and I'll see you in the halls."

I stood, liking that she didn't waste any time. Did I dare hope this could be the end of all the drama this year?

"Um, okay."

She smiled again as I tried not to trip over my feet on my way out. How strange. This year really had come full circle.

Only when I'd shut myself in my dorm did I open the box. Caramels, Tootsie Rolls, taffy, mints—hundreds of individually wrapped pieces of candy stared up at me.

I sat down heavily on my bed. My mom hated candy. Was this a peace offering? I picked up a handful and let them fall between my fingers back into the box. Mom never admitted when she was wrong, but this was… I didn't even know how to process it. I spied a note nestled in the corner of the pile. I snatched it up and read the single sentence written in shaky handwriting, like maybe the author was crying when she penned it.

I love you more than anything.

Tears flooded my vision as I slowly unwrapped a pink Starburst. The sweetness exploding on my tongue wasn't enough to get rid of everything sour between us, but it was a start.

Xander sat with Agnes and me at lunch that day, which was crazy. When Trent and Jenna slid their trays next to ours too, I almost fell out of my chair.

"What?" Jenna said. "Don't make it a thing."

So I didn't, but I couldn't help my smile. It was kind of cool. Agnes seemed to think so, too. It never occurred to me that we might have been isolating ourselves by sitting alone the way we did. That I might have been isolating Agnes. And now, suddenly, we had friends.

Out of the corner of my eye, I spied Trent snag Jenna's hand under the table and thread his fingers through hers. She gave him a small smile, nothing like her stage persona. Somehow, I wasn't surprised when she laid her head on his shoulder and closed her eyes. Who better for Jenna than someone who wasn't afraid to face life head on? It made sense. They were so alike.

Not like Xander and me, I mused, watching him talk with Agnes about her day. Was that boy ever going to cut his hair? I imagined him with it pulled back into a bun or ponytail. That was where he was headed in a few months if he continued to let it grow. His shirt was half-untucked from his pants again. Had it ever seen the flat side of an iron? But God, he was so sexy. Maybe I could learn how to relax from him. Not much, but, like...a little.

As if he could feel me watching him, his eyes flicked toward mine, and he gave me that knowing smile that annoyed me so much. I kicked him under the table, and he chuckled.

"You kinda have a thing for me," he said.

"Nah," I dipped a carrot stick into ranch dressing.

His mouth compressed into an annoyed line.

I grinned. "There's no 'kinda'."

He chuckled.

"Ugh, get a room," Agnes groaned.

Chad's lumbering body squeezed in beside her, and she couldn't talk about anyone getting a room anymore. The way she draped herself over that guy was almost physically impossible. He was somehow still able to eat around her cuddling. I remembered Chad telling me how I wasn't as "scary" as the person threatening me, and I pursed my lips. He was talking about her. Then Agnes giggled as she whispered in his ear, and he snorted over whatever she'd just said. They were too cute to hate. Much.

I went back to eating, the simple penne pasta tasting less like cafeteria food and more like freedom with every forkful.

On the way to class, Xander pulled me back by my backpack. "You know what I love about you?" he asked as he fell into step with me.

I rubbed my shoulder, scowling. "My strong back and forgiving nature?"

"Shut up." He laughed. Then he kissed me.

We never finished that conversation, but I think I knew the answer, anyway.

ACKNOWLEDGMENTS

This book has had such a long and interesting journey, and it wouldn't be possible without all of the hands and hearts that have touched it over the years.

Thank you to my friends on Scribophile who, when I asked if the alliteration in the mini-golf scene was maybe too much, laughed uproariously and told me to keep going. You're horrible influences, and the book is funnier for it.

To Jay Heltzer for lending your fencing expertise a few years ago, thank you. I was able to revise with so much more confidence once I understood an instructor's point of view.

Thank you to my sister Valerie who reads so much more than I could ever hope to—your knowledge as a beta reader is so, so necessary. Sisters tell it how it is.

To Maren Jenner, a wonderful author friend who never fails to give me quick feedback and champions my flawed cinnamon rolls like no other, you rock.

A big thank you to Michael and Suzan at Winding Road Stories for accepting my manuscript and helping me shape it into a better version for public consumption. Your support is so valuable to me.

To Sterling and Samson, my beautiful sons, my everything. It is so cool to be your mom. You both inspire me daily.

And to Andrew. You and me against the world forever. I couldn't write love if I didn't feel it so deeply every single day with you.

ABOUT THE AUTHOR

Jessica K. Foster is the author of Young Adult Romance titles including *Andy and the Extroverts* and *Andy and the Summer of Something.* When she's not writing, you can find her teaching middle schoolers about subordinating conjunctions or sunning herself at the lake with a beach read in her hand. Jessica lives in West Michigan with her husband, two boys, and their ragtag crew of rescue animals. Visit her website at https://jessicakfoster.com for more information.

www.ingramcontent.com/pod-product-compliance
Lightning Source LLC
Chambersburg PA
CBHW030905060726

47591CB00005B/1423